The Library of Indiana Classics

" *'You better be givin' some of these berries the eye so they'll ask you to dance.'* "

ALICE ADAMS

Booth Tarkington

Illustrated by Arthur William Brown

Introduction by Donald Gray

Bloomington & Indianapolis

The Library of Indiana Classics is available in a special clothbound library-quality edition and in a paperback edition.

This book is a publication of
Indiana University Press
601 North Morton Street
Bloomington, IN 47404-3797 USA

http://iupress.indiana.edu

Telephone orders 800-842-6796
Fax orders 812-855-7931
Orders by e-mail iuporder@indiana.edu

The paper used in this publication meets the minimum requirements of American National Standard for Information Sciences—Permanence of Paper for Printed Library Materials, ANSI Z39.48-1984.

MANUFACTURED IN THE UNITED STATES OF AMERICA

Library of Congress Cataloging-in-Publication Data

Tarkington, Booth, 1869–1946.
Alice Adams / Booth Tarkington ; illustrated by Arthur William Brown ; introduction by Donald Gray.
p. cm. — (The library of Indiana classics)
ISBN 0-253-34227-9 (alk. paper) — ISBN 0-253-21593-5 (pbk. : alk. paper)
1. Young women—Fiction. 2. Social classes—Fiction. 3. Middle class families—Fiction. 4. Indiana—Fiction. I. Title. II. Series.
PS2972 .A42 2003
813'.52—dc21
2002152864

1 2 3 4 5 08 07 06 05 04 03

To

S. S. McClure

List of Illustrations

Introduction

For nearly the entire first half of the twentieth century Booth Tarkington sustained a remarkable popularity as a writer of fiction. Exactly at the turn of the century, his first two novels were serialized almost consecutively, the first installment of the second novel appearing only a couple of months after the final installment of the first, in one of the most successful of the new monthly magazines edited to attract a large general readership. One of the owners and editors of the magazine told him—as Tarkington wrote in a letter to his parents and sister (1 Feb. 1899), which is part of the extensive collection of Tarkington papers in the Princeton University Library—that the publication of his novels would make him "the most famous young man in America." Whether or not this prediction came true, their publication did put his name prominently before a large public. Tarkington kept it there for the rest of his life.

By the time of his death in 1946 he had produced thirty-nine volumes of fiction. This work always first appeared as short stories or serials in one of the mass-circulation magazines which served readers for whom magazine fiction was a principal form of entertainment: the *Saturday Evening Post, Harper's, Colliers,* the *Ladies' Home Journal, Redbook, Cosmopolitan.* In the first half of his long career Tarkington also collaborated on plays which ran on Broadway and sometimes for years in the repertories of touring companies; and he wrote for radio and, in their early years, for movies. Many of his novels became plays or movies, or both; *Alice Adams* was made into a movie twice, the second time, in 1935, with Katharine Hepburn in the leading role. One of his first novels to be published, *Monsieur Beaucaire* (1900), was still in print in the 1940s, principally because a movie of that name starring Bob Hope was released in 1946. His last novel to be published before his death, *Image of Josephine* (1945), was selected by one of the big book clubs, a decision that, he was assured by his editor, meant an additional sale of 400,000 copies (letter from Lee Barker of Doubleday Doran, 5 Dec. 1944).

Tarkington wanted to be an esteemed as well as a popular writer. In a letter written in 1914 he considered the work of some of his competitors for popularity and judged that their writing would "perish because their appeal is not to the people who preserve the memory of books" (letter to Julian Street, 18 June 1914). He constantly referred in his letters and essays to writers like Thomas Hardy, George Meredith, Henry James, and William Dean Howells, novelists of distinction in his youth who might have fallen out of fashion in the first quarter of the new century but whose books held their places in schools, libraries, and the conversation of literary critics and scholars.

He achieved his ambition, although even during his lifetime he began to slip down in the rankings of important American novelists. Two of his novels—*The Magnificent Ambersons* in 1918 and *Alice Adams* in 1921—won Pulitzer Prizes. Several times in the 1920s his name appeared high on lists of the most significant American contemporary writers. Because of the popularity of his stories of youth and adolescence in the Penrod books (1914, 1916, 1929) and *Seventeen*, his books became part of the furnishings of schoolrooms. (He regarded this distinction wryly: "I'm so darn dignified," he wrote to Julian Street in 1924, "that the only alleviating thing about my reputation nowadays is the fact that most of the schoolchildren under the 7th grade in the country, think that I'm the man that killed Abraham Lincoln.") He liked being good at the business of popular fiction while writing books that were thought to be good by the people who delivered such honors. When he was elected to the American Academy of Arts and Letters in 1920 he celebrated his identity as "an innovation: an academic who writes for any old Red Book or Pictorial Review that pays most" (letter to Julian Street, 22 Mar. 1920).

Tarkington served a dutiful apprenticeship to his popularity and eminence. Born into a modestly affluent Indianapolis family of midwestern patrician standing—a social position more like that of the Palmers and the Lambs than that of Alice Adams's family—he was sent east to prep school, returned for a couple of years of study at Purdue, and completed his education at Princeton. He did not receive a degree from Princeton because he lacked some courses in classical language and literature, but he left as a member of the class of 1893, an association he cherished. He lived for a while in New York, while he revised a play that was never produced, but for most of the next six years he lived in his parents' house in Indianapolis. He worked on plays and his two novels, and unrelentingly submitted sketches, stories, drawings, and even jokes to magazines. All but one (a drawing sent to a comic magazine) were rejected so rapidly, he wrote in an autobiographical sketch that was serialized in the *Saturday Evening Post* in 1941, "that sometimes I thought my poor things must have been stopped and returned from Philadelphia; they didn't seem to have time to get all the way to New York and back" (July–August 1941).

Even after Tarkington broke through into print and popularity, it took him another fifteen years before he consistently began to write the kind of books that won prizes. He spent much of the first decade of the century in Europe, living on Capri, then in a country house in France, and finally in Paris. He had become popular by writing versions of romance, and he continued to use its tactics. His second novel, *Monsieur Beaucaire* (1900), is a romantic comedy set in eighteenth-century England, and he followed its success with two more historical romances. He set some of his stories and plays in Europe, and arranged their plots so that conventionally innocent Americans show up or escape cunning Continentals who scheme to fleece them. With one exception, when he wrote about contemporary America, he ornamented and resolved his stories with the melodramatic turns of his first novel, *The Gentleman from Indiana* (1899), whose hero survives an assassination attempt by a lower-class gang dressed like the Ku Klux Klan and marries a plucky, resourceful young woman on his way to election to Congress.

The exception is Tarkington's best book in these years, *In the Arena* (1905), a set of sketches about corrupt American politics based on his one-term (1902–1903) experience as a member of the Indiana legislature. Later he said that these sketches marked the beginning of his "realism" (letter to Julian Street, 14 Feb. 1922). Whatever the name for the manner of his mature practice as a novelist, he did not settle into it until a few years after he moved back to the United States in 1910. He returned to Indianapolis and took over his parents' house, beginning a routine, which he maintained for the rest of his life, of living about half the year in Indiana and the other half in a house in Maine. The interests of his fiction began to shift decisively from the past and Europe to the American present, and from happily resolved confrontations of place and class to stories about the much less certain consequences of change in contemporary midwestern cities.

Alice Adams first appeared in the spring of 1921 as a four-part serial in the *Pictorial Review*, a big-circulation monthly magazine directed primarily to women. On the first page of the second installment (March 1921) the editors included a synopsis of the story so far that points to one of the principal reasons for the popularity of Tarkington's fiction.

> What young girl hasn't lived through the tragedy of going to a dance in a made-over organdy dress only to find all the others in brocade and silver? What small-town boy of seventeen hasn't been lured into the pool-room in the rough section of town? What proud mother

> hasn't struggled beyond her means and strength to give to her son and daughter all the luxuries and happiness other children have? These are the people in the story of Alice Adams—a girl like all other young girls in the world, eager for love, hungry for good times, groping about helplessly for that indefinite something that older folk call "life."

This invitation to the magazine's readers (over a million of them in the 1920s) to put themselves into Alice's story assumes, or insists, that they and Tarkington share important information and attitudes. They all agree on the meaning of poolrooms and made-over organdy dresses. They recognize the social geography of towns and cities like the one in which Alice gropes for love and moves into life. They probably know too what might be called their social geology, the clear striations of speech, dress, interior decoration, and pedigree that distinguish one caste from another in the extensive American middle classes. Most remarkably, the synopsis advises readers to identify not just with Alice's embarrassment and her mother's struggles, but also with their ambition, their hungry idea that happiness and love come dressed in brocade and silver, and accompanied by luxuries and good times.

Tarkington probably would have regarded it as a sign of his seriousness as a novelist that his story does not endorse or reward this ambition. Neither does it finally condemn it. True, the novel describes the attempt of Alice and her family to rise in the world as a wishful enterprise conducted by show and founded in delusion. Alice sometimes seems to think that she can make her wishes come true by literally waving her hands, which someone has told her are pretty. "On exhibition she led a life of gestures," Tarkington writes (15). She goes for a walk in a kind of costume, carrying a cane; she acts out a pantomime of waiting for an absent companion when she is abandoned at a dance; she offers to her father as a plan for her future her desire to be an actress.

Her more practical mother knows that gesture is not enough. Alice's predicament, she tells her husband, is that her family is poor, "and she hasn't got any background" (70). Money will provide background; "the way the world is now, money *is* family" (210). But Mrs. Adams invests her ambition in a fantasy of her own, the "fairy godmother" (167), in Alice's phrase, of a glue factory that will transform her husband from a salaried employee to an owner and capitalist. It is an unlikely transformation of a man who begins the novel so resistant to change that he is suspicious of such improvements as window screens. Nonetheless, Adams goes along with the scheme, nourished by his own delusion that he possesses a valuable secret.

In another of her moods Alice wants only to stop and rest. She tells the man who looks to be her best chance of rising in the world that she would like to stay out of it. She wishes that she and he could remain on her porch, apart from the parties and gossip in which she knows she will be humbled, outside the shabby, smoke-stained living room and its testimony to where her family stands in society. "But *wouldn't* it be pleasant if two people could ever just keep themselves *to* themselves, so far as they two were concerned? I mean, if they could just manage to be friends without people talking about it, or talking to *them* about it?" (230–31).

An ambition like Alice's, however, permits no rest. Even in her moments of withdrawal the world is busy with schemes to fulfill identical ambitions. Alice's street is lined with young women sitting on verandas and stoops, "cheerful as young fishermen on the banks of a stream" (190). Other mothers—Mrs. Dowling, for example—hustle to promote the chances of their children. Mrs. Palmer, having dismissed Alice as "a pushing sort of girl" (334), almost literally pushes her daughter out to a conservatory to capture the allegiance, if perhaps not the affection, of the young man who has shared Alice's retreat on her porch. Mr. Lamb, the beneficent employer who supports Alice's father during his illness, pauses not for a moment to try to push him to the wall when he becomes a business competitor.

For in Tarkington's view, Alice's ambition has taken over the country to which he returned in 1910. *Alice Adams* can be read as one of a suite of novels in which Tarkington dramatizes the character and effect of what in the first of these novels, *The Turmoil* (1915), he calls Bigness.

> Year by year the longing increased until it became an accumulated force: We must Grow! We must be Bigger! Bigness means Money! . . . Blow! Boost! Brag! Kill the fault-finder! Scream and bellow to the Most High: Bigness is patriotism and honour! Bigness is love and life and happiness!

Tarkington later put *The Turmoil* with *The Magnificent Ambersons* (1918) and *The Midlander* (1924) into a trilogy he titled *Growth* (1927). Growth had polluted American cities with smoke and the smell of glue factories. It pushed city boundaries into the countryside, leaving the center of the city a blighted place "too full of everybody," as he wrote in *Alice Adams*, "without anybody being home" (242). Grand old families like the Ambersons declined. Their great houses became boardinghouses and the meeting rooms of fraternal lodges; their high social rank was taken over by real-estate developers and pump manufacturers and the owners of automobile factories.

One of the questions of *Alice Adams* is whether Alice and her family belong with these small-city tycoons. I don't want to give away the ending of a novel to which I am offering an introduction. But whether the Adamses rise or fall, they live in the ruin and promise created by the energy of the prosperous agents of Bigness. More important, in a modest way they share their ambition, along with the many readers of their story, then and now. Tarkington's observation and supple prose in *Alice Adams* masterfully render the look and sound of the experience of these modest strivers. He gives his readers not just the clothing and furniture among which they move every day, but also small and deeply resonant details such as Alice's violets at the dance and the one picture of which she is proud in her living room. He lets us hear the tense yearning that bobs through Alice's chatter, the desperation that ultimately breaks through her brother's breeziness, the old disappointments and grievances that move beneath the quarrels of her parents. His achievement in *Alice Adams* is to organize and render a social reality that is still familiar, and to raise discomfiting questions about it.

How readers answer the questions about ambition raised in the novel will depend on what they make of Alice at the end. The writers of the script of the 1935 movie of *Alice Adams* make it simple: Alice ends in the arms of a young man who is at home among the gracious comforts for which Alice yearns. By the time he wrote his novel, Tarkington had learned to prepare more complicated responses to the stories he told. In a comment he wrote as a reader of his own novel, Tarkington suggests two ways to understand Alice and her story. Either, and both, fully respond to the restlessness that makes Alice interesting, gets her in trouble, and keeps her story moving.

The collection of Tarkington's papers at Princeton contains the galley proofs of the serial of the novel. In the margin of the last page of proof Tarkington has written in pencil a judgment of Alice: "incorrigible in dramatizing herself." The word "incorrigible" carries a reproach. The reproach, extended beyond Alice to those who share even as they frustrate her ambition—to the Palmers and Arthur Russell as well as to Alice and her family—turns the novel against her and those who yearn to rise in the world, and against too the smugness and casual cruelty of those who have already risen.

This judgment would come easily to Tarkington. One reason for the decline in his literary standing from its eminence in the 1920s may be that he sometimes seems too tightly bound within the attitudes of his time and the biases of his place in its social hierarchy. That shows most uncomfortably in his representation of black characters. He took over without reflection or refinement the degrading caricatures of his period, using craps-shooting chauffeurs and a slovenly servant as nothing more than markers of the Adamses' unfitness for the station to which the women of the family aspire.

So too, Tarkington's ease in the station to which he was born, and which he markedly improved by his talents, perhaps limited his sympathy for aspirations that begin so far down and are prosecuted by women, with their small and shallow desires for nice things and the good marriages that will provide them. In the novels which he wrote around the time he wrote *Alice Adams*, Tarkington imagines that Bigness and change can be made to yield beneficent as well as destructive effects. But he has that constructive work done always by young men of good family, sons and grandsons of lawyers or owners of land and factories, and not the wife and daughter of a man on salary. Read in this way, *Alice Adams* becomes a kind of cautionary tale, advice to all of Tarkington's contemporaries to ennoble their hunger to grow and rise, and to those in the lower precincts of the middle classes to curb ambition, to refashion desire so that it fits their place.

But Tarkington's recognition of the persistence of Alice's self-invention allows for a kind of admiration as well as, or instead of, reproach. Arthur Russell, who has been away to the war and is just adventurous enough to break from the expectations of his caste and sit on the porch with Alice, thinks when he meets her on her parade downtown: "Never had he seen a creature so plastic and so wistful."

> Here was a contrast to his cousin Mildred, who was not wistful, and controlled any impulses towards plasticity, if she had them. "By George!" he said. "But you *are* different!" (147)

A second way to read the novel is to ask whether in its ending Tarkington preserves Alice's difference. Alice can be brought to earth not just by a summary judgment of her fault; she can be diminished and changed by pity, our pity and self-pity, that converts her wistfulness into pathos, that lets us feel sorry for her without really liking her. But with an Alice not just diminished but extinguished, without the wistful yearning that softens her desire, the mobile identities she tries out before her mirror, the inventions that keep her going at and after the dance, life in middle-class, midland America will flatten and dim. Failure will sound like the tiresome quarrels in the bedroom of Alice's parents; success will look like a party to which only duplicates of Mildred are invited.

Alice can imagine possibilities more various, if less plausible, than these. So can Tarkington, who imagined Alice. It is difficult for a novelist, and for novel-readers, utterly to turn against fiction. Alice begins the novel trying to make something grand out of a stolen bouquet of what her brother calls dead flowers. Suppose that she does end, as Tarkington suggests, still practicing her bad habit of improvising improvements upon her circumstances. That is her charm, and one of the reasons we read her story. By the time he wrote *Alice Adams*, Tarkington had graduated from the kinds of satisfaction provided by his early novels, and now by the movies, which had become the truly popular entertainment of the half-century in which he did his work. If he allows Alice to walk out of her story still possessed of the comforts and powers of imagining, that can be understood not just as her fault. Alice's persistence, her preservation of the possibilities of fiction, may also be what she, and we, now get as a happy ending.

Donald Gray
Indiana University

Quotations from letters and other material in the Booth Tarkington papers housed in the Manuscripts Division of the Department of Rare Books and Special Collections of the Princeton University Library are published with the permission of the Library. I am grateful for this permission and for the assistance and courtesy of the librarians of the Manuscripts Division.

ALICE ADAMS

ALICE ADAMS

CHAPTER I

THE patient, an old-fashioned man, thought the nurse made a mistake in keeping both of the windows open, and her sprightly disregard of his protests added something to his hatred of her. Every evening he told her that anybody with ordinary gumption ought to realize that night air was bad for the human frame. "The human frame won't stand everything, Miss Perry," he warned her, resentfully. "Even a child, if it had just ordinary gumption, ought to know enough not to let the night air blow on sick people—yes, nor well people, either! 'Keep out of the night air, no matter how well you feel.' That's what my mother used to tell me when I was a boy. 'Keep out of the night air, Virgil,' she'd say. 'Keep out of the night air.'"

"I expect probably her mother told her the same thing," the nurse suggested.

"Of course she did. My grandmother——"

"Oh, I guess your *grand*mother thought so, Mr. Adams! That was when all this flat central country was swampish and hadn't been drained off yet. I guess the truth must been the swamp mosquitoes bit people and gave 'em malaria, especially before they began to put screens in their windows. Well, we got screens in these windows, and no mosquitoes are goin' to bite us; so just you be a good boy and rest your mind and go to sleep like you need to."

"Sleep?" he said. "Likely!"

He thought the night air worst of all in April; he hadn't a doubt it would kill him, he declared. "It's miraculous what the human frame *will* survive," he admitted on the last evening of that month. "But you and the doctor ought to both be taught it won't stand too dang much! You poison a man and poison and poison him with this April night air——"

"Can't poison you with much more of it," Miss Perry interrupted him, indulgently. "To-morrow it'll be May night air, and I expect that'll be a lot better for you, don't you? Now let's just sober down and be a good boy and get some nice sound sleep."

She gave him his medicine, and, having set the

glass upon the center table, returned to her cot, where, after a still interval, she snored faintly. Upon this, his expression became that of a man goaded out of overpowering weariness into irony.

"Sleep? Oh, *certainly*, thank you!"

However, he did sleep intermittently, drowsed between times, and even dreamed; but, forgetting his dreams before he opened his eyes, and having some part of him all the while aware of his discomfort, he believed, as usual, that he lay awake the whole night long. He was conscious of the city as of some single great creature resting fitfully in the dark outside his windows. It lay all round about, in the damp cover of its night cloud of smoke, and tried to keep quiet for a few hours after midnight, but was too powerful a growing thing ever to lie altogether still. Even while it strove to sleep it muttered with digestions of the day before, and these already merged with rumblings of the morrow. "Owl" cars, bringing in last passengers over distant trolley-lines, now and then howled on a curve; far-away metallic stirrings could be heard from factories in the sooty suburbs on the plain outside the city; east, west, and south, switch-engines chugged and snorted on sidings; and everywhere in the air there seemed to be a faint, voluminous hum as of innumerable wires trembling overhead to vibration of machinery underground.

In his youth Adams might have been less resentful of sounds such as these when they interfered with his night's sleep: even during an illness he might have taken some pride in them as proof of his citizenship in a "live town"; but at fifty-five he merely hated them because they kept him awake. They "pressed on his nerves," as he put it; and so did almost everything else, for that matter.

He heard the milk-wagon drive into the cross-street beneath his windows and stop at each house. The milkman carried his jars round to the "back porch," while the horse moved slowly ahead to the gate of the next customer and waited there. "He's gone into Pollocks'," Adams thought, following this progress. "I hope it'll sour on 'em before breakfast. Delivered the Andersons'. Now he's getting out ours. Listen to the darn brute! What's *he* care who wants to sleep!" His complaint was of the horse, who casually shifted weight with a clink of steel shoes on the worn brick pavement of the street, and then heartily shook himself in his harness, perhaps to dislodge a fly far ahead of its season. Light had just filmed the windows; and with that the first sparrow woke, chirped instantly, and roused neighbours in the trees of the small yard, including a loud-voiced robin. Vociferations began irregularly, but were soon unanimous.

"Sleep? Dang likely now, ain't it!"

Night sounds were becoming day sounds; the far-away hooting of freight-engines seemed brisker than an hour ago in the dark. A cheerful whistler passed the house, even more careless of sleepers than the milkman's horse had been; then a group of coloured workmen came by, and although it was impossible to be sure whether they were homeward bound from night-work or on their way to day-work, at least it was certain that they were jocose. Loose, aboriginal laughter preceded them afar, and beat on the air long after they had gone by.

The sick-room night-light, shielded from his eyes by a newspaper propped against a water-pitcher, still showed a thin glimmering that had grown offensive to Adams. In his wandering and enfeebled thoughts, which were much more often imaginings than reasonings, the attempt of the night-light to resist the dawn reminded him of something unpleasant, though he could not discover just what the unpleasant thing was. Here was a puzzle that irritated him the more because he could not solve it, yet always seemed just on the point of a solution. However, he may have lost nothing cheerful by remaining in the dark upon the matter; for if he had been a little sharper in this introspection he might have concluded that the squalor of the night-light, in its seeming effort to show against the forerunning of the sun itself, had stimulated some half-buried perception within him to sketch the painful little synopsis of an autobiography.

In spite of noises without, he drowsed again, not knowing that he did; and when he opened his eyes the nurse was just rising from her cot. He took no pleasure in the sight, it may be said. She exhibited to him a face mismodelled by sleep, and set like a clay face left on its cheek in a hot and dry studio. She was still only in part awake, however, and by the time she had extinguished the night-light and given her patient his tonic, she had recovered enough plasticity. "Well, isn't that grand! We've had another good night," she said as she departed to dress in the bathroom.

"Yes, you had another!" he retorted, though not until after she had closed the door.

Presently he heard his daughter moving about in her room across the narrow hall, and so knew that she had risen. He hoped she would come in to see him soon, for she was the one thing that didn't press on his nerves, he felt; though the thought of her hurt him, as, indeed, every thought hurt him. But it was his wife who came first.

She wore a lank cotton wrapper, and a crescent of gray hair escaped to one temple from beneath the handkerchief she had worn upon her head for the night and still retained; but she did everything possible to make her expression cheering.

"Oh, you're better again! I can see that, as soon as I look at you," she said. "Miss Perry tells me you've had another splendid night."

He made a sound of irony, which seemed to dispose unfavourably of Miss Perry, and then, in order to be more certainly intelligible, he added, "She slept well, as usual!"

But his wife's smile persisted. "It's a good sign to be cross; it means you're practically convalescent right now."

"Oh, I am, am I?"

"No doubt in the world!" she exclaimed. "Why, you're practically a well man, Virgil—all except getting your strength back, of course, and that isn't going to take long. You'll be right on your feet in a couple of weeks from now."

"Oh, I will?"

"Of course you will!" She laughed briskly, and, going to the table in the center of the room, moved his glass of medicine an inch or two, turned a book over so that it lay upon its other side, and for a few moments occupied herself with similar futilities, having taken on the air of a person who makes things neat, though she produced no such actual effect upon them. "Of course you will," she repeated, absently. "You'll be as strong as you ever were; maybe stronger." She paused for a moment, not looking at him, then added, cheerfully, "So that you can fly around and find something really good to get into."

Something important between them came near the surface here, for though she spoke with what seemed but a casual cheerfulness, there was a little betraying break in her voice, a trembling just perceptible in the utterance of the final word. And she still kept up the affectation of being helpfully preoccupied with the table, and did not look at her husband—perhaps because they had been married so many years that without looking she knew just what his expression would be, and preferred to avoid the actual sight of it as long as possible. Meanwhile, he stared hard at her, his lips beginning to move with little distortions not lacking in the pathos of a sick man's agitation.

"So that's it," he said. "That's what you're hinting at."

"'Hinting?'" Mrs. Adams looked surprised and indulgent. "Why, I'm not doing any hinting, Virgil."

"What did you say about my finding 'something good to get into?'" he asked, sharply. "Don't you call that hinting?"

Mrs. Adams turned toward him now; she came to the bedside and would have taken his hand, but he quickly moved it away from her.

"You mustn't let yourself get nervous," she said. "But of course when you get well there's only one thing to do. You mustn't go back to that old hole again."

"'Old hole?' That's what you call it, is it?" In spite of his weakness, anger made his voice strident, and upon this stimulation she spoke more urgently.

"You just mustn't go back to it, Virgil. It's not fair to any of us, and you know it isn't."

"Don't tell me what I know, please!"

She clasped her hands, suddenly carrying her urgency to plaintive entreaty. "Virgil, you *won't* go back to that hole?"

"That's a nice word to use to me!" he said. "Call a man's business a hole!"

"Virgil, if you don't owe it to me to look for something different, don't you owe it to your children? Don't tell me you won't do what we all want you to, and what you know in your heart you ought to! And if you *have* got into one of your stubborn fits and are bound to go back there for no other reason except to have your own way, don't tell me so, for I can't bear it!"

He looked up at her fiercely. "You've got a fine way to cure a sick man!" he said; but she had concluded her appeal—for that time—and instead of making any more words in the matter, let him see that there were tears in her eyes, shook her head, and left the room.

Alone, he lay breathing rapidly, his emaciated chest proving itself equal to the demands his emotion put upon it. "Fine!" he repeated, with husky indignation. "Fine way to cure a sick man! Fine!" Then, after a silence, he gave forth whispering sounds as of laughter, his expression the while remaining sore and far from humour.

"And give us our daily bread!" he added, meaning that his wife's little performance was no novelty.

CHAPTER II

IN FACT, the agitation of Mrs. Adams was genuine, but so well under her control that its traces vanished during the three short steps she took to cross the narrow hall between her husband's door and the one opposite. Her expression was matter-of-course, rather than pathetic, as she entered the pretty room where her daughter, half dressed, sat before a dressing-table and played with the reflections of a three-leafed mirror framed in blue enamel. That is, just before the moment of her mother's entrance, Alice had been playing with the mirror's reflections—posturing her arms and her expressions, clasping her hands behind her neck, and tilting back her head to foreshorten the face in a tableau conceived to represent sauciness, then one of smiling weariness, then one of scornful toleration, and all very piquant; but as the door opened she hurriedly resumed the practical, and occupied her hands in the arrangement of her plentiful brownish hair.

They were pretty hands, of a shapeliness delicate and fine. "The best things she's got!" a cold-blooded girl friend said of them, and meant to include Alice's mind and character in the implied list of possessions surpassed by the notable hands. However that may have been, the rest of her was well enough. She was often called "a right pretty girl"—temperate praise meaning a girl rather pretty than otherwise, and this she deserved, to say the least. Even in repose she deserved it, though repose was anything but her habit, being seldom seen upon her except at home. On exhibition she led a life of gestures, the unkind said to make her lovely hands more memorable; but all of her usually accompanied the gestures of the hands, the shoulders ever giving them their impulses first, and even her feet being called upon, at the same time, for eloquence.

So much liveliness took proper place as only accessory to that of the face, where her vivacity reached its climax; and it was unfortunate that an ungifted young man, new in the town, should have attempted to define the effect upon him of all this generosity of emphasis. He said that "the way she used her cute hazel eyes and the wonderful glow of her facial expression gave her a mighty spiritual quality." His actual rendition of the word was "spirichul"; but it was not his pronunciation that embalmed this outburst in the perennial laughter of Alice's girl friends; they made the misfortune far less his than hers.

Her mother comforted her too heartily, insisting that Alice had "plenty enough spiritual qualities," certainly more than possessed by the other girls who flung the phrase at her, wooden things, jealous of everything they were incapable of themselves; and then Alice, getting more championship than she sought, grew uneasy lest Mrs. Adams should repeat such defenses "outside the family"; and Mrs. Adams ended by weeping because the daughter so distrusted her intelligence. Alice frequently thought it necessary to instruct her mother.

Her morning greeting was an instruction to-day; or, rather, it was an admonition in the style of an entreaty, the more petulant as Alice thought that Mrs. Adams might have had a glimpse of the posturings to the mirror. This was a needless worry; the mother had caught a thousand such glimpses, with Alice unaware, and she thought nothing of the one just flitted.

"For heaven's sake, mama, come clear inside the room and shut the door! *Please* don't leave it open for everybody to look at me!"

"There isn't anybody to see you," Mrs. Adams explained, obeying. "Miss Perry's gone downstairs, and——"

"Mama, I heard you in papa's room," Alice said, not dropping the note of complaint. "I could hear both of you, and I don't think you ought to get poor old papa so upset—not in his present condition, anyhow."

Mrs. Adams seated herself on the edge of the bed. "He's better all the time," she said, not disturbed. "He's almost well. The doctor says so and Miss Perry says so; and if we don't get him into the right frame of mind now we never will. The first day he's outdoors he'll go back to that old hole—you'll see! And if he once does that, he'll settle down there and it'll be too late and we'll never get him out."

"Well, anyhow, I think you could use a little more tact with him."

"I do try to," the mother sighed. "It never was much use with him. I don't think you understand him as well as I do, Alice."

"There's one thing I don't understand about either of you," Alice returned, crisply. "Before people get married they can do anything they want to with each other. Why can't they do the same thing after they're married? When you and papa were young people and engaged, he'd have done anything you wanted him to. That must have been because you knew how to manage him then. Why can't you go at him the same way now?"

Mrs. Adams sighed again, and laughed a little, making no other response; but Alice persisted. "Well, *why* can't you? Why can't you ask him to do things the way you used to ask him when you were just in love with each other? Why don't you anyhow try it, mama, instead of ding-donging at him?"

"'Ding-donging at him,' Alice?" Mrs. Adams said, with a pathos somewhat emphasized. "Is that how my trying to do what I can for you strikes you?"

"Never mind that; it's nothing to hurt your feelings." Alice disposed of the pathos briskly. "Why don't you answer my question? What's the matter with using a little more tact on papa? Why can't you treat him the way you probably did when you were young people, before you were married? I never have understood why people can't do that."

"Perhaps you *will* understand some day," her mother said, gently. "Maybe you will when you've been married twenty-five years."

"You keep evading. Why don't you answer my question right straight out?"

"There are questions you can't answer to young people, Alice."

"You mean because we're too young to understand the answer? I don't see that at all. At twenty-two a girl's supposed to have some intelligence, isn't she? And intelligence is the ability to understand, isn't it? Why do I have to wait till I've lived with a man twenty-five years to understand why you can't be tactful with papa?"

"You may understand some things before that," Mrs. Adams said, tremulously. "You may understand how you hurt me sometimes. Youth can't know everything by being intelligent, and by the time you could understand the answer you're asking for you'd know it, and wouldn't need to ask. You don't understand your father, Alice; you don't know what it takes to change him when he's made up his mind to be stubborn."

Alice rose and began to get herself into a skirt. "Well, I don't think making scenes ever changes anybody," she grumbled. "I think a little jolly persuasion goes twice as far, myself."

"'A little jolly persuasion!'" Her mother turned the echo of this phrase into an ironic lament. "Yes, there was a time when I thought that, too! It didn't work; that's all."

"Perhaps you left the 'jolly' part of it out, mama."

For the second time that morning—it was now a little after seven o'clock—tears seemed about to offer their solace to Mrs. Adams. "I might have expected you to say that, Alice; you never do miss a chance," she said, gently. "It seems queer you don't some time miss just *one* chance!"

But Alice, progressing with her toilet, appeared to be little concerned. "Oh, well, I think there are better ways of managing a man than just hammering at him."

Mrs. Adams uttered a little cry of pain. "'Hammering,' Alice?"

"If you'd left it entirely to me," her daughter went on, briskly, "I believe papa'd already be willing to do anything we want him to."

"That's it; tell me I spoil everything. Well, I

won't interfere from now on, you can be sure of it."

"Please don't talk like that," Alice said, quickly. "I'm old enough to realize that papa may need pressure of all sorts; I only think it makes him more obstinate to get him cross. You probably do understand him better, but that's one thing I've found out and you haven't. There!" She gave her mother a friendly tap on the shoulder and went to the door. "I'll hop in and say hello to him now."

As she went, she continued the fastening of her blouse, and appeared in her father's room with one hand still thus engaged, but she patted his forehead with the other.

"Poor old papa-daddy!" she said, gaily. "Every time he's better somebody talks him into getting so mad he has a relapse. It's a shame!"

Her father's eyes, beneath their melancholy brows, looked up at her wistfully. "I suppose you heard your mother going for me," he said.

"I heard you going for her, too!" Alice laughed. "What was it all about?"

"Oh, the same danged old story!"

"You mean she wants you to try something new when you get well?" Alice asked, with cheerful innocence. "So we could all have a lot more money?"

At this his sorrowful forehead was more sorrowful than ever. The deep horizontal lines moved upward to a pattern of suffering so familiar to his daughter that it meant nothing to her; but he spoke quietly. "Yes; so we wouldn't have any money at all, most likely."

"Oh, no!" she laughed, and, finishing with her blouse, patted his cheeks with both hands. "Just think how many grand openings there must be for a man that knows as much as you do! I always did believe you could get rich if you only cared to, papa."

But upon his forehead the painful pattern still deepened. "Don't you think we've always had enough, the way things are, Alice?"

"Not the way things *are!*" She patted his cheeks again; laughed again. "It used to be enough, maybe—anyway we did skimp along on it—but the way things are now I expect mama's really pretty practical in her ideas, though, I think it's a shame for her to bother you about it while you're so weak. Don't you worry about it, though; just think about other things till you get strong."

"You know," he said; "you know it isn't exactly the easiest thing in the world for a man of my age to find these grand openings you speak of. And when you've passed half-way from fifty to sixty you're apt to see some risk in giving up what you know how to do and trying something new."

"My, what a frown!" she cried, blithely. "Didn't I tell you to stop thinking about it till you get *all* well?" She bent over him, giving him a gay little kiss on the bridge of his nose. "There! I must run to breakfast. Cheer up now! *Au 'voir!*" And with her pretty hand she waved further encouragement from the closing door as she departed.

Lightsomely descending the narrow stairway, she whistled as she went, her fingers drumming time on the rail; and, still whistling, she came into the dining-room, where her mother and her brother were already at the table. The brother, a thin and sallow boy of twenty, greeted her without much approval as she took her place.

"Nothing seems to trouble you!" he said.

"No; nothing much," she made airy response. "What's troubling yourself, Walter?"

"Don't let that worry you!" he returned, seeming to consider this to be repartee of an effective sort;

for he furnished a short laugh to go with it, and turned to his coffee with the manner of one who has satisfactorily closed an episode.

"Walter always seems to have so many secrets!" Alice said, studying him shrewdly, but with a friendly enough amusement in her scrutiny. "Everything he does or says seems to be acted for the benefit of some mysterious audience inside himself, and he always gets its applause. Take what he said just now: he seems to think it means something, but if it does, why, that's just another secret between him and the secret audience inside of him! We don't really know anything about Walter at all, do we, mama?"

Walter laughed again, in a manner that sustained her theory well enough; then after finishing his coffee, he took from his pocket a flattened packet in glazed blue paper; extracted with stained fingers a bent and wrinkled little cigarette, lighted it, hitched up his belted trousers with the air of a person who turns from trifles to things better worth his attention, and left the room.

Alice laughed as the door closed. "He's *all* secrets," she said. "Don't you think you really ought to know more about him, mama?"

"I'm sure he's a good boy," Mrs. Adams returned,

thoughtfully. "He's been very brave about not being able to have the advantages that are enjoyed by the boys he's grown up with. I've never heard a word of complaint from him."

"About his not being sent to college?" Alice cried. "I should think you wouldn't! He didn't even have enough ambition to finish high school!"

Mrs. Adams sighed. "It seemed to me Walter lost his ambition when nearly all the boys he'd grown up with went to Eastern schools to prepare for college, and we couldn't afford to send him. If only your father would have listened——"

Alice interrupted: "What nonsense! Walter hated books and studying, and athletics, too, for that matter. He doesn't care for anything nice that I ever heard of. What do you suppose he does like, mama? He must like something or other somewhere, but what do you suppose it is? What does he do with his time?"

"Why, the poor boy's at Lamb and Company's all day. He doesn't get through until five in the afternoon; he doesn't *have* much time."

"Well, we never have dinner until about seven, and he's always late for dinner, and goes out, heaven knows where, right afterward!" Alice shook her head. "He used to go with our friends' boys, but I don't think he does now."

"Why, how could he?" Mrs. Adams protested. "That isn't *his* fault, poor child! The boys he knew when he was younger are nearly all away at college."

"Yes, but he doesn't see anything of 'em when they're here at holiday-time or vacation. None of 'em come to the house any more."

"I suppose he's made other friends. It's natural for him to want companions, at his age."

"Yes," Alice said, with disapproving emphasis. "But who are they? I've got an idea he plays pool at some rough place down-town."

"Oh, no; I'm sure he's a steady boy," Mrs. Adams protested, but her tone was not that of thorough-going conviction, and she added, "Life might be a very different thing for him if only your father can be brought to see——"

"Never mind, mama! It isn't me that has to be convinced, you know; and we can do a lot more with papa if we just let him alone about it for a day or two. Promise me you won't say any more to him until—well, until he's able to come downstairs to table. Will you?"

Mrs. Adams bit her lip, which had begun to tremble. "I think you can trust me to know a *few* things, Alice," she said. "I'm a little older than you, you know."

"That's a good girl!" Alice jumped up, laughing. "Don't forget it's the same as a promise, and do just cheer him up a little. I'll say good-bye to him before I go out."

"Where are you going?"

"Oh, I've got lots to do. I thought I'd run out to Mildred's to see what she's going to wear to-night, and then I want to go down and buy a yard of chiffon and some narrow ribbon to make new bows for my slippers—you'll have to give me some money——"

"If he'll give it to me!" her mother lamented, as they went toward the front stairs together; but an hour later she came into Alice's room with a bill in her hand.

"He has some money in his bureau drawer," she said. "He finally told me where it was."

There were traces of emotion in her voice, and Alice, looking shrewdly at her, saw moisture in her eyes.

"Mama!" she cried. "You didn't do what you

promised me you wouldn't, did you—*not* before Miss Perry!"

"Miss Perry's getting him some broth," Mrs. Adams returned, calmly. "Besides, you're mistaken in saying I promised you anything; I said I thought you could trust me to know what is right."

"So you did bring it up again!" And Alice swung away from her, strode to her father's door, flung it open, went to him, and put a light hand soothingly over his unrelaxed forehead.

"Poor old papa!" she said. "It's a shame how everybody wants to trouble him. He shan't be bothered any more at all! He doesn't need to have everybody telling him how to get away from that old hole he's worked in so long and begin to make us all nice and rich. *He* knows how!"

Thereupon she kissed him a consoling good-bye, and made another gay departure, the charming hand again fluttering like a white butterfly in the shadow of the closing door.

CHAPTER III

MRS. ADAMS had remained in Alice's room, but her mood seemed to have changed, during her daughter's little more than momentary absence.

"What did he *say?*" she asked, quickly, and her tone was hopeful.

"'Say?'" Alice repeated, impatiently. "Why, nothing. I didn't let him. Really, mama, I think the best thing for you to do would be to just keep out of his room, because I don't believe you can go in there and not talk to him about it, and if you do talk we'll never get him to do the right thing. Never!"

The mother's response was a grieving silence; she turned from her daughter and walked to the door.

"Now, for goodness' sake!" Alice cried. "Don't go making tragedy out of my offering you a little practical advice!"

"I'm not," Mrs. Adams gulped, halting. "I'm just—just going to dust the downstairs, Alice."

And with her face still averted, she went out into the little hallway, closing the door behind her. A moment later she could be heard descending the stairs, the sound of her footsteps carrying somehow an effect of resignation.

Alice listened, sighed, and, breathing the words, "Oh, murder!" turned to cheerier matters. She put on a little apple-green turban with a dim gold band round it, and then, having shrouded the turban in a white veil, which she kept pushed up above her forehead, she got herself into a tan coat of soft cloth fashioned with rakish severity. After that, having studied herself gravely in a long glass, she took from one of the drawers of her dressing-table a black leather card-case cornered in silver filigree, but found it empty.

She opened another drawer wherein were two white pasteboard boxes of cards, the one set showing simply "Miss Adams," the other engraved in Gothic characters, "Miss Alys Tuttle Adams." The latter belonged to Alice's "Alys" period—most girls go through it; and Alice must have felt that she had graduated, for, after frowning thoughtfully at the exhibit this morning, she took the box with its contents, and let the white shower fall from her fingers into the waste-basket beside her small desk. She replenished the card-case from the "Miss Adams" box; then, having found a pair of fresh white gloves, she tucked an ivory-topped Malacca walking-stick under her arm and set forth.

She went down the stairs, buttoning her gloves and still wearing the frown with which she had put "Alys" finally out of her life. She descended slowly, and paused on the lowest step, looking about her with an expression that needed but a slight deepening to betoken bitterness. Its connection with her dropping "Alys" forever was slight, however.

The small frame house, about fifteen years old, was already inclining to become a new Colonial relic. The Adamses had built it, moving into it from the "Queen Anne" house they had rented until they took this step in fashion. But fifteen years is a long time to stand still in the midland country, even for a house, and this one was lightly made, though the Adamses had not realized how flimsily until they had lived in it for some time. "Solid, compact, and convenient" were the instructions to the architect; and he had made it compact successfully. Alice, pausing at the foot of the stairway, was at the same time fairly in the "living-room," for the only separation between the "living room" and the hall was a demarcation suggested to willing imaginations by a pair of wooden columns painted white. These columns, pine under the paint, were bruised and chipped at the base; one of them showed a crack that threatened to become a split; the "hard-wood" floor had become uneven; and in a corner the walls apparently failed of solidity, where the wall-paper had declined to accompany some staggerings of the plaster beneath it.

The furniture was in great part an accumulation begun with the wedding gifts; though some of it was older, two large patent rocking-chairs and a foot-stool having belonged to Mrs. Adams's mother in the days of hard brown plush and veneer. For decoration there were pictures and vases. Mrs. Adams had always been fond of vases, she said, and every year her husband's Christmas present to her was a vase of one sort or another—whatever the clerk showed him, marked at about twelve or fourteen dollars. The pictures were some of them etchings framed in gilt: Rheims, Canterbury, schooners grouped against a wharf; and Alice could remember how, in her childhood, her father sometimes pointed out the watery reflections in this last as very fine. But it was a long time since he had shown interest in such things—"or in anything much," as she thought.

Other pictures were two water-colours in baroque frames; one being the Amalfi monk on a pergola wall, while the second was a yard-wide display of iris blossoms, painted by Alice herself at fourteen, as a birthday gift to her mother. Alice's glance paused upon it now with no great pride, but showed more approval of an enormous photograph of the Colosseum. This she thought of as "the only good thing in the room"; it possessed and bestowed distinction, she felt; and she did not regret having won her struggle to get it hung in its conspicuous place of honour over the mantelpiece. Formerly that place had been held for years by a steel-engraving, an accurate representation of the Suspension Bridge at Niagara Falls. It was almost as large as its successor, the "Colosseum," and it had been presented to Mr. Adams by colleagues in his department at Lamb and Company's. Adams had shown some feeling when Alice began to urge its removal to obscurity in the "upstairs hall"; he even resisted for several days after she had the "Colosseum" charged to him, framed in oak, and sent to the house. She cheered him up, of course, when he gave way; and her heart never misgave her that there might be a doubt which of the two pictures was the more dismaying.

Over the pictures, the vases, the old brown plush rocking-chairs and the stool, over the three gilt chairs, over the new chintz-covered easy chair and the gray velure sofa—over everything everywhere, was the familiar coating of smoke grime. It had worked into every fibre of the lace curtains, dingying them to an unpleasant gray; it lay on the window-sills and it dimmed the glass panes; it covered the walls, covered the ceiling, and was smeared darker and thicker in all corners. Yet here was no fault of housewifery; the curse could not be lifted, as the ingrained smudges permanent on the once white woodwork proved. The grime was perpetually renewed; scrubbing only ground it in.

This particular ugliness was small part of Alice's discontent, for though the coating grew a little deeper each year she was used to it. Moreover, she knew that she was not likely to find anything better in a thousand miles, so long as she kept to cities, and that none of her friends, however opulent, had any advantage of her here. Indeed, throughout all the great soft-coal country, people who consider themselves comparatively poor may find this consolation: cleanliness has been added to the virtues and beatitudes that money can not buy.

Alice brightened a little as she went forward to the front door, and she brightened more when the spring breeze met her there. Then all depression left her as she walked down the short brick path to the sidewalk, looked up and down the street, and saw how bravely the maple shade-trees, in spite of the black powder they breathed, were flinging out their thousands of young green particles overhead.

She turned north, treading the new little shadows on the pavement briskly, and, having finished buttoning her gloves, swung down her Malacca stick from under her arm to let it tap a more leisurely accompaniment to her quick, short step. She had to step quickly if she was to get anywhere; for the closeness of her skirt, in spite of its little length, permitted no natural stride; but she was pleased to be impeded, these brevities forming part of her show of fashion.

Other pedestrians found them not without charm, though approval may have been lacking here and there; and at the first crossing Alice suffered what she might have accounted an actual injury, had she allowed herself to be so sensitive. An elderly woman in fussy black silk stood there, waiting for a street-car; she was all of a globular modelling, with a face patterned like a frost-bitten peach; and that the approaching gracefulness was uncongenial she naïvely made too evident. Her round, wan eyes seemed roused to bitter life as they rose from the curved high heels of the buckled slippers to the tight little skirt, and thence with startled ferocity to the Malacca cane, which plainly appeared to her as a decoration not more astounding than it was insulting.

Perceiving that the girl was bowing to her, the globular lady hurriedly made shift to alter her injurious expression. "Good morning, Mrs. Dowling," Alice said, gravely. Mrs. Dowling returned the salutation with a smile as convincingly benevolent as the ghastly smile upon a Santa Claus face; and then, while Alice passed on, exploded toward her a single compacted breath through tightened lips.

The sound was eloquently audible, though Mrs. Dowling remained unaware that in this or any manner whatever she had shed a light upon her thoughts; for it was her lifelong innocent conviction that other people saw her only as she wished to be seen, and heard from her only what she intended to be heard. At home it was always her husband who pulled down the shades of their bedroom window.

Alice looked serious for a few moments after the little encounter, then found some consolation in the behaviour of a gentleman of forty or so who was coming toward her. Like Mrs. Dowling, he had begun to show consciousness of Alice's approach while she was yet afar off; but his tokens were of a kind pleasanter to her. He was like Mrs. Dowling again, however, in his conception that Alice would not realize the significance of what he did. He passed his hand over his neck-scarf to see that it lay neatly to his collar, smoothed a lapel of his coat, and adjusted his hat, seeming to be preoccupied the while with problems that kept his eyes to the pavement; then, as he came within a few feet of her, he looked up, as in a surprised recognition almost dramatic, smiled winningly, lifted his hat decisively, and carried it to the full arm's length.

Alice's response was all he could have asked. The cane in her right hand stopped short in its swing, while her left hand moved in a pretty gesture as if an impulse carried it toward the heart; and she smiled, with her under lip caught suddenly between her teeth. Months ago she had seen an actress use this smile in a play, and it came perfectly to Alice now, without conscious direction, it had been so well acquired; but the pretty hand's little impulse toward the heart was an original bit all her own, on the spur of the moment.

The gentleman went on, passing from her forward vision as he replaced his hat. Of himself he was nothing to Alice, except for the gracious circumstance that he had shown strong consciousness of a pretty girl. He was middle-aged, substantial, a family man, securely married; and Alice had with him one of those long acquaintances that never become emphasized by so much as five minutes of talk; yet for this inconsequent meeting she had enacted a little part like a fragment in a pantomime of Spanish wooing.

It was not for him—not even to impress him, except as a messenger. Alice was herself almost unaware of her thought, which was one of the running thousands of her thoughts that took no deliberate form in words. Nevertheless, she had it, and it was the impulse of all her pretty bits of pantomime when she met other acquaintances who made their appreciation visible, as this substantial gentleman did. In Alice's unworded thought, he was to be thus encouraged as in some measure a champion to speak well of her to the world; but more than this: he was to tell some magnificent unknown bachelor how wonderful, how mysterious, she was.

She hastened on gravely, a little stirred reciprocally with the supposed stirrings in the breast of that shadowy ducal mate, who must be somewhere "waiting," or perhaps already seeking her; for she more often thought of herself as "waiting" while he sought her; and sometimes this view of things became so definite that it shaped into a murmur on her lips. "Waiting. Just waiting." And she might add, "For him!" Then, being twenty-two, she was apt to conclude the mystic interview by laughing at herself, though not without a continued wistfulness.

She came to a group of small coloured children playing waywardly in a puddle at the mouth of a muddy alley; and at sight of her they gave over their pastime in order to stare. She smiled brilliantly upon them, but they were too struck with wonder to comprehend that the manifestation was friendly; and as Alice picked her way in a little detour to keep from the mud, she heard one of them say, "Lady got cane! Jeez'!"

She knew that many coloured children use impieties familiarly, and she was not startled. She was disturbed, however, by an unfavourable hint in the speaker's tone. He was six, probably, but the sting of a criticism is not necessarily allayed by knowledge of its ignoble source, and Alice had already begun to feel a slight uneasiness about her cane. Mrs. Dowling's stare had been strikingly projected at it; other women more than merely glanced, their brows and lips contracting impulsively; and Alice was aware that one or two of them frankly halted as soon as she had passed.

She had seen in several magazines pictures of ladies with canes, and on that account she had bought this one, never questioning that fashion is recognized, even in the provinces, as soon as beheld. On the contrary, tnese staring women obviously failed to realize that what they were being shown was not an eccentric outburst, but the bright harbinger of an illustrious mode. Alice had applied a bit of artificial pigment to her lips and cheeks before she set forth this morning; she did not need it, having a ready colour of her own, which now mounted high with annoyance.

Then a splendidly shining closed black automobile, with windows of polished glass, came silently down the street toward her. Within it, as in a luxurious little apartment, three comely ladies in mourning sat and gossiped; but when they saw Alice they clutched one another. They instantly recovered, bowing to her solemnly as they were borne by, yet were not gone from her sight so swiftly but the edge of her side glance caught a flash of teeth in mouths suddenly opened, and the dark glisten of black gloves again clutching to share mirth.

The colour that outdid the rouge on Alice's cheek extended its area and grew warmer as she realized how all too cordial had been her nod and smile to these humorous ladies. But in their identity lay a significance causing her a sharper smart, for they were of the family of that Lamb, chief of Lamb and Company, who had employed her father since before she was born.

"And know his salary! They'd be *sure* to find out about that!" was her thought, coupled with another bitter one to the effect that they had probably made instantaneous financial estimates of what she wore—though certainly her walking-stick had most fed their hilarity.

She tucked it under her arm, not swinging it again; and her breath became quick and irregular as emotion beset her. She had been enjoying her walk, but within the space of the few blocks she had gone since she met the substantial gentleman, she found that more than the walk was spoiled: suddenly her life seemed to be spoiled, too; though she did not view the ruin with complaisance. These Lamb women thought her and her cane ridiculous, did they? she said to herself. That was their parvenu blood: to think because a girl's father worked for their grandfather she had no right to be rather striking in style, especially when the striking *was* her style. Probably all the other girls and women would agree with them and would laugh at her when they got together, and, what might be fatal, would try to make all the men think her a silly pretender. Men were just like sheep, and nothing was easier than for women to set up as shepherds and pen them in a fold. "To keep out outsiders," Alice thought. "And make 'em believe I *am* an outsider. What's the use of living?"

All seemed lost when a trim young man appeared, striding out of a cross-street not far before her, and, turning at the corner, came toward her. Visibly, he slackened his gait to lengthen the time of his approach, and, as he was a stranger to her, no motive could be ascribed to him other than a wish to have a longer time to look at her.

She lifted a pretty hand to a pin at her throat, bit her lip—not with the smile, but mysteriously—and at the last instant before her shadow touched the stranger, let her eyes gravely meet his. A moment later, having arrived before the house which was her destination, she halted at the entrance to a driveway leading through fine lawns to the intentionally important mansion. It was a pleasant and impressive place to be seen entering, but Alice did not enter at once. She paused, examining a tiny bit of mortar which the masons had forgotten to scrape from a brick in one of the massive gate-posts. She frowned at this tiny defacement, and with an air of annoyance scraped it away, using the ferrule of her cane—an act of fastidious proprietorship. If any one had looked back over his shoulder he would not have doubted that she lived there.

Alice did not turn to see whether anything of the

sort happened or not, but she may have surmised that it did. At all events, it was with an invigorated step that she left the gateway behind her and went cheerfully up the drive to the house of her friend Mildred.

CHAPTER IV

ADAMS had a restless morning, and toward noon he asked Miss Perry to call his daughter; he wished to say something to her.

"I thought I heard her leaving the house a couple of hours ago—maybe longer," the nurse told him. "I'll go see." And she returned from the brief errand, her impression confirmed by information from Mrs. Adams. "Yes. She went up to Miss Mildred Palmer's to see what she's going to wear to-night."

Adams looked at Miss Perry wearily, but remained passive, making no inquiries; for he was long accustomed to what seemed to him a kind of jargon among ladies, which became the more incomprehensible when they tried to explain it. A man's best course, he had found, was just to let it go as so much sound. His sorrowful eyes followed the nurse as she went back to her rocking-chair by the window; and her placidity showed him that there was no mystery for her in the fact that Alice walked two miles to ask so simple a question when there was a telephone in the house. Obviously Miss Perry also comprehended why Alice thought it important to know what Mildred meant to wear. Adams understood why Alice should be concerned with what she herself wore—"to look neat and tidy and at her best, why, of course she'd want to," he thought—but he realized that it was forever beyond him to understand why the clothing of other people had long since become an absorbing part of her life.

Her excursion this morning was no novelty; she was continually going to see what Mildred meant to wear, or what some other girl meant to wear; and when Alice came home from wherever other girls or women had been gathered, she always hurried to her mother with earnest descriptions of the clothing she had seen. At such times, if Adams was present, he might recognize "organdie," or "taffeta," or "chiffon," as words defining certain textiles, but the rest was too technical for him, and he was like a dismal boy at a sermon, just waiting for it to get itself finished. Not the least of the mystery was his wife's interest: she was almost indifferent about her own clothes, and when she consulted Alice about them spoke hurriedly and with an air of apology;

but when Alice described other people's clothes, Mrs. Adams listened as eagerly as the daughter talked.

"There they go!" he muttered to-day, a moment after he heard the front door closing, a sound recognizable throughout most of the thinly built house. Alice had just returned, and Mrs. Adams called to her from the upper hallway, not far from Adams's door

"What did she *say?*"

"She was sort of snippy about it," Alice returned, ascending the stairs. "She gets that way sometimes, and pretended she hadn't made up her mind, but I'm pretty sure it'll be the maize Georgette with Malines flounces."

"Didn't you say she wore that at the Pattersons'?" Mrs. Adams inquired, as Alice arrived at the top of the stairs. "And didn't you tell me she wore it again at the——"

"Certainly not," Alice interrupted, rather petulantly. "She's never worn it but once, and of course she wouldn't want to wear anything to-night that people have seen her in a lot."

Miss Perry opened the door of Adams's room and stepped out. "Your father wants to know if you'll come and see him a minute, Miss Adams."

"Poor old thing! Of course!" Alice exclaimed, and went quickly into the room, Miss Perry remaining outside. "What's the matter, papa? Getting awful sick of lying on his tired old back, I expect."

"I've had kind of a poor morning," Adams said, as she patted his hand comfortingly. "I been thinking——"

"Didn't I tell you not to?" she cried, gaily. "Of course you'll have poor times when you go and do just exactly what I say you mustn't. You stop thinking this very minute!"

He smiled ruefully, closing his eyes; was silent for a moment, then asked her to sit beside the bed. "I been thinking of something I wanted to say," he added.

"What like, papa?"

"Well, it's nothing—much," he said, with something deprecatory in his tone, as if he felt vague impulses toward both humour and apology. "I just thought maybe I ought to've said more to you some time or other about—well, about the way things *are*, down at Lamb and Company's, for instance."

"Now, papa!" She leaned forward in the chair she had taken, and pretended to slap his hand crossly. "Isn't that exactly what I said you couldn't think one single think about till you get *all* well?"

"Well——" he said, and went on slowly, not looking at her, but at the ceiling. "I just thought maybe it wouldn't been any harm if some time or other I told you something about the way they sort of depend on me down there."

"Why don't they show it, then?" she asked, quickly. "That's just what mama and I have been feeling so much; they don't appreciate you."

"Why, yes, they do," he said. "Yes, they do. They began h'isting my salary the second year I went in there, and they've h'isted it a little every two years all the time I've worked for 'em. I've been head of the sundries department for seven years now, and I could hardly have more authority in that department unless I was a member of the firm itself."

"Well, why don't they make you a member of the firm? That's what they ought to've done! Yes, and long ago!"

Adams laughed, but sighed with more heartiness than he had laughed. "They call me their 'oldest stand-by' down there." He laughed again, apologetically, as if to excuse himself for taking a little pride in this title. "Yes, sir; they say I'm their 'oldest stand-by'; and I guess they know they can count on my department's turning in as good a report as they look for, at the end of every month; but they don't have to take a man into the firm to get him to do my work, dearie."

"But you said they depended on you, papa."

"So they do; but of course not so's they couldn't get along without me." He paused, reflecting. "I don't just seem to know how to put it—I mean how to put what I started out to say. I kind of wanted to tell you—well, it seems funny to me, these last few years, the way your mother's taken to feeling about it. I'd like to see a better established wholesale drug business than Lamb and Company this side the Alleghanies—I don't say bigger, I say better established—and it's kind of funny for a man that's been with a business like that as long as I have to hear it called a 'hole.' It's kind of funny when you think, yourself, you've done pretty fairly well in a business like that, and the men at the head of it seem to think so, too, and put your salary just about as high as anybody could consider customary—well, what I mean, Alice, it's kind of funny to have your mother think it's mostly just—mostly just a failure, so to speak."

His voice had become tremulous in spite of him; and this sign of weakness and emotion had sufficient effect upon Alice. She bent over him suddenly, with her arm about him and her cheek against his. "Poor papa!" she murmured. "Poor papa!"

"No, no," he said. "I didn't mean anything to trouble you. I just thought——" He hesitated. "I just wondered—I thought maybe it wouldn't be any harm if I said something about how things *are* down there. I got to thinking maybe you didn't understand it's a pretty good place. They're fine people to work for; and they've always seemed to think something of me;—the way they took Walter on, for instance, soon as I asked 'em, last year. Don't you think that looked a good deal as if they thought something of me, Alice?"

"Yes, papa," she said, not moving.

"And the work's right pleasant," he went on. "Mighty nice boys in our department, Alice. Well, they are in all the departments, for that matter. We have a good deal of fun down there some days."

She lifted her head. "More than you do at home 'some days,' I expect, papa!" she said.

He protested feebly. "Now, I didn't mean that—I didn't want to trouble you——"

She looked at him through winking eyelashes. "I'm sorry I called it a 'hole,' papa."

"No, no," he protested, gently. "It was your mother said that."

"No. I did, too."

"Well, if you did, it was only because you'd heard her."

She shook her head, then kissed him. "I'm going to talk to her," she said, and rose decisively.

But at this, her father's troubled voice became quickly louder: "You better let her alone. I just wanted to have a little talk with you. I didn't mean to start any—your mother won't——"

"Now, papa!" Alice spoke cheerfully again, and smiled upon him. "I want you to quit worrying! Everything's going to be all right and nobody's going to bother you any more about anything. You'll see!"

She carried her smile out into the hall, but after she had closed the door her face was all pity; and her mother, waiting for her in the opposite room, spoke sympathetically.

"What's the matter, Alice? What did he say that's upset you?"

"Wait a minute, mama." Alice found a handkerchief, used it for eyes and suffused nose, gulped, then suddenly and desolately sat upon the bed. "Poor, poor, *poor* papa!" she whispered.

"Why?" Mrs. Adams inquired, mildly. "What's the matter with him? Sometimes you act as if he weren't getting well. What's he been talking about?"

"Mama—well, I think I'm pretty selfish. Oh, I do!"

"Did he say you were?"

"Papa? No, indeed! What I mean is, maybe we're both a little selfish to try to make him go out and hunt around for something new."

Mrs. Adams looked thoughtful. "Oh, that's what he was up to!"

"Mama, I think we ought to give it up. I didn't dream it had really hurt him."

"Well, doesn't he hurt us?"

"Never that I know of, mama."

"I don't mean by *saying* things," Mrs. Adams explained, impatiently. "There are more ways than that of hurting people. When a man sticks to a salary that doesn't provide for his family, isn't that hurting them?"

"Oh, it 'provides' for us well enough, mama. We have what we need—if I weren't so extravagant. Oh, *I* know I am!"

But at this admission her mother cried out sharply. "'Extravagant!' You haven't one tenth of what the other girls you go with have. And you *can't* have what you ought to as long as he doesn't get out of that horrible place. It provides bare food and shelter for us, but what's that?"

"I don't think we ought to try any more to change him."

"You don't?" Mrs. Adams came and stood before her. "Listen, Alice: your father's asleep; that's his trouble, and he's got to be waked up. He doesn't know that things have changed. When you and Walter were little children we did have enough—at least it seemed to be about as much as most of the people we knew. But the town isn't what it was in those days, and times aren't what they were then, and these fearful *prices* aren't the old prices. Everything else but your father has changed, and all the time he's stood still. He doesn't know it; he thinks because they've given him a hundred dollars more every two years he's quite a prosperous man! And he thinks that because his children cost him more than he and I cost our parents he gives them—enough!"

"But Walter——" Alice faltered. "Walter doesn't cost him anything at all any more." And she concluded, in a stricken voice, "It's all—me!"

"Why shouldn't it be?" her mother cried. "You're young—you're just at the time when your life should be fullest of good things and happiness. Yet what do you get?"

Alice's lip quivered; she was not unsusceptible to such an appeal, but she contrived the semblance of a protest. "I don't have such a bad time—not a good *deal* of the time, anyhow. I've got a good *many* of the things other girls have——"

"You have?" Mrs. Adams was piteously satirical. "I suppose you've got a limousine to go to that dance to-night? I suppose you've only got to call a florist and tell him to send you some orchids? I suppose you've——"

But Alice interrupted this list. Apparently in a single instant all emotion left her, and she became businesslike, as one in the midst of trifles reminded of really serious matters. She got up from the bed and went to the door of the closet where she kept her dresses. "Oh, see here," she said, briskly. "I've decided to wear my white organdie if you could put in a new lining for me. I'm afraid it'll take you nearly all afternoon."

She brought forth the dress, displayed it upon the bed, and Mrs. Adams examined it attentively.

"Do you think you could get it done, mama?"

"I don't see why not," Mrs. Adams answered, passing a thoughtful hand over the fabric. "It oughtn't to take more than four or five hours."

"It's a shame to have you sit at the machine that long," Alice said, absently, adding, "And I'm sure we ought to let papa alone. Let's just give it up, mama."

Mrs. Adams continued her thoughtful examination of the dress. "Did you buy the chiffon and ribbon, Alice?"

"Yes. I'm sure we oughtn't to talk to him about it any more, mama."

"Well, we'll see."

"Let's both agree that we'll *never* say another single word to him about it," said Alice. "It'll be a great deal better if we just let him make up his mind for himself."

CHAPTER V

WITH this, having more immediately practical questions before them, they dropped the subject, to bend their entire attention upon the dress; and when the lunch-gong sounded downstairs Alice was still sketching repairs and alterations. She continued to sketch them, not heeding the summons.

"I suppose we'd better go down to lunch," Mrs. Adams said, absently. "She's at the gong again."

In a minute, mama. Now about the sleeves——" And she went on with her planning. Unfortunately the gong was inexpressive of the mood of the person who beat upon it. It consisted of three little metal bowls upon a string; they were unequal in size, and, upon being tapped with a padded stick, gave forth vibrations almost musically pleasant. It was Alice who had substituted this contrivance for the brass "dinner-bell" in use throughout her childhood; and neither she nor the others of her family realized that the substitution of sweeter sounds had made the life of that household more difficult. In spite of dismaying increases in wages, the Adamses still strove to keep a cook; and, as they were unable to pay the higher rates demanded by a good one, what they usually had was a whimsical coloured woman of nomadic impulses. In the hands of such a person the old-fashioned "dinner-bell" was satisfying; life could instantly be made intolerable for any one dawdling on his way to a meal; the bell was capable of every desirable profanity and left nothing bottled up in the breast of the ringer. But the chamois-covered stick might whack upon Alice's little Chinese bowls for a considerable length of time and produce no great effect of urgency upon a hearer, nor any other effect, except fury in the cook. The ironical impossibility of expressing indignation otherwise than by sounds of gentle harmony proved exasperating; the cook was apt to become surcharged, so that explosive resignations, never rare, were somewhat more frequent after the introduction of the gong.

Mrs. Adams took this increased frequency to be only another manifestation of the inexplicable new difficulties that beset all housekeeping. You paid a cook double what you had paid one a few years before; and the cook knew half as much of cookery, and had no gratitude. The more you gave these people, it seemed, the worse they behaved—a condition not to be remedied by simply giving them less, because you couldn't even get the worst unless you paid her what she demanded. Nevertheless, Mrs. Adams remained fitfully an optimist in the matter. Brought up by her mother to speak of a female cook as "the girl," she had been instructed by Alice to drop that definition in favour of one not an improvement in accuracy: "the maid." Almost always, during the first day or so after every cook came, Mrs. Adams would say, at intervals, with an air of triumph: "I believe—of course it's a little soon to be sure—but I do really believe this new maid is the treasure we've been looking for so long!" Much in the same way that Alice dreamed of a mysterious perfect mate for whom she "waited," her mother had a fairy theory that hidden somewhere in the universe there was the treasure, the perfect "maid," who would come and cook in the Adamses' kitchen, not four days or four weeks, but forever.

The present incumbent was not she. Alice, profoundly interested herself, kept her mother likewise so preoccupied with the dress that they were but vaguely conscious of the gong's soft warnings, though these were repeated and protracted unusually. Finally the sound of a hearty voice, independent and enraged, reached the pair. It came from the hall below.

"I says goo'-*bye!*" it called. "Da'ss all!"

Then the front door slammed.

"Why, what——" Mrs. Adams began.

They went down hurriedly to find out. Miss Perry informed them.

"I couldn't make her listen to reason," she said. "She rang the gong four or five times and got to talking to herself; and then she went up to her room and packed her bag. I told her she had no business to go out the front door, anyhow."

Mrs. Adams took the news philosophically. "I thought she had something like that in her eye when I paid her this morning, and I'm not surprised. Well, we won't let Mr. Adams know anything's the matter till I get a new one."

They lunched upon what the late incumbent had left chilling on the table, and then Mrs. Adams prepared to wash the dishes; she would "have them done in a jiffy," she said, cheerfully. But it was Alice who washed the dishes.

"I *don't* like to have you do that, Alice," her mother protested, following her into the kitchen. "It roughens the hands, and when a girl has hands like yours——"

"I know, mama." Alice looked troubled, but shook her head. "It can't be helped this time; you'll need every minute to get that dress done."

Mrs. Adams went away lamenting, while Alice, no expert, began to splash the plates and cups and saucers in the warm water. After a while, as she worked, her eyes grew dreamy: she was making little gay-coloured pictures of herself, unfounded prophecies of how she would look and what would happen to her that evening. She saw herself, charming and demure, wearing a fluffy idealization of the dress her mother now determinedly struggled with upstairs; she saw herself framed in a garlanded archway, the entrance to a ballroom, and saw the people on the shining floor turning dramatically to look at her; then from all points a rush of young men shouting for dances with her; and she constructed a superb stranger, tall, dark, masterfully smiling, who swung her out of the clamouring group as the music began. She saw herself dancing with him, saw the half-troubled smile she would give him; and she accurately smiled that smile as she rinsed the knives and forks.

These hopeful fragments of drama were not to be realized, she knew; but she played that they were true, and went on creating them. In all of them she wore or carried flowers—her mother's sorrow for her in this detail but made it the more important—and she saw herself glamorous with orchids; discarded these for an armful of long-stemmed, heavy roses; tossed them away for a great bouquet of white camellias; and so wandered down a lengthening hothouse gallery of floral beauty, all costly and beyond her reach except in such a wistful day-dream. And upon her present whole horizon, though she searched it earnestly, she could discover no figure of a sender of flowers.

Out of her fancies the desire for flowers to wear that night emerged definitely and became poignant; she began to feel that it might be particularly important to have them. "This might be the night!" She was still at the age to dream that the night of any dance may be the vital point in destiny. No matter how commonplace or disappointing other dance nights have been this one may bring the great meeting. The unknown magnifico may be there.

Alice was almost unaware of her own reveries in which this being appeared—reveries often so transitory that they developed and passed in a few seconds. And in some of them the being was not wholly a stranger; there were moments when he seemed to be composed of recognizable fragments of young men she knew—a smile she had liked, from one; the figure of another, the hair of another—and sometimes she thought he might be concealed, so to say, within the person of an actual acquaintance, someone she had never suspected of being the right seeker for her, someone who had never suspected that it was she who "waited" for him. Anything might reveal them to each other: a look, a turn of the head, a singular word—perhaps some flowers upon her breast or in her hand.

She wiped the dishes slowly, concluding the operation by dropping a saucer upon the floor and dreamily sweeping the fragments under the stove. She sighed and replaced the broom near a window, letting her glance wander over the small yard outside. The grass, repulsively besooted to the colour of coal-smoke all winter, had lately come to life again and now sparkled with green, in the midst of which a tiny shot of blue suddenly fixed her absent eyes. They remained upon it for several moments, becoming less absent.

It was a violet.

Alice ran upstairs, put on her hat, went outdoors and began to search out the violets. She found twenty-two, a bright omen—since the number was that of her years—but not enough violets. There were no more; she had ransacked every foot of the yard.

She looked dubiously at the little bunch in her hand, glanced at the lawn next door, which offered no favourable prospect; then went thoughtfully into the house, left her twenty-two violets in a bowl of water, and came quickly out again, her brow marked with a frown of decision. She went to a trolley-line and took a car to the outskirts of the city where a new park had been opened.

Here she resumed her search, but it was not an easily rewarded one, and for an hour after her arrival she found no violets. She walked conscientiously over the whole stretch of meadow, her eyes roving discontentedly; there was never a blue dot in the groomed expanse; but at last, as she came near the borders of an old grove of trees, left untouched by the municipal landscapers, the little flowers appeared, and she began to gather them. She picked them carefully, loosening the earth round each tiny plant, so as to bring the roots up with it, that it might live the longer; and she had brought a napkin, which she drenched at a hydrant, and kept loosely wrapped about the stems of her collection.

The turf was too damp for her to kneel; she worked patiently, stooping from the waist; and when she got home in a drizzle of rain at five o'clock her knees were tremulous with strain, her back ached, and she was tired all over, but she had three hundred violets. Her mother moaned when Alice showed them to her, fragrant in a basin of water.

"Oh, you *poor* child! To think of your having to work so hard to get things that other girls only need lift their little fingers for!"

"Never mind," said Alice, huskily. "I've got 'em and I *am* going to have a good time to-night!"

"You've just got to!" Mrs. Adams agreed, intensely sympathetic. "The Lord knows you deserve to, after picking all these violets, poor thing, and He wouldn't be mean enough to keep you from it. I may have to get dinner before I finish the dress, but I can get it done in a few minutes afterward, and it's going to look right pretty. Don't you worry about *that!* And with all these lovely violets——"

"I wonder——" Alice began, paused, then went on, fragmentarily: "I suppose—well, I wonder—do you suppose it would have been better policy to have told Walter before——"

"No," said her mother. "It would only have given him longer to grumble."

"But he might——"

"Don't worry," Mrs. Adams reassured her. "He'll be a little cross, but he won't be stubborn; just let me talk to him and don't you say anything at all, no matter what *he* says."

These references to Walter concerned some necessary manœuvres which took place at dinner, and were conducted by the mother, Alice having accepted her advice to sit in silence. Mrs. Adams began by laughing cheerfully. "I wonder how much longer it took me to cook this dinner than it does Walter to eat it?" she said. "Don't gobble, child! There's no hurry."

In contact with his own family Walter was no squanderer of words. "Is for me," he said. "Got date."

"I know you have, but there's plenty of time."

He smiled in benevolent pity. "*You* know, do you? If you made any coffee—don't bother if you didn't. Get some down-town." He seemed about to rise and depart; whereupon Alice, biting her lip, sent a panic-stricken glance at her mother.

But Mrs. Adams seemed not at all disturbed; and laughed again. "Why, what nonsense, Walter! I'll bring your coffee in a few minutes, but we're going to have dessert first."

"What sort?"

"Some lovely peaches."

"Doe' want 'ny canned peaches," said the frank Walter, moving back his chair. "G'-night."

"Walter! It doesn't begin till about nine o'clock at the earliest."

He paused, mystified. "What doesn't?"

"The dance."

"What dance?"

"Why, Mildred Palmer's dance, of course."

Walter laughed briefly. "What's that to me?"

"Why, you haven't forgotten it's *to-night*, have you?" Mrs. Adams cried. "What a boy!"

"I told you a week ago I wasn't going to that ole dance," he returned, frowning. "You heard me."

"Walter!" she exclaimed. "Of *course* you're going. I got your clothes all out this afternoon, and brushed them for you. They'll look very nice, and——"

"They won't look nice on *me*," he interrupted. "Got date down-town, I tell you."

"But of course you'll——"

"See here!" Walter said, decisively. "Don't get any wrong ideas in your head. I'm just as liable to go up to that ole dance at the Palmers' as I am to eat a couple of barrels of broken glass."

"But, Walter——"

Walter was beginning to be seriously annoyed. "Don't 'Walter' me! I'm no s'ciety snake. I wouldn't jazz with that Palmer crowd if they coaxed me with diamonds."

"Walter——"

"Didn't I tell you it's no use to 'Walter' me?" he demanded.

"My dear child——"

"Oh, Glory!"

At this Mrs. Adams abandoned her air of amusement, looked hurt, and glanced at the demure Miss Perry across the table. "I'm afraid Miss Perry won't think you have very good manners, Walter."

"You're right she won't," he agreed, grimly.

"Not if I haf to hear any more about me goin' to——"

But his mother interrupted him with some asperity: "It seems very strange that you always object to going anywhere among *our* friends, Walter."

"*Your* friends!" he said, and, rising from his chair, gave utterance to an ironical laugh strictly monosyllabic. "*Your* friends!" he repeated, going to the door. "Oh, yes! Certainly! Good-*night!*"

And looking back over his shoulder to offer a final brief view of his derisive face, he took himself out of the room.

Alice gasped: "Mama——"

"I'll stop him!" her mother responded, sharply; and hurried after the truant, catching him at the front door with his hat and raincoat on.

"Walter——"

"Told you had a date down-town," he said, gruffly; and would have opened the door, but she caught his arm and detained him.

"Walter, please come back and finish your dinner. When I take all the trouble to cook it for you, I think you might at least——"

"Now, now!" he said. "That isn't what you're

up to. You don't want to make me eat; you want to make me listen."

"Well, you *must* listen!" She retained her grasp upon his arm, and made it tighter. "Walter, please!" she entreated, her voice becoming tremulous. "*Please* don't make me so much trouble!"

He drew back from her as far as her hold upon him permitted, and looked at her sharply. "Look here!" he said. "I *get* you, all right! What's the matter of Alice goin' to that party by herself?"

"She just *can't!*"

"Why not?"

"It makes things too *mean* for her, Walter. All the other girls have somebody to depend on after they get there."

"Well, why doesn't she have somebody?" he asked, testily. "Somebody besides *me*, I mean! Why hasn't somebody asked her to go? She ought to be *that* popular, anyhow, I sh'd think—she *tries* enough!"

"I don't understand how you can be so hard," his mother wailed, huskily. "You know why they don't run after her the way they do the other girls she goes with, Walter. It's because we're poor, and she hasn't got any background."

"'Background?'" Walter repeated. "'Background?' What kind of talk is that?"

"You *will* go with her to-night, Walter?" his mother pleaded, not stopping to enlighten him. "You don't understand how hard things are for her and how brave she is about them, or you *couldn't* be so selfish! It'd be more than I can bear to see her disappointed to-night! She went clear out to Belleview Park this afternoon, Walter, and spent hours and hours picking violets to wear. You *will*——"

Walter's heart was not iron, and the episode of the violets may have reached it. "Oh, *blub!*" he said, and flung his soft hat violently at the wall.

His mother beamed with delight. "*That's* a good boy, darling! You'll never be sorry you——"

"Cut it out," he requested. "If I take her, will you pay for a taxi?"

"Oh, Walter!" And again Mrs. Adams showed distress. "Couldn't you?"

"No, I couldn't; I'm not goin' to throw away my good money like that, and you can't tell what time o' night it'll be before she's willin' to come home. What's the matter you payin' for one?"

"I haven't any money."

"Well, father——"

She shook her head dolefully. "I got some from him this morning, and I can't bother him for any more; it upsets him. He's *always* been so terribly close with money——"

"I guess he couldn't help that," Walter observed. "We're liable to go to the poorhouse the way it is. Well, what's the matter our walkin' to this rotten party?"

"In the rain, Walter?"

"Well, it's only a drizzle and we can take a street-car to within a block of the house."

Again his mother shook her head. "It wouldn't do."

"Well, darn the luck, all *right!*" he consented, explosively. "I'll get her something to ride in. It means seventy-five cents."

"Why, Walter!" Mrs. Adams cried, much pleased. "Do you know how to get a cab for that little? How splendid!"

"Tain't a cab," Walter informed her crossly. "It's a tin Lizzie, but you don't haf' to tell her what it is till I get her into it, do you?"

Mrs. Adams agreed that she didn't.

CHAPTER VI

ALICE was busy with herself for two hours after dinner; but a little before nine o'clock she stood in front of her long mirror, completed, bright-eyed and solemn. Her hair, exquisitely arranged, gave all she asked of it; what artificialities in colour she had used upon her face were only bits of emphasis that made her prettiness the more distinct; and the dress, not rumpled by her mother's careful hours of work, was a white cloud of loveliness. Finally there were two triumphant bouquets of violets, each with the stems wrapped in tin-foil shrouded by a bow of purple chiffon; and one bouquet she wore at her waist and the other she carried in her hand.

Miss Perry, called in by a rapturous mother for the free treat of a look at this radiance, insisted that Alice was a vision. "Purely and simply a vision!" she said, meaning that no other definition whatever would satisfy her. "I never saw anybody look a vision if she don't look one to-night," the admiring nurse declared. "Her papa'll think the same I do about it. You see if he doesn't say she's purely and simply a vision."

Adams did not fulfil the prediction quite literally when Alice paid a brief visit to his room to "show" him and bid him good-night; but he chuckled feebly. "Well, well, well!" he said. "You look mighty fine—*mighty* fine!" And he waggled a bony finger at her two bouquets. "Why, Alice, who's your beau?"

"Never you mind!" she laughed, archly brushing his nose with the violets in her hand. "He treats me pretty well, doesn't he?"

"Must like to throw his money around! These violets smell mighty sweet, and they ought to, if they're going to a party with *you*. Have a good time, dearie."

"I mean to!" she cried; and she repeated this gaily, but with an emphasis expressing sharp determination as she left him. "I *mean* to!"

"What was he talking about?" her mother inquired, smoothing the rather worn and old evening wrap she had placed on Alice's bed. "What were you telling him you 'mean to?'"

Alice went back to her triple mirror for the last

time, then stood before the long one. "That I mean to have a good time to-night," she said; and as she turned from her reflection to the wrap Mrs. Adams held up for her, "It looks as though I *could*, don't you think so?"

"You'll just be a queen to-night," her mother whispered in fond emotion. "You mustn't doubt yourself."

"Well, there's one thing," said Alice. "I think I do look nice enough to get along without having to dance with that Frank Dowling! All I ask is for it to happen just *once;* and if he comes near me to-night I'm going to treat him the way the other girls do. Do you suppose Walter's got the taxi out in front?"

"He—he's waiting down in the hall," Mrs. Adams answered, nervously; and she held up another garment to go over the wrap.

Alice frowned at it. "What's that, mama?"

"It's—it's your father's raincoat. I thought you'd put it on over——"

"But I won't need it in a taxicab."

"You will to get in and out, and you needn't take it into the Palmers'. You can leave it in the—in the —— It's drizzling, and you'll need it."

"Oh, well," Alice consented; and a few minutes later, as with Walter's assistance she climbed into the vehicle he had provided, she better understood her mother's solicitude.

"What on earth *is* this, Walter?" she asked.

"Never mind; it'll keep you dry enough with the top up," he returned, taking his seat beside her. Then for a time, as they went rather jerkily up the street, she was silent; but finally she repeated her question: "What *is* it, Walter?"

"What's what?"

"This—this *car?*"

"It's a ottomobile."

"I mean—what kind is it?"

"Haven't you got eyes?"

"It's too dark."

"It's a second-hand tin Lizzie," said Walter. "D'you know what that means? It means a flivver."

"Yes, Walter."

"Got 'ny 'bjections?"

"Why, no, dear," she said, placatively. "Is it yours, Walter? Have you bought it?"

"Me?" he laughed. "*I* couldn't buy a used wheelbarrow. I rent this sometimes when I'm goin' out among 'em. Costs me seventy-five cents and the price o' the gas."

"That seems very moderate."

"I guess it is! The feller owes me some money, and this is the only way I'd ever get it off him."

"Is he a garage-keeper?"

"Not exactly!" Walter uttered husky sounds of amusement. "You'll be just as happy, I guess, if you don't know who he is," he said.

His tone misgave her; and she said truthfully that she was content not to know who owned the car. "I joke sometimes about how you keep things to yourself," she added, "but I really never do pry in your affairs, Walter."

"Oh, no, you don't!"

"Indeed, I don't."

"Yes, you're mighty nice and cooing when you got me where you want me," he jeered. "Well, *I* just as soon tell you where I get this car."

"I'd just as soon you wouldn't, Walter," she said, hurriedly. "Please don't."

But Walter meant to tell her. "Why, there's nothin' exactly *criminal* about it," he said. "It belongs to old J. A. Lamb himself. He keeps it for their coon chauffeur. I rent it from him."

"From Mr. *Lamb?*"

"No; from the coon chauffeur."

"Walter!" she gasped.

"Sure I do! I can get it any night when the coon isn't goin' to use it himself. He's drivin' their limousine to-night—that little Henrietta Lamb's goin' to the party, no matter if her father *has* only been dead less'n a year!" He paused, then inquired: "Well, how d'you like it?"

She did not speak, and he began to be remorseful for having imparted so much information, though his way of expressing regret was his own. "Well, you *will* make the folks make me take you to parties!" he said. "I got to do it the best way I *can*, don't I?"

Then as she made no response, "Oh, the car's *clean* enough," he said. "This coon, he's as particular as any white man; you needn't worry about that." And as she still said nothing, he added gruffly, "I'd of had a better car if I could afforded it. You needn't get so upset about it."

"I don't understand—" she said in a low voice—"I don't understand how you know such people."

"Such people as who?"

"As—coloured chauffeurs."

"Oh, look here, now!" he protested, loudly. "Don't you know this is a democratic country?"

"Not quite that democratic, is it, Walter?"

"The trouble with you," he retorted, "you don't know there's anybody in town except just this silk-shirt crowd." He paused, seeming to await a refutation; but as none came, he expressed himself definitely: "They make me sick."

They were coming near their destination, and the glow of the big, brightly lighted house was seen before them in the wet night. Other cars, not like theirs, were approaching this center of brilliance; long triangles of light near the ground swept through the fine drizzle; small red tail-lights gleamed again from the moist pavement of the street; and, through the myriads of little glistening leaves along the curving driveway, glimpses were caught of lively colours moving in a white glare as the limousines released their occupants under the shelter of the porte-cochère.

Alice clutched Walter's arm in a panic; they were just at the driveway entrance. "Walter, we mustn't go in there."

"What's the matter?"

"Leave this awful car outside."

"Why, I——"

"Stop!" she insisted, vehemently. "You've got to! Go back!"

"Oh, Glory!"

The little car was between the entrance posts; but Walter backed it out, avoiding a collision with an impressive machine which swerved away from them and passed on toward the porte-cochère, showing a man's face grinning at the window as it went by. "Flivver runabout got the wrong number!" he said.

"Did he *see* us?" Alice cried.

"Did who see us?"

"Harvey Malone—in that foreign coupé."

"No; he couldn't tell who we were under this top," Walter assured her as he brought the little car to a standstill beside the curbstone, out in the street. "What's it matter if he did, the big fish?"

Alice responded with a loud sigh, and sat still.

"Well, want to go on back?" Walter inquired. "You bet I'm willing!"

"No."

"Well, then, what's the matter our drivin' on up to the porte-cochère? There's room for me to park just the other side of it."

"No, *no!*"

"What you expect to do? Sit *here* all night?"

"No, leave the car here."

"*I* don't care where we leave it," he said. "Sit still till I lock her, so none o' these millionaires around here'll run off with her." He got out with a padlock and chain; and, having put these in place, offered Alice his hand. "Come on, if you're ready."

"Wait," she said, and, divesting herself of the raincoat, handed it to Walter. "Please leave this with your things in the men's dressing-room, as if it were an extra one of your own, Walter."

He nodded; she jumped out; and they scurried through the drizzle. As they reached the porte-cochère she began to laugh airily, and spoke to the impassive man in livery who stood there. "Joke on us!" she said, hurrying by him toward the door of the house. "Our car broke down outside the gate."

The man remained impassive, though he responded with a faint gleam as Walter, looking back at him, produced for his benefit a cynical distortion of countenance which offered little confirmation of Alice's account of things. Then the door was swiftly opened to the brother and sister; and they came into a marble-floored hall, where a dozen sleeked young men lounged, smoked cigarettes and fastened their gloves, as they waited for their ladies. Alice nodded to one or another of these, and went quickly on, her face uplifted and smiling; but Walter detained her at the door to which she hastened.

"Listen here," he said. "I suppose you want me to dance the first dance with you——"

"If you please, Walter," she said, meekly.

"How long you goin' to hang around fixin' up in that dressin'-room?"

"I'll be out before you're ready yourself," she promised him; and kept her word, she was so eager for her good time to begin. When he came for her, they went down the hall to a corridor opening upon three great rooms which had been thrown open together, with the furniture removed and the broad floors waxed. At one end of the corridor musicians sat in a green grove, and Walter, with some interest, turned toward these; but his sister, pressing his arm, impelled him in the opposite direction.

"What's the matter now?" he asked. "That's Jazz Louie and his half-breed bunch—three white and four mulatto. Let's——?"

"No, no," she whispered. "We must speak to Mildred and Mr. and Mrs. Palmer."

"'Speak' to 'em? I haven't got a thing to say to *those* berries!"

"Walter, won't you *please* behave?"

He seemed to consent, for the moment, at least, and suffered her to take him down the corridor toward a floral bower where the hostess stood with her father and mother. Other couples and groups were moving in the same direction, carrying with them a hubbub of laughter and fragmentary chatterings; and Alice, smiling all the time, greeted people on every side of her eagerly—a little more eagerly than most of them responded—while Walter nodded in a non-committal manner to one or two, said nothing, and yawned audibly, the last resource of a person who finds himself nervous in a false situation. He repeated his yawn and was beginning another when a convulsive pressure upon his arm made him understand that he must abandon this method of reassuring himself. They were close upon the floral bower.

Mildred was giving her hand to one and another of her guests as rapidly as she could, passing them on to her father and mother, and at the same time resisting the efforts of three or four detached bachelors who besought her to give over her duty in favour of the dance-music just beginning to blare.

She was a large, fair girl, with a kindness of eye somewhat withheld by an expression of fastidiousness; at first sight of her it was clear that she would never in her life do anything "incorrect," or wear anything "incorrect." But her correctness was of the finer sort, and had no air of being studied or achieved; conduct would never offer her a problem to be settled from a book of rules, for the rules were so deep within her that she was unconscious of them. And behind this perfection there was an even ampler perfection of what Mrs. Adams called "background." The big, rich, simple house was part of it, and Mildred's father and mother were part of it. They stood beside her, large, serene people, murmuring graciously and gently inclining their handsome heads as they gave their hands to the guests; and even the youngest and most ebullient of these took on a hushed mannerliness with a closer approach to the bower.

When the opportunity came for Alice and Walter to pass within this precinct, Alice, going first, leaned forward and whispered in Mildred's ear. "You *didn't* wear the maize georgette! That's what I thought you were going to. But you look simply *darling!* And those *pearls*——"

Others were crowding decorously forward, anxious

to be done with ceremony and get to the dancing; and Mildred did not prolong the intimacy of Alice's enthusiastic whispering. With a faint accession of colour and a smile tending somewhat in the direction of rigidity, she carried Alice's hand immediately onward to Mrs. Palmer's. Alice's own colour showed a little heightening as she accepted the suggestion thus implied; nor was that emotional tint in any wise decreased, a moment later, by an impression that Walter, in concluding the brief exchange of courtesies between himself and the stately Mr. Palmer, had again reassured himself with a yawn.

But she did not speak of it to Walter; she preferred not to confirm the impression and to leave in her mind a possible doubt that he had done it. He followed her out upon the waxed floor, said resignedly: "Well, come on," put his arm about her, and they began to dance.

Alice danced gracefully and well, but not so well as Walter. Of all the steps and runs, of all the whimsical turns and twirlings, of all the rhythmic swayings and dips commanded that season by such blarings as were the barbaric product, loud and wild, of the Jazz Louies and their half-breed bunches, the thin and sallow youth was a master. Upon his face could be seen contempt of the easy marvels he performed as he moved in swift precision from one smooth agility to another; and if some too-dainty or jealous cavalier complained that to be so much a stylist in dancing was "not quite like a gentleman," at least Walter's style was what the music called for. No other dancer in the room could be thought comparable to him. Alice told him so.

"It's wonderful!" she said. "And the mystery is, where you ever learned to *do* it! You never went to dancing-school, but there isn't a man in the room who can dance half so well. I don't see why, when you dance like this, you always make such a fuss about coming to parties."

He sounded his brief laugh, a jeering bark out of one side of the mouth, and swung her miraculously through a closing space between two other couples. "You know a lot about what goes on, don't you? You prob'ly think there's no other place to dance in this town except these frozen-face joints."

"'Frozen face?'" she echoed, laughing. "Why, everybody's having a splendid time. Look at them."

"Oh, they holler loud enough," he said. "They do it to make each other think they're havin' a good time. You don't call that Palmer family frozen-face berries, I s'pose. No?"

"Certainly not. They're just dignified and——"

"Yeuh!" said Walter. "They're dignified, 'specially when you tried to whisper to Mildred to show how *in* with her you were, and she moved you on that way. *She's* a hot friend, isn't she!"

"She didn't mean anything by it. She——"

"Ole Palmer's a hearty, slap you-on-the-back ole berry," Walter interrupted; adding in a casual tone, "All I'd like, I'd like to hit him."

"Walter! By the way, you mustn't forget to ask Mildred for a dance before the evening is over."

"Me?" He produced the lop-sided appearance of his laugh, but without making it vocal. "You watch me do it!"

"She probably won't have one left, but you must ask her, anyway."

"Why must I?"

"Because, in the first place, you're supposed to, and, in the second place, she's my most intimate friend."

"Yeuh? Is she? I've heard you pull that 'most-intimate-friend' stuff often enough about her. What's *she* ever do to show she is?"

"Never mind. You really must ask her, Walter. I want you to; and I want you to ask several other girls afterwhile; I'll tell you who."

"Keep on wanting; it'll do you good."

"Oh, but you really——"

"Listen!" he said. "I'm just as liable to dance with any of these fairies as I am to buy a bucket o' rusty tacks and eat 'em. Forget it! Soon as I get rid of you I'm goin' back to that room where I left my hat and overcoat and smoke myself to death."

"Well," she said, a little ruefully, as the frenzy of Jazz Louie and his half-breeds was suddenly abated to silence, "you mustn't—you mustn't get rid of me *too* soon, Walter."

They stood near one of the wide doorways, remaining where they had stopped. Other couples, everywhere, joined one another, forming vivacious clusters, but none of these groups adopted the brother and sister, nor did any one appear to be hurrying in Alice's direction to ask her for the next dance. She looked about her, still maintaining that jubilance of look and manner she felt so necessary—for it is to the girls who are "having a good time" that partners are attracted—and, in order to lend greater colour to her impersonation of a lively belle, she began to chatter loudly, bringing into play an accompaniment of frolicsome gesture. She brushed Walter's nose saucily with the bunch of violets in her hand, tapped him on the shoulder, shook her pretty forefinger in his face, flourished her arms, kept her shoulders moving, and laughed continuously as she spoke.

"You *naughty* old Walter!" she cried. "*Aren't* you ashamed to be such a wonderful dancer and then only dance with your own little sister! You could dance on the stage if you wanted to. Why, you could made your *fortune* that way! Why don't you? Wouldn't it be just lovely to have all the rows and rows of people clapping their hands and shouting, 'Hurrah! Hurrah, for Walter Adams! Hurrah! Hurrah! Hurrah!"

He stood looking at her in stolid pity.

"Cut it out," he said. "You better be givin' some of these berries the eye so they'll ask you to dance."

She was not to be so easily checked, and laughed loudly, flourishing her violets in his face again. "You *would* like it; you know you would; you needn't pretend! Just think! A whole big audience shouting, 'Hurrah! *Hurrah! Hur——*'"

"The place 'll be pulled if you get any noisier,"

he interrupted, not ungently. "Besides, I'm no muley cow."

"A '*cow*?'" she laughed. "What on earth——"

"I can't eat dead violets," he explained. "So don't keep tryin' to make me do it."

This had the effect he desired, and subdued her; she abandoned her unsisterly coquetries, and looked beamingly about her, but her smile was more mechanical than it had been at first.

At home she had seemed beautiful; but here, where the other girls competed, things were not as they had been there, with only her mother and Miss Perry to give contrast. These crowds of other girls had all done their best, also, to look beautiful, though not one of them had worked so hard for such a consummation as Alice had. They did not need to; they did not need to get their mothers to make old dresses over; they did not need to hunt violets in the rain.

At home her dress had seemed beautiful; but that was different, too, where there were dozens of brilliant fabrics, fashioned in new ways—some of these new ways startling, which only made the wearers centers of interest and shocked no one. And Alice remembered that she had heard a girl say, not long before, "Oh, *organdie!* Nobody wears organdie for evening gowns except in midsummer." Alice had thought little of this; but as she looked about her and saw no organdie except her own, she found greater difficulty in keeping her smile as arch and spontaneous as she wished it. In fact, it was beginning to make her face ache a little.

Mildred came in from the corridor, heavily attended. She carried a great bouquet of violets laced with lilies-of-the-valley; and the violets were lusty, big purple things, their stems wrapped in cloth of gold, with silken cords dependent, ending in long tassels. She and her convoy passed near the two young Adamses; and it appeared that one of the convoy besought his hostess to permit "cutting in"; they were "doing it other places" of late, he urged; but he was denied and told to console himself by holding the bouquet, at intervals, until his third of the sixteenth dance should come. Alice looked dubiously at her own bouquet.

Suddenly she felt that the violets betrayed her; that any one who looked at them could see how rustic, how innocent of any florist's craft they were. "I can't eat dead violets," Walter said. The little wild flowers, dying indeed in the warm air, were drooping in a forlorn mass; and it seemed to her that whoever noticed them would guess that she had picked them herself. She decided to get rid of them.

Walter was becoming restive. "Look here!" he said. "Can't you flag one o' these long-tailed birds to take you on for the next dance? You came to have a good time; why don't you get busy and have it? I want to get out and smoke."

"You *mustn't* leave me, Walter," she whispered, hastily. "Somebody'll come for me before long, but until they do——"

"Well, couldn't you sit somewhere?"

"No, no! There isn't any one I could sit with."

"Well, why not? Look at those ole dames in the corners. What's the matter your tyin' up with some o' them for a while?"

"*Please,* Walter; no!"

In fact, that indomitable smile of hers was the more difficult to maintain because of these very elders to whom Walter referred. They were mothers of girls among the dancers, and they were there to fend and contrive for their offspring; to keep them in countenance through any trial; to lend them diplomacy in the carrying out of all enterprises; to be "background" for them; and in these essentially biological functionings to imitate their own matings and renew the excitement of their nuptial periods. Older men, husbands of these ladies and fathers of eligible girls, were also to be seen, most of them with Mr. Palmer in a billiard-room across the corridor.

Mr. and Mrs. Adams had not been invited. "Of course papa and mama just barely know Mildred Palmer," Alice thought, "and most of the other girls' fathers and mothers are old friends of Mr. and Mrs. Palmer, but I do think she might have *asked* papa and mama, anyway—she needn't have been afraid just to ask them; she knew they couldn't come." And her smiling lip twitched a little threateningly, as she concluded the silent monologue. "I suppose she thinks I ought to be glad enough she asked Walter!"

Walter was, in fact, rather noticeable. He was not Mildred's only guest to wear a short coat and to appear without gloves; but he was singular (at least in his present surroundings) on account of a kind of coiffuring he favoured, his hair having been shaped after what seemed a Mongol inspiration. Only upon the top of the head was actual hair perceived, the rest appearing to be nudity. And even more than by any difference in mode he was set apart by his look and manner, in which there seemed to be a brooding, secretive and jeering superiority; and this was most vividly expressed when he felt called upon for his loud, short, lop-sided laugh. Whenever he uttered it Alice laughed, too, as loudly as she could, to cover it.

"Well," he said. "How long we goin' to stand here? My feet are sproutin' roots."

Alice took his arm, and they began to walk aimlessly through the rooms, though she tried to look as if they had a definite destination, keeping her eyes eager and her lips parted;—people had called jovially to them from the distance, she meant to imply, and they were going to join these merry friends. She was still upon this ghostly errand when a furious outbreak of drums and saxophones sounded a prelude for the second dance.

Walter danced with her again, but he gave her a warning. "I don't want to leave you high and dry," he told her, "but I can't stand it. I got to get somewhere I don't haf' to hurt my eyes with these berries; I'll go blind if I got to look at any more of 'em. I'm goin' out to smoke as soon as the music begins the next time, and you better get fixed for it."

Alice tried to get fixed for it. As they danced she nodded sunnily to every man whose eye she caught, smiled her smile with the under lip caught between her teeth; but it was not until the end of the intermission after the dance that she saw help coming.

Across the room sat the globular lady she had encountered that morning, and beside the globular lady sat a round-headed, round-bodied girl; her daughter, at first glance. The family contour was also as evident a characteristic of the short young man who stood in front of Mrs. Dowling, engaged with her in a discussion which was not without evidences of an earnestness almost impassioned. Like Walter, he was declining to dance a third time with sister; he wished to go elsewhere.

Alice from a sidelong eye watched the controversy: she saw the globular young man glance toward her, over his shoulder; whereupon Mrs. Dowling, following this glance, gave Alice a look of open fury, became much more vehement in the argument, and even struck her knee with a round, fat fist for emphasis.

"I'm on my way," said Walter. "There's the music startin' up again, and I told you——"

She nodded gratefully. "It's all right—but come back before long, Walter."

The globular young man, red with annoyance, had torn himself from his family and was hastening across the room to her. "C'n I have this dance?"

"Why, you nice Frank Dowling!" Alice cried "How lovely!"

CHAPTER VII

THEY danced. Mr. Dowling should have found other forms of exercise and pastime. Nature has not designed everyone for dancing, though sometimes those she has denied are the last to discover her niggardliness. But the round young man was at least vigorous enough—too much so, when his knees collided with Alice's—and he was too sturdy to be thrown off his feet, himself, or to allow his partner to fall when he tripped her. He held her up valiantly, and continued to beat a path through the crowd of other dancers by main force.

He paid no attention to anything suggested by the efforts of the musicians, and appeared to be unaware that there should have been some connection between what they were doing and what he was doing; but he may have listened to other music of his own, for his expression was of high content; he seemed to feel no doubt whatever that he was dancing. Alice kept as far away from him as under the circumstances she could; and when they stopped she glanced down, and found the execution of unseen manœuvres, within the protection of her skirt, helpful to one of her insteps and to the toes of both of her slippers.

Her cheery partner was paddling his rosy brows with a fine handkerchief. "That was great!" he said. "Let's go out and sit in the corridor; they've got some comfortable chairs out there."

"Well—let's not," she returned. "I believe I'd rather stay in here and look at the crowd."

"No; that isn't it," he said, chiding her with a waggish forefinger. "You think if you go out there you'll miss a chance of someone else asking you for the next dance, and so you'll have to give it to me."

"How absurd!" Then, after a look about her that revealed nothing encouraging, she added graciously, "You can have the next if you want it."

"Great!" he exclaimed, mechanically. "Now let's get out of here—out of *this* room, anyhow."

"Why? What's the matter with——"

"My mother," Mr. Dowling explained. "But don't look at her. She keeps motioning me to come and see after Ella, and I'm simply *not* going to do it, you see!"

Alice laughed. "I don't believe it's so much that," she said, and consented to walk with him to a point in the next room from which Mrs. Dowling's continuous signalling could not be seen. "Your mother hates me."

"Oh, no; I wouldn't say that. No, she don't," he protested, innocently. "She don't know you more than just to speak to, you see. So how could she?"

"Well, she does. I can tell."

A frown appeared upon his rounded brow. "No; I'll tell you the way she feels. It's like this: Ella isn't *too* popular, you know—it's hard to see why, because she's a right nice girl, in her way—and mother thinks I ought to look after her, you see. She thinks I ought to dance a whole lot with her myself, and stir up other fellows to dance with her—it's simply impossible to make mother understand you *can't* do that, you see. And then about me, you see, if she had her way I wouldn't get to dance with anybody at all except girls like Mildred Palmer and Henrietta Lamb. Mother wants to run my whole programme for me, you understand, but the trouble of it is—about girls like that, you see—well, I couldn't do what she wants, even if I wanted to myself, because you take those girls, and by the time I get Ella off my hands for a minute, why, their dances are always every last one taken, and where do I come in?"

Alice nodded, her amiability undamaged. "I see. So that's why you dance with me."

"No, I like to," he protested. "I rather dance with you than I do with those girls." And he added with a retrospective determination which showed that he had been through quite an experience with Mrs. Dowling in this matter. "I *told* mother I would, too!"

"Did it take all your courage, Frank?"

He looked at her shrewdly. "Now you're trying to tease me," he said. "I don't care; I *would* rather dance with you! In the first place, you're a perfectly beautiful dancer, you see, and in the second, a man feels a lot more comfortable with you than he does with them. Of course I know almost all the other fellows get along with those girls all right; but I don't waste any time on 'em I don't have to. *I* like people that are always cordial to everybody, you see—the way you are."

"Thank you," she said, thoughtfully.

"Oh, I *mean* it," he insisted. "There goes the band again. Shall we——?"

"Suppose we sit it out?" she suggested. "I believe I'd like to go out in the corridor, after all—it's pretty warm in here."

Assenting cheerfully, Dowling conducted her to a pair of easy-chairs within a secluding grove of box-trees, and when they came to this retreat they found Mildred Palmer just departing, under escort of a well-favoured gentleman about thirty. As these two walked slowly away, in the direction of the dancing-floor, they left it not to be doubted that they were on excellent terms with each other; Mildred was evidently willing to make their progress even slower, for she halted momentarily, once or twice; and her upward glances to her tall companion's face were of a gentle, almost blushing deference. Never before had Alice seen anything like this in her friend's manner.

"How queer!" she murmured.

"What's queer?" Dowling inquired as they sat down.

"Who was that man?"

"Haven't you met him?"

"I never saw him before. Who is he?"

"Why, it's this Arthur Russell."

"What Arthur Russell? I never heard of him."

Mr. Dowling was puzzled. "Why, *that's* funny!

Only the last time I saw you, you were telling me how awfully well you knew Mildred Palmer."

"Why, certainly I do," Alice informed him. "She's my most intimate friend."

"That's what makes it seem so funny you haven't heard anything about this Russell, because everybody says even if she isn't engaged to him right now, she most likely will be before very long. I must say it looks a good deal that way to me, myself."

"What nonsense!" Alice exclaimed. "She's never even mentioned him to me."

The young man glanced at her dubiously and passed a finger over the tiny prong that dashingly composed the whole substance of his moustache. "Well, you see, Mildred *is* pretty reserved," he remarked. "This Russell is some kind of cousin of the Palmer family, I understand."

"He is?"

"Yes—second or third or something, the girls say. You see, my sister Ella hasn't got much to do at home, and don't read anything, or sew, or play solitaire, you see; and she hears about pretty much everything that goes on, you see. Well, Ella says a lot of the girls have been talking about Mildred and this Arthur Russell for quite a while back, you see.

They were all wondering what he was going to look like, you see; because he only got here yesterday; and that proves she must have been talking to some of 'em, or else how——"

Alice laughed airily, but the pretty sound ended abruptly with an audible intake of breath. "Of course, while Mildred *is* my most intimate friend," she said, "I don't mean she tells me everything—and naturally she has other friends besides. What else did your sister say she told them about this Mr. Russell?"

"Well, it seems he's *very* well off; at least Henrietta Lamb told Ella he was. Ella says——"

Alice interrupted again, with an increased irritability. "Oh, never mind what Ella says! Let's find something better to talk about than Mr. Russell!"

"Well, *I'm* willing," Mr. Dowling assented, ruefully. "What you want to talk about?"

But this liberal offer found her unresponsive; she sat leaning back, silent, her arms along the arms of her chair, and her eyes, moist and bright, fixed upon a wide doorway where the dancers fluctuated. She was disquieted by more than Mildred's reserve, though reserve so marked had certainly the significance of a warning that Alice's definition, "my most intimate friend," lacked sanction. Indirect notice to this effect could not well have been more emphatic, but the sting of it was left for a later moment. Something else preoccupied Alice: she had just been surprised by an odd experience. At first sight of this Mr. Arthur Russell, she had said to herself instantly, in words as definite as if she spoke them aloud, though they seemed more like words spoken to her by some unknown person within her: "There! That's exactly the kind of looking man I'd like to marry!"

In the eyes of the restless and the longing, Providence often appears to be worse than inscrutable: an unreliable Omnipotence given to haphazard whimsies in dealing with its own creatures, choosing at random some among them to be rent with tragic deprivations and others to be petted with blessing upon blessing. In Alice's eyes, Mildred had been blessed enough; something ought to be left over, by this time, for another girl. The final touch to the heaping perfection of Christmas-in-everything for Mildred was that this Mr. Arthur Russell, good-looking, kind-looking, graceful, the perfect fiancé, should be also "*very* well off." Of course! These rich always married one another. And while the Mildreds danced with their Arthur Russells the best an outsider could do for herself was to sit with Frank Dowling—the one last course left her that was better than dancing with him.

"Well, what *do* you want to talk about?" he inquired.

"Nothing," she said. "Suppose we just sit, Frank." But a moment later she remembered something, and, with a sudden animation, began to prattle. She pointed to the musicians down the corridor. "Oh, look at them! Look at the leader! Aren't they *funny?* Someone told me they're called 'Jazz Louie and his half-breed bunch.' Isn't that just crazy? Don't you *love* it? Do watch them, Frank."

She continued to chatter, and, while thus keeping his glance away from herself, she detached the forlorn bouquet of dead violets from her dress and laid it gently beside the one she had carried The latter already reposed in the obscurity selected for it at the base of one of the box-trees.

Then she was abruptly silent.

"You certainly are a funny girl," Dowling remarked. "You say you don't want to talk about anything at all, and all of a sudden you break out and talk a blue streak; and just about the time I begin to get interested in what you're saying you shut off! What's the matter with girls, anyhow, when they do things like that?"

"I don't know; we're just queer, I guess."

"I say so! Well, what'll we do *now?* Talk, or just sit?"

"Suppose we just sit some more."

"Anything to oblige," he assented. "I'm willing to sit as long as you like."

But even as he made his amiability clear in this matter, the peace was threatened—his mother came down the corridor like a rolling, ominous cloud. She was looking about her on all sides, in a fidget of annoyance, searching for him, and to his dismay she saw him. She immediately made a horrible face at his companion, beckoned to him imperiously with a dumpy arm, and shook her head reprovingly. The unfortunate young man tried to repulse her with an icy stare, but this effort having obtained little to encourage his feeble hope of driving her away, he shifted his chair so that his back was toward her discomfiting pantomime. He should have known better, the instant result was Mrs. Dowling in motion at an impetuous waddle.

She entered the box-tree seclusion with the lower rotundities of her face hastily modelled into the resemblance of an over-benevolent smile—a contortion which neglected to spread its intended geniality upward to the exasperated eyes and anxious forehead.

"I think your mother wants to speak to you, Frank," Alice said, upon this advent.

Mrs. Dowling nodded to her. "Good evening, Miss Adams," she said. "I just thought as you and Frank weren't dancing you wouldn't mind my disturbing you——"

"Not at all," Alice murmured.

Mr. Dowling seemed of a different mind. "Well, what *do* you want?" he inquired, whereupon his mother struck him roguishly with her fan.

"Bad fellow!" She turned to Alice. "I'm sure you won't mind excusing him to let him do something for his old mother, Miss Adams."

"What *do* you want?" the son repeated.

"Two very nice things," Mrs. Dowling informed him. "Everybody is so anxious for Henrietta Lamb to have a pleasant evening, because it's the very first time she's been anywhere since her father's death, and of course her dear grandfather's an old friend of ours, and——"

"Well, well!" her son interrupted. "Miss Adams isn't interested in all this, mother."

"But Henrietta came to speak to Ella and me, and I told her you were so anxious to dance with her——"

"Here!" he cried. "Look here! I'd rather do my own——"

"Yes; that's just it," Mrs. Dowling explained. "I just thought it was such a good opportunity; and Henrietta said she had most of her dances taken, but she'd give you one if you asked her before they were all gone. So I thought you'd better see her as soon as possible."

Dowling's face had become rosy. "I refuse to do anything of the kind."

"Bad fellow!" said his mother, gaily. "I thought this would be the best time for you to see Henrietta, because it won't be long till all her dances are gone, and you've promised on your *word* to dance the next with Ella, and you mightn't have a chance to do it then. I'm sure Miss Adams won't mind if you——"

"Not at all," Alice said.

"Well, *I* mind!" he said. "I wish you *could* understand that when I want to dance with any girl I don't need my mother to ask her for me. I really *am* more than six years old!"

He spoke with too much vehemence, and Mrs. Dowling at once saw how to have her way. As with husbands and wives, so with many fathers and daughters, and so with some sons and mothers: the man will himself be cross in public and think nothing of it, nor will he greatly mind a little crossness on the part of the woman; but let her show agitation before any spectator, he is instantly reduced to a coward's slavery. Women understand that ancient weakness, of course; for it is one of their most important means of defense, but can be used ignobly.

Mrs. Dowling permitted a tremulousness to become audible in her voice. "It isn't very—very pleasant—to be talked to like that by your own son—before strangers!"

"Oh, my! Look here!" the stricken Dowling protested. "*I* didn't say anything, mother. I was just joking about how you never get over thinking I'm a little boy. I only——"

Mrs. Dowling continued: "I just thought I was doing you a little favour. I didn't think it would make you so angry."

"Mother, for goodness' sake! Miss Adams'll think——"

"I suppose," Mrs. Dowling interrupted, piteously, "I suppose it doesn't matter what *I* think!"

"Oh, gracious!"

Alice interfered; she perceived that the ruthless Mrs. Dowling meant to have her way. "I think you'd better go, Frank. Really."

"There!" his mother cried. "Miss Adams says so, herself! What more do you want?"

"Oh, gracious!" he lamented again, and, with a sick look over his shoulder at Alice, permitted his mother to take his arm and propel him away. Mrs. Dowling's spirits had strikingly recovered even before the pair passed from the corridor: she moved almost bouncingly beside her embittered son, and her eyes and all the convolutions of her abundant face were blithe.

Alice went in search of Walter, but without much hope of finding him. What he did with himself at frozen-face dances was one of his most successful mysteries, and her present excursion gave her no clue leading to its solution. When the musicians again lowered their instruments for an interval she had returned, alone, to her former seat within the partial shelter of the box-trees.

She had now to practise an art that affords but a

limited variety of methods, even to the expert: the art of seeming to have an escort or partner when there is none. The practitioner must imply, merely by expression and attitude, that the supposed companion has left her for only a few moments, that she herself has sent him upon an errand; and, if possible, the minds of observers must be directed toward a conclusion that this errand of her devising is an amusing one; at all events, she is alone temporarily and of choice, not deserted. She awaits a devoted man who may return at any instant.

Other people desired to sit in Alice's nook, but discovered her in occupancy. She had moved the vacant chair closer to her own, and she sat with her arm extended so that her hand, holding her lace kerchief, rested upon the back of this second chair, claiming it. Such a preëmption, like that of a traveller's bag in the rack, was unquestionable; and, for additional evidence, sitting with her knees crossed, she kept one foot continuously moving a little, in cadence with the other, which tapped the floor. Moreover, she added a fine detail: her half-smile, with the under lip caught, seemed to struggle against repression, as if she found the service engaging her absent companion even more amusing than she would let him see when he returned: there was jovial intrigue of some sort afoot, evidently. Her eyes, beaming with secret fun, were averted from intruders, but sometimes, when couples approached, seeking possession of the nook, her thoughts about the absentee appeared to threaten her with outright laughter; and though one or two girls looked at her skeptically, as they turned away, their escorts felt no such doubts, and merely wondered what importantly funny affair Alice Adams was engaged in. She had learned to do it perfectly.

She had learned it during the last two years; she was twenty when for the first time she had the shock of finding herself without an applicant for one of her dances. When she was sixteen "all the nice boys in town," as her mother said, crowded the Adamses' small veranda and steps, or sat near by, cross-legged on the lawn, on summer evenings; and at eighteen she had replaced the boys with "the older men." By this time most of "the other girls," her contemporaries, were away at school or college, and when they came home to stay, they "came out"—that feeble revival of an ancient custom offering the maiden to the ceremonial inspection of the tribe. Alice neither went away nor "came out," and, in contrast with those who did, she may have seemed to lack freshness of lustre—jewels are richest when revealed all new in a white velvet box. And Alice may have been too eager to secure new retainers, too kind in her efforts to keep the old ones. She had been a belle too soon.

CHAPTER VIII

THE device of the absentee partner has the defect that it cannot be employed for longer than ten or fifteen minutes at a time, and it may not be repeated more than twice in one evening: a single repetition, indeed, is weak, and may prove a betrayal. Alice knew that her present performance could be effective during only this interval between dances; and though her eyes were guarded, she anxiously counted over the partnerless young men who lounged together in the doorways within her view. Every one of them ought to have asked her for dances, she thought, and although she might have been put to it to give a reason why any of them "ought," her heart was hot with resentment against them.

For a girl who has been a belle, it is harder to live through these bad times than it is for one who has never known anything better. Like a figure of painted and brightly varnished wood, Ella Dowling sat against the wall through dance after dance with glassy imperturbability; it was easier to be wooden, Alice thought, if you had your mother with you, as Ella had. You were left with at least the shred of a pretense that you came to sit with your mother as a spectator, and not to offer yourself to be danced with by men who looked you over and rejected you—not for the first time. "Not for the first time": there lay a sting! Why had you thought this time might be different from the other times? Why had you broken your back picking those hundreds of violets?

Hating the fatuous young men in the doorways more bitterly for every instant that she had to maintain her tableau, the smiling Alice knew fierce impulses to spring to her feet and shout at them, "You *idiots!*" Hands in pockets, they lounged against the pilasters, or faced one another, laughing vaguely, each one of them seeming to Alice no more than so much mean beef in clothes. She wanted to tell them they were no better than that; and it seemed a cruel thing of heaven to let them go on believing themselves young lords. They were doing nothing, killing time. Wasn't she at her lowest value at least a means of killing time? Evidently the mean beeves thought not. And when one of them finally lounged across the corridor and spoke to her, he was the very one to whom she preferred her loneliness.

"Waiting for somebody, Lady Alicia?" he asked, negligently; and his easy burlesque of her name was like the familiarity of the rest of him. He was one of those full-bodied, grossly handsome men who are powerful and active, but never submit themselves to the rigour of becoming athletes, though they shoot and fish from expensive camps. Gloss is the most shining outward mark of the type. Nowadays these men no longer use brilliantine on their moustaches, but they have gloss bought from manicure-girls, from masseurs, and from automobile-makers; and their eyes, usually large, are glossy. None of this is allowed to interfere with business; these are "good business men," and often make large fortunes. They are men of imagination about two things—women and money, and, combining their imaginings about both, usually make a wise first marriage. Later, however, they are apt to imagine too much about some little woman without whom life seems duller than need be. They run away, leaving the first wife well enough dowered. They are never intentionally unkind to women, and in the end they usually make the mistake of thinking they have had their money's worth of life. Here was Mr. Harvey Malone, a young specimen in an earlier stage of development, trying to marry Henrietta Lamb, and now sauntering over to speak to Alice, as a time-killer before his next dance with Henrietta.

Alice made no response to his question, and he dropped lazily into the vacant chair, from which she sharply withdrew her hand. "I might as well use his chair till he comes, don't you think? You don't *mind*, do you, old girl?"

"Oh, no," Alice said. "It doesn't matter one way or the other. Please don't call me that."

"So that's how you feel?" Mr. Malone laughed indulgently, without much interest. "I've been meaning to come to see you for a long time—honestly I have—because I wanted to have a good talk with you about old times. I know you think it was funny, after the way I used to come to your house two or three times a week, and sometimes oftener—well, I don't blame you for being hurt, the way I stopped without explaining or anything. The truth is there wasn't any reason: I just happened to have a lot of important things to do and couldn't find the time. But I *am* going to call on you some evening—honestly I am. I don't wonder you think——"

"You're mistaken," Alice said. "I've never thought anything about it at all."

"Well, well!" he said, and looked at her languidly. "What's the use of being cross with this old man? He always means well." And, extending his arm, he would have given her a friendly pat upon the shoulder but she evaded it. "Well, well!" he said. "Seems to me you're getting awful tetchy! Don't you like your old friends any more?"

"Not all of them."

"Who's the new one?" he asked, teasingly. "Come on and tell us, Alice. Who is it you were holding this chair for?"

"Never mind."

"Well, all I've got to do is to sit here till he comes back; then I'll see who it is."

"He may not come back before you have to go."

"Guess you got me *that* time," Malone admitted, laughing as he rose. "They're tuning up, and I've got this dance. I *am* coming around to see you some evening." He moved away, calling back over his shoulder, "Honestly, I am!"

Alice did not look at him.

She had held her tableau as long as she could; it was time for her to abandon the box-trees; and she stepped forth frowning, as if a little annoyed with the absentee for being such a time upon her errand; whereupon the two chairs were instantly seized by a coquetting pair who intended to "sit out" the dance. She walked quickly down the broad corridor, turned into the broader hall, and hurriedly entered the dressing-room where she had left her wraps.

She stayed here as long as she could, pretending to arrange her hair at a mirror, then fidgeting with one of her slipper-buckles; but the intelligent elderly woman in charge of the room made an indefinite sojourn impracticable. "Perhaps I could help you with that buckle, Miss," she suggested, approaching. "Has it come loose?" Alice wrenched desperately; then it was loose. The competent woman, producing needle and thread, deftly made the buckle fast; and there was nothing for Alice to do but to express her gratitude and go.

She went to the door of the cloak-room opposite, where a coloured man stood watchfully in the doorway. "I wonder if you know which of the gentlemen is my brother, Mr. Walter Adams," she said.

"Yes'm; I know him."

"Could you tell me where he is?"

"No'm; I couldn't say."

"Well, if you see him, would you please tell him that his sister, Miss Adams, is looking for him and very anxious to speak to him?"

"Yes'm. Sho'ly, sho'ly!"

As she went away he stared after her and seemed to swell with some bursting emotion. In fact, it was too much for him, and he suddenly retired within the room, releasing strangulated laughter.

Walter remonstrated. Behind an excellent screen of coats and hats, in a remote part of the room, he was kneeling on the floor, engaged in a game of chance with a second coloured attendant; and the laughter became so vehement that it not only interfered with the pastime in hand, but threatened to attract frozen-face attention.

"I cain' he'p it, man," the laughter explained. "I cain' he'p it! You sut'n'y the beatin'es' white boy 'n 'is city!"

The dancers were swinging into an "encore" as Alice halted for an irresolute moment in a doorway. Across the room, a cluster of matrons sat chatting absently, their eyes on their dancing daughters; and Alice, finding a refugee's courage, dodged through the scurrying couples, seated herself in a chair on the outskirts of this colony of elders, and began to talk eagerly to the matron nearest her. The matron seemed unaccustomed to so much vivacity, and responded but dryly, whereupon Alice was more vivacious than ever; for she meant now to present the picture of a jolly girl too much interested in these wise older women to bother about every foolish young man who asked her for a dance.

Her matron was constrained to go so far as to supply a tolerant nod, now and then, in complement to the girl's animation, and Alice was grateful for the nods. In this fashion she supplemented the exhausted resources of the dressing-room and the box-tree nook; and lived through two more dances, when again Mr. Frank Dowling presented himself as a partner.

She needed no pretense to seek the dressing-room for repairs after that number; this time they were necessary and genuine. Dowling waited for her, and when she came out he explained for the fourth or fifth time how the accident had happened. "It was entirely those other people's fault," he said. "They got me in a kind of a corner, because neither of those fellows knows the least thing about guiding; they just jam ahead and expect everybody to get out of *their* way. It was Charlotte Thom's diamond crescent pin that got caught on your dress in the back and made such a——"

"Never mind," Alice said in a tired voice. "The maid fixed it so that she says it isn't very noticeable."

"Well, it isn't," he returned. "You could hardly tell there'd been anything the matter. Where do you want to go? Mother's been interfering in my affairs some more and I've got the next taken."

"I was sitting with Mrs. George Dresser. You might take me back there."

He left her with the matron, and Alice returned to her picture-making, so that once more, while two numbers passed, whoever cared to look was offered the sketch of a jolly, clever girl preoccupied with her elders. Then she found her friend Mildred standing before her, presenting Mr. Arthur Russell, who asked her to dance with him.

Alice looked uncertain, as though not sure what her engagements were; but her perplexity cleared; she nodded, and swung rhythmically away with the tall applicant. She was not grateful to her hostess for this alms. What a young hostess does with a fiancé, Alice thought, is to make him dance with the unpopular girls. She supposed that Mr. Arthur Russell had already danced with Ella Dowling.

The loan of a lover, under these circumstances, may be painful to the lessee, and Alice, smiling never more brightly, found nothing to say to Mr. Russell, though she thought he might have found something to say to her. "I wonder what Mildred told him," she thought. "Probably she said, 'Dearest, there's one more girl you've got to help me out with. You wouldn't like her much, but she dances well enough and she's having a rotten time. Nobody ever goes near her any more.'"

When the music stopped, Russell added his applause to the hand-clapping that encouraged the uproarious instruments to continue, and as they renewed the tumult, he said heartily, "That's splendid!"

Alice gave him a glance, necessarily at short range, and found his eyes kindly and pleased. Here was a friendly soul, it appeared, who probably "liked everybody." No doubt he had applauded for an "encore" when he danced with Ella Dowling, gave Ella the same genial look, and said, "That's splendid!"

When the "encore" was over, Alice spoke to him for the first time.

"Mildred will be looking for you," she said.

"I think you'd better take me back to where you found me."

He looked surprised. "Oh, if you——"

"I'm sure Mildred will be needing you," Alice said, and as she took his arm and they walked toward Mrs. Dresser, she thought it might be just possible to make a further use of the loan. "Oh, I wonder if you——" she began.

"Yes?" he said, quickly.

"You don't know my brother, Walter Adams," she said. "But he's somewhere—I think possibly he's in a smoking-room or some place where girls aren't expected, and if you wouldn't think it too much trouble to inquire——"

"I'll find him," Russell said, promptly. "Thank you so much for that dance. I'll bring your brother in a moment."

It was to be a long moment, Alice decided, presently. Mrs. Dresser had grown restive; and her nods and vague responses to her young dependent's gaieties were as meager as they could well be. Evidently the matron had no intention of appearing to her world in the light of a chaperone for Alice Adams; and she finally made this clear. With a word or two of excuse, breaking into something Alice was saying, she rose and went to sit next to Mildred's mother, who had become the nucleus of the cluster. So Alice was left very much against the wall, with short stretches of vacant chairs on each side of her. She had come to the end of her picture-making, and could only pretend that there was something amusing the matter with the arm of her chair.

She supposed that Mildred's Mr. Russell had forgotten Walter by this time. "I'm not even an intimate enough friend of Mildred's for him to have thought he ought to bother to tell me he couldn't find him," she thought. And then she saw Russell coming across the room toward her, with Walter beside him. She jumped up gaily.

"Oh, thank you!" she cried. "I know this naughty boy must have been terribly hard to find. Mildred'll *never* forgive me! I've put you to so much——"

"Not at all," he said, amiably, and went away, leaving the brother and sister together.

"Walter, let's dance just once more," Alice said, touching his arm placatively. "I thought—well, perhaps we might go home then."

But Walter's expression was that of a person upon whom an outrage has just been perpetrated. "No," he said. "We've stayed *this* long, I'm goin' to wait and see what they got to eat. And you look here!" He turned upon her angrily. "Don't you ever do that again!"

"Do what?"

"Send somebody after me that pokes his nose into every corner of the house till he finds me! 'Are you Mr. Walter Adams?' he says. I guess he must asked everybody in the place if they were Mr. Walter Adams! Well, I'll bet a few iron men you wouldn't send anybody to hunt for me again if you knew where he found me!"

"Where was it?"

Walter decided that her fit punishment was to know. "I was shootin' dice with those coons in the cloak-room."

"And he *saw* you?"

"Unless he was blind!" said Walter. "Come on, I'll dance this one more dance with you. Supper comes after that, and *then* we'll go home."

Mrs. Adams heard Alice's key turning in the front door and hurried down the stairs to meet her.

"Did you get wet coming in, darling?" she asked. "Did you have a good time?"

"Just lovely!" Alice said, cheerily; and after she had arranged the latch for Walter, who had gone to return the little car, she followed her mother upstairs and hummed a dance-tune on the way.

"Oh, I'm so glad you had a nice time," Mrs. Adams said, as they reached the door of her daughter's room together. "You *deserved* to, and it's lovely to think——"

But at this, without warning, Alice threw herself into her mother's arms, sobbing so loudly that in his room, close by, her father, half drowsing through the night, started to full wakefulness.

CHAPTER IX

ON A morning, a week after this collapse of festal hopes, Mrs. Adams and her daughter were concluding a three-days' disturbance, the "Spring house-cleaning"—postponed until now by Adams's long illness—and Alice, on her knees before a chest of drawers, in her mother's room, paused thoughtfully after dusting a packet of letters wrapped in worn muslin. She called to her mother, who was scrubbing the floor of the hallway just beyond the open door,

"These old letters you had in the bottom drawer, weren't they some papa wrote you before you were married?"

Mrs. Adams laughed and said, "Yes. Just put 'em back where they were—or else up in the attic—anywhere you want to."

"Do you mind if I read one, mama?"

Mrs. Adams laughed again. "Oh, I guess you can if you want to. I expect they're pretty funny!"

Alice laughed in response, and chose the topmost

letter of the packet. "My dear, beautiful girl," it began; and she stared at these singular words. They gave her a shock like that caused by overhearing some bewildering impropriety; and, having read them over to herself several times, she went on to experience other shocks.

My dear, beautiful girl:

This time yesterday I had a mighty bad case of blues because I had not had a word from you in two whole long days and when I do not hear from you every day things look mighty down in the mouth to me. Now it is all so different because your letter has arrived and besides I have got a piece of news I believe you will think as fine as I do. Darling, you will be surprised, so get ready to hear about a big effect on our future. It is this way. I had sort of a suspicion the head of the firm kind of took a fancy to me from the first when I went in there, and liked the way I attended to my work and so when he took me on this business trip with him I felt pretty sure of it and now it turns out I was about right. In return I guess I have got about the best boss in this world and I believe you will think so too. Yes, sweetheart, after the talk I have just had with him if J. A. Lamb asked me to cut my hand off for him I guess I would come pretty near doing it because what he says means the end of our waiting to be together. From New Years on he is going to put me in entire charge of the sundries dept. and what do you think is going to be my salary? Eleven hundred cool dollars a year ($1,100.00). That's all! Just only a cool eleven hundred per annum! Well, I guess that will show your mother whether I can take care of you or not. And oh how I would like to see your dear, beautiful, loving face when you get this news.

I would like to go out on the public streets and just dance and shout and it is all I can do to help doing it, especially when I know we will be talking it all over together this time next week, and oh my darling, now that your folks have no excuse for putting it off any longer we might be in our own little home before Xmas. Would you be glad?

Well, darling, this settles everything and makes our future just about as smooth for us as anybody could ask. I can hardly realize after all this waiting life's troubles are over for you and me and we have nothing to do but to enjoy the happiness granted us by this wonderful, beautiful thing we call life. I know I am not any poet and the one I tried to write about you the day of the picnic was fearful but the way I *think* about you is a poem.

Write me what you think of the news. I know but write me anyhow. I'll get it before we start home and I can be reading it over all the time on the train.

Your always loving

VIRGIL.

The sound of her mother's diligent scrubbing in the hall came back slowly to Alice's hearing, as she restored the letter to the packet, wrapped the packet in its muslin covering, and returned it to the drawer. She had remained upon her knees while she read the letter; now she sank backward, sitting upon the floor with her hands behind her, an unconscious relaxing for better ease to think. Upon her face there had fallen a look of wonder.

For the first time she was vaguely perceiving that life is everlasting movement. Youth really believes what is running water to be a permanent crystallization and sees time fixed to a point: some people have dark hair, some people have blond hair, some people have gray hair. Until this moment, Alice had no conviction that there was a universe before she came into it. She had always thought of it as the background of herself: the moon was something to make her prettier on a summer night.

But this old letter, through which she saw still flickering an ancient starlight of young love, astounded her. Faintly before her it revealed the whole lives of her father and mother, who had been young, after all—they *really* had—and their youth was now so utterly passed from them that the picture of it, in the letter, was like a burlesque of them. And so she, herself, must pass to such changes, too, and all that now seemed vital to her would be nothing.

When her work was finished, that afternoon, she went into her father's room. His recovery had progressed well enough to permit the departure of Miss Perry; and Adams, wearing one of Mrs. Adams's wrappers over his night-gown, sat in a high-backed chair by a closed window. The weather was warm, but the closed window and the flannel wrapper had not sufficed him: round his shoulders he had an old crocheted scarf of Alice's; his legs were wrapped in a heavy comfort; and, with these swathings about him, and his eyes closed, his thin and grizzled head making but a slight indentation in the pillow supporting it, he looked old and little and queer.

Alice would have gone out softly, but without opening his eyes, he spoke to her: "Don't go, dearie. Come sit with the old man a little while."

She brought a chair near his. "I thought you were napping."

"No. I don't hardly ever do that. I just drift a little sometimes."

"How do you mean you drift, papa?"

He looked at her vaguely. "Oh, I don't know. Kind of pictures. They get a little mixed up—old times with times still ahead, like planning what to do, you know. That's as near a nap as I get—when the pictures mix up some. I suppose it's sort of drowsing."

She took one of his hands and stroked it. "What do you mean when you say you have pictures like 'planning what to do'?" she asked.

"I mean planning what to do when I get out and able to go to work again."

"But that doesn't need any planning," Alice said, quickly. "You're going back to your old place at Lamb's, of course."

Adams closed his eyes again, sighing heavily, but made no other response.

"Why, of *course* you are!" she cried. "What are you talking about?"

His head turned slowly toward her, revealing the eyes, open in a haggard stare. "I heard you the other night when you came from the party," he said. "I know what was the matter."

"Indeed, you don't," she assured him. "You don't know anything about it, because there wasn't anything the matter at all."

"Don't you suppose I heard you crying? What'd you cry for if there wasn't anything the matter?"

"Just nerves, papa. It wasn't anything else in the world."

"Never mind," he said. "Your mother told me."

"She promised me not to!"

At that Adams laughed mournfully. "It wouldn't be very likely I'd hear you so upset and not ask about it, even if she didn't come and tell me on her own hook. You needn't try to fool me; I tell you I know what was the matter."

"The only matter was I had a silly fit," Alice protested. "It did me good, too."

"How's that?"

"Because I've decided to do something about it, papa."

"That isn't the way your mother looks at it," Adams said, ruefully. "She thinks it's our place to do something about it. Well, I don't know—I don't know; everything seems so changed these days. You've always been a good daughter, Alice, and you ought to have as much as any of these girls you go with; she's convinced me she's right about *that*. The trouble is——" He faltered, apologetically, then went on, "I mean the question is—how to get it for you."

"No!" she cried. "I had no business to make such a fuss just because a lot of idiots didn't break their necks to get dances with me and because I got mortified about Walter—Walter *was* pretty terrible——"

"Oh, me, my!" Adams lamented. "I guess that's something we just have to leave work out itself. What you going to do with a boy nineteen or twenty years old that makes his own living? Can't whip him. Can't keep him locked up in the house. Just got to hope he'll learn better, I suppose."

"Of course he didn't want to go to the Palmers'," Alice explained, tolerantly—"and as mama and I made him take me, and he thought that was pretty selfish in me, why, he felt he had a right to amuse himself any way he could. Of course it was awful that this—that this Mr. Russell should——" In spite of her, the recollection choked her.

"Yes, it was awful," Adams agreed. "Just awful. Oh, me, my!"

But Alice recovered herself at once, and showed him a cheerful face. "Well, just a few years from now I probably won't even remember it! I believe hardly anything amounts to as much as we think it does at the time."

"Well—sometimes it don't."

"What I've been thinking, papa: it seems to me I ought to *do* something."

"What like?"

She looked dreamy, but was obviously serious as she told him: "Well, I mean I ought to be something besides just a kind of nobody. I ought to——" She paused.

"What, dearie?"

"Well—there's one thing I'd like to do. I'm sure I *could* do it, too."

"What?"

"I want to go on the stage: I know I could act."

At this, her father abruptly gave utterance to a feeble cackling of laughter; and when Alice, surprised and a little offended, pressed him for his reason, he tried to evade, saying, "Nothing, dearie. I just thought of something." But she persisted until he had to explain.

"It made me think of your mother's sister, your Aunt Flora, that died when you were little," he said. "She was always telling how she was going on the stage, and talking about how she was certain she'd make a great actress, and all so on; and one day your mother broke out and said *she* ought 'a' gone on the stage, herself, because she always knew she had the talent for it—and, well, they got into kind of a spat about which one'd make the best actress. I had to go out in the hall to laugh!"

"Maybe you were wrong," Alice said, gravely. "If they both felt it, why wouldn't that look as if there was talent in the family? I've *always* thought——"

"No, dearie," he said, with a final chuckle. "Your mother and Flora weren't different from a good many others. I expect ninety per cent. of all the women I ever knew were just sure they'd be mighty fine actresses if they ever got the chance. Well, I guess it's a good thing; they enjoy thinking about it and it don't do anybody any harm."

Alice was piqued. For several days she had thought almost continuously of a career to be won by her own genius. Not that she planned details, or concerned herself with first steps; her picturings overleaped all that. Principally, she saw her name great on all the bill-boards of that unkind city, and herself, unchanged in age but glamorous with fame and Paris clothes, returning in a private car. No doubt the pleasantest development of her vision was a dialogue with Mildred; and this became so real that, as she projected it, Alice assumed the proper expressions for both parties to it, formed words with her lips, and even spoke some of them aloud. "No, I haven't forgotten you, Mrs. Russell. I remember you quite pleasantly, in fact. You were a Miss Palmer, I recall, in those funny old days. Very kind of you, I'm shaw. I appreciate your eagerness to do something for me in your own little home. As you say, a reception *would* renew my acquaintanceship with many old friends—but I'm shaw you won't mind my mentioning that

I don't find much inspiration in these provincials. I really must ask you not to press me. An artist's time is not her own, though of course I could hardly expect you to understand——"

Thus Alice illuminated the dull time; but she retired from the interview with her father still manfully displaying an outward cheerfulness, while depression grew heavier within, as if she had eaten soggy cake. Her father knew nothing whatever of the stage, and she was aware of his ignorance, yet for some reason his innocently skeptical amusement reduced her bright project almost to nothing. Something like this always happened, it seemed; she was continually making these illuminations, all gay with gildings and colourings; and then as soon as anybody else so much as glanced at them—even her father, who loved her—the pretty designs were stricken with a desolating pallor. "Is this *life?*" Alice wondered, not doubting that the question was original and all her own. "Is it life to spend your time imagining things that aren't so, and never will be? Beautiful things happen to other people; why should I be the only one they never *can* happen to?"

The mood lasted overnight; and was still upon her

"She looked dreamy but was obviously serious . . . . 'I want to go on the stage. I know I could act.' "

the next afternoon when an errand for her father took her down-town. Adams had decided to begin smoking again, and Alice felt rather degraded, as well as embarrassed, when she went into the large shop her father had named, and asked for the cheap tobacco he used in his pipe. She fell back upon an air of amused indulgence, hoping thus to suggest that her purchase was made for some faithful old retainer, now infirm; and although the calmness of the clerk who served her called for no such elaboration of her sketch, she ornamented it with a little laugh and with the remark, as she dropped the package into her coat-pocket, "I'm sure it'll please him; they tell me it's the kind he likes."

Still playing Lady Bountiful, smiling to herself in anticipation of the joy she was bringing to the simple old negro or Irish follower of the family, she left the shop; but as she came out upon the crowded pavement her smile vanished quickly.

Next to the door of the tobacco-shop, there was the open entrance to a stairway, and, above this rather bleak and dark aperture, a sign-board displayed in begrimed gilt letters the information that Frincke's Business College occupied the upper floors of the building. Furthermore, Frincke here publicly offered "personal instruction and training in practical mathematics, bookkeeping, and all branches of the business life, including stenography, typewriting, etc."

Alice halted for a moment, frowning at this signboard as though it were something surprising and distasteful which she had never seen before. Yet it was conspicuous in a busy quarter; she almost always passed it when she came down-town, and never without noticing it. Nor was this the first time she had paused to lift toward it that same glance of vague misgiving.

The building was not what the changeful city defined as a modern one, and the dusty wooden stairway, as seen from the pavement, disappeared upward into a smoky darkness. So would the footsteps of a girl ascending there lead to a hideous obscurity, Alice thought; an obscurity as dreary and as permanent as death. And like dry leaves falling about her she saw her wintry imaginings in the May air: pretty girls turning into withered creatures as they worked at typing-machines; old maids "taking dictation" from men with double chins; Alice saw old maids of a dozen different kinds "taking dictation." Her mind's eye was crowded with them, as it always was when she passed that stairway entrance; and though they were all different from one another, all of them looked a little like herself.

She hated the place, and yet she seldom hurried by it or averted her eyes. It had an unpleasant fascination for her, and a mysterious reproach, which she did not seek to fathom. She walked on thoughtfully to-day; and when, at the next corner, she turned into the street that led toward home, she was given a surprise. Arthur Russell came rapidly from behind her, lifting his hat as she saw him.

"Are you walking north, Miss Adams?" he asked. "Do you mind if I walk with you?"

She was not delighted, but seemed so. "How charming!" she cried, giving him a little flourish of the shapely hands; and then, because she wondered if he had seen her coming out of the tobacco-shop, she laughed and added, "I've just been on the most ridiculous errand!"

"What was that?"

"To order some cigars for my father. He's been quite ill, poor man, and he's so particular—but what in the world do *I* know about cigars?"

Russell laughed. "Well, what *do* you know about 'em? Did you select by the price?"

"Mercy, no!" she exclaimed, and added, with an afterthought, "Of course he wrote down the name of the kind he wanted and I gave it to the shopman. I could never have pronounced it."

CHAPTER X

IN HER pocket as she spoke her hand rested upon the little sack of tobacco, which responded accusingly to the touch of her restless fingers; and she found time to wonder why she was building up this fiction for Mr. Arthur Russell. His discovery of Walter's device for whiling away the dull evening had shamed and distressed her; but she would have suffered no less if almost any other had been the discoverer. In this gentleman, after hearing that he was Mildred's Mr. Arthur Russell, Alice felt not the slightest "personal interest"; and there was yet to develop in her life such a thing as an interest not personal. At twenty-two this state of affairs is not unique.

So far as Alice was concerned Russell might have worn a placard, "Engaged." She looked upon him as diners entering a restaurant look upon tables marked "Reserved": the glance, slightly discontented, passes on at once. Or so the eye of a prospector wanders querulously over staked and established claims on the mountainside, and seeks the virgin land beyond; unless, indeed, the prospector be dishonest. But Alice was no claim-jumper—so long as the notice of ownership was plainly posted.

Though she was indifferent now, habit ruled her: and, at the very time she wondered why she created fictitious cigars for her father, she was also regretting that she had not boldly carried her Malacca stick down-town with her. Her vivacity increased automatically.

"Perhaps the clerk thought you wanted the cigars for yourself," Russell suggested. "He may have taken you for a Spanish countess."

"I'm sure he did!" Alice agreed, gaily; and she hummed a bar or two of "La Paloma," snapping her fingers as castanets, and swaying her body a little, to suggest the accepted stencil of a "Spanish Dancer." "Would you have taken me for one, Mr. Russell?" she asked, as she concluded the impersonation.

"I? Why, yes," he said. "*I'd* take you for anything you wanted me to."

"Why, what a speech!" she cried, and, laughing, gave him a quick glance in which there glimmered some real surprise. He was looking at her quizzically, but with the liveliest ap ɔreciation. Her surprise increased; and she was glad that he had joined her.

To be seen walking with such a companion added to her pleasure. She would have described him as "altogether quite stunning-looking"; and she liked his tall, dark thinness, his gray clothes, his soft hat, and his clean brown shoes; she liked his easy swing of the stick he carried.

"Shouldn't I have said it?" he asked. "Would you rather not be taken for a Spanish countess?"

"That isn't it," she explained. "You said——"

"I said I'd take you for whatever you wanted me to. Isn't that all right?"

"It would all depend, wouldn't it?"

"Of course it would depend on what you wanted."

"Oh, no!" she laughed. "It might depend on a lot of things."

"Such as?"

"Well——" She hesitated, having the mischievous impulse to say, "Such as Mildred!" But she decided to omit this reference, and became serious, remembering Russell's service to her at Mildred's house. "Speaking of what I want to be taken for," she said;—"I've been wondering ever since the other night what you did take me for! You must have taken me for the sister of a professional gambler, I'm afraid!"

Russell's look of kindness was the truth about him, she was to discover; and he reassured her now by the promptness of his friendly chuckle. "Then your young brother told you where I found him, did he? I kept my face straight at the time, but I laughed afterward—to myself. It struck me as original, to say the least: his amusing himself with those darkies."

"Walter *is* original," Alice said; and, having adopted this new view of her brother's eccentricities, she impulsively went on to make it more plausible. "He's a very odd boy, and I was afraid you'd misunderstand. He tells wonderful 'darky stories,' and he'll do anything to draw coloured people out and make them talk; and that's what he was doing at Mildred's when you found him for me—he says he wins their confidence by playing dice with them. In the family we think he'll probably write about them some day. He's rather literary."

"Are you?" Russell asked, smiling.

"I? Oh——" She paused, lifting both hands in a charming gesture of helplessness. "Oh, I'm just—me!"

His glance followed the lightly waved hands with

keen approval, then rose to the lively and colourful face, with its hazel eyes, its small and pretty nose, and the lip-caught smile which seemed the climax of her decorative transition. Never had he seen a creature so plastic or so wistful.

Here was a contrast to his cousin Mildred, who was not wistful, and controlled any impulses toward plasticity, if she had them. "By George!" he said. "But you *are* different!"

With that, there leaped in her such an impulse of roguish gallantry as she could never resist. She turned her head, and, laughing and bright-eyed, looked him full in the face.

"From whom?" she cried.

"From—everybody!" he said. "Are you a mind-reader?"

"Why?"

"How did you know I was thinking you were different from my cousin, Mildred Palmer?"

"What makes you think I *did* know it?"

"Nonsense!" he said. "You knew what I was thinking and I knew you knew."

"Yes," she said with cool humour. "How intimate that seems to make us all at once!"

Russell left no doubt that he was delighted with

these gaieties of hers. "By George!" he exclaimed again. "I thought you were this sort of girl the first moment I saw you!"

"What sort of girl? Didn't Mildred tell you what sort of girl I am when she asked you to dance with me?"

"She didn't ask me to dance with you—I'd been looking at you. You were talking to some old ladies, and I asked Mildred who you were."

"Oh, so Mildred *didn't*——" Alice checked herself. "Who did she tell you I was?"

"She just said you were a Miss Adams, so I——"

"'A' Miss Adams?" Alice interrupted.

"Yes. Then I said I'd like to meet you."

"I see. You thought you'd save me from the old ladies."

"No. I thought I'd save myself from some of the girls Mildred was getting me to dance with. There was a Miss Dowling——"

"Poor man!" Alice said, gently, and her impulsive thought was that Mildred had taken few chances, and that as a matter of self-defense her carefulness might have been well founded. This Mr. Arthur Russell was a much more responsive person than one had supposed.

"So, Mr. Russell, you don't know anything about me except what you thought when you first saw me?"

"Yes, I know I was right when I thought it."

"You haven't told me what you thought."

"I thought you were like what you *are* like."

"Not very definite, is it? I'm afraid you shed more light a minute or so ago, when you said how different from Mildred you thought I was. That *was* definite, unfortunately!"

"I didn't say it," Russell explained. "I thought it, and you read my mind. That's the sort of girl I thought you were—one that could read a man's mind. Why do you say 'unfortunately' you're not like Mildred?"

Alice's smooth gesture seemed to sketch Mildred. "Because she's perfect—why, she's *perfectly* perfect! She never makes a mistake, and everybody looks up to her—oh, yes, we all fairly adore her! She's like some big, noble, cold statue—'way above the rest of us—and she hardly ever does anything mean or treacherous. Of all the girls I know I believe she's played the fewest really petty tricks. She's——"

Russell interrupted; he looked perplexed. "You

say she's perfectly perfect, but that she does play *some*——"

Alice laughed, as if at his sweet innocence. "Men are so funny!" she informed him. "Of course girls *all* do mean things sometimes. My own career's just one long brazen smirch of 'em! What I mean is, Mildred's perfectly perfect compared to the rest of us."

"I see," he said, and seemed to need a moment or two of thoughtfulness. Then he inquired, "What sort of treacherous things do *you* do?"

"I? Oh, the very worst kind! Most people bore me—particularly the men in this town—and I show it."

"But I shouldn't call that treacherous, exactly."

"Well, *they* do," Alice laughed. "It's made me a terribly unpopular character! I do a lot of things they hate. For instance, at a dance I'd a lot rather find some clever old woman and talk to her than dance with nine-tenths of these nonentities. I usually do it, too."

"But you danced as if you liked it. You danced better than any other girl I——"

"This flattery of yours doesn't quite turn my head, Mr. Russell," Alice interrupted. "Particularly since

Mildred only gave you Ella Dowling to compare with me!"

"Oh, no," he insisted. "There were others—and of course Mildred, herself."

"Oh, of course, yes. I forgot that. Well——" She paused, then added, "I certainly *ought* to dance well."

"Why is it so much a duty?"

"When I think of the dancing-teachers and the expense to papa! All sorts of fancy instructors—I suppose that's what daughters have fathers for, though, isn't it? To throw money away on them?"

"You don't——" Russell began, and his look was one of alarm. "You haven't taken up——"

She understood his apprehension and responded merrily, "Oh, murder, no! You mean you're afraid I break out sometimes in a piece of cheesecloth and run around a fountain thirty times, and then, for an encore, show how much like snakes I can make my arms look."

"I *said* you were a mind-reader!" he exclaimed. "That's exactly what I was pretending to be afraid you might do."

"'Pretending?' That's nicer of you. No; it's not my mania."

"What is?"

"Oh, nothing in particular that I know of just now. Of course I've had the usual one: the one that every girl goes through."

"What's that?"

"Good heavens, Mr. Russell, you can't expect me to believe you're really a man of the world if you don't know that every girl has a time in her life when she's positive she's divinely talented for the stage! It's the only universal rule about women that hasn't got an exception. I don't mean we all want to go on the stage, but we all think we'd be wonderful if we did. Even Mildred. Oh, she wouldn't confess it to you: you'd have to know her a great deal better than any man can ever know her to find out."

"I see," he said. "Girls are always telling us we can't know them. I wonder if you——"

She took up his thought before he expressed it, and again he was fascinated by her quickness, which indeed seemed to him almost telepathic. "Oh, but *don't* we know one another, though!" she cried. "Such things we have to keep secret—things that go on right before *your* eyes!"

"Why don't some of you tell us?" he asked.

"We can't tell you."

"Too much honour?"

"No. Not even too much honour among thieves, Mr. Russell. We don't tell you about our tricks against one another because we know it wouldn't make any impression on you. The tricks aren't played against you, and you have a soft side for cats with lovely manners!"

"What about your tricks against us?"

"Oh, those!" Alice laughed. "We think they're rather cute!"

"Bravo!" he cried, and hammered the ferrule of his stick upon the pavement.

"What's the applause for?"

"For you. What you said was like running up the black flag to the masthead."

"Oh, no. It was just a modest little sign in a pretty flower-bed: 'Gentlemen, beware!'"

"I see I must," he said, gallantly.

"Thanks! But I mean, beware of the whole bloomin' garden!" Then, picking up a thread that had almost disappeared: "You needn't think you'll ever find out whether I'm right about Mildred's not being an exception by asking her," she said. "She won't tell you: she's not the sort that ever makes a confession."

But Russell had not followed her shift to the

former topic. "'Mildred's not being an exception?'" he said, vaguely. "I don't——"

"An exception about thinking she could be a wonderful thing on the stage if she only cared to. If you asked her I'm pretty sure she'd say, 'What nonsense!' Mildred's the dearest, finest thing anywhere, but you won't find out many things about her by asking her."

Russell's expression became more serious, as it did whenever his cousin was made their topic. "You think not?" he said. "You think she's——"

"No. But it's not because she isn't sincere exactly. It's only because she has such a lot to live up to. She has to live up to being a girl on the grand style—to herself, I mean, of course." And without pausing Alice rippled on, "You ought to have seen *me* when I had the stage-fever! I used to play 'Juliet' all alone in my room.' She lifted her arms in graceful entreaty, pleading musically,

> "O, swear not by the moon, the inconstant moon,
> That monthly changes in her circled orb,
> Lest thy love prove——"

She broke off abruptly with a little flourish, snapping thumb and finger of each outstretched hand, then laughed and said, "Papa used to make such fun of me! Thank heaven, I was only fifteen; I was all over it by the next year."

"No wonder you had the fever," Russell observed. "You do it beautifully. Why didn't you finish the line?"

"Which one? 'Lest thy love prove likewise variable'? Juliet was saying it to a *man*, you know. She seems to have been ready to worry about his constancy pretty early in their affair!"

Her companion was again thoughtful. "Yes," he said, seeming to be rather irksomely impressed with Alice's suggestion. "Yes; it does appear so."

Alice glanced at his serious face, and yielded to an audacious temptation. "You mustn't take it so hard," she said, flippantly. "It isn't about you: it's only about Romeo and Juliet."

"See here!" he exclaimed. "You aren't at your mind-reading again, are you? There are times when it won't do, you know!"

She leaned toward him a little, as if companionably: they were walking slowly, and this geniality of hers brought her shoulder in light contact with his for a moment. "Do you dislike my mind-reading?" she asked, and, across their two just touching shoulders, gave him her sudden look of smiling wistfulness. "Do you hate it?"

He shook his head. "No, I don't," he said, gravely. "It's quite—pleasant. But I think it says, 'Gentlemen, beware!'"

She instantly moved away from him, with the lawless and frank laugh of one who is delighted to be caught in a piece of hypocrisy. "How lovely!" she cried. Then she pointed ahead. "Our walk is nearly over. We're coming to the foolish little house where I live. It's a queer little place, but my father's so attached to it the family have about given up hope of getting him to build a real house farther out. He doesn't mind our being extravagant about anything else, but he won't let us alter one single thing about his precious little old house. Well!" She halted, and gave him her hand. "Adieu!"

"I couldn't," he began; hesitated, then asked: "I couldn't come in with you for a little while?"

"Not now," she said, quickly. "You can come——" She paused.

"When?"

"Almost any time." She turned and walked slowly up the path, but he waited. "You can come in the evening if you like," she called back to him over her shoulder.

"Soon?"

"As soon as you like!" She waved her hand; then ran indoors and watched him from a window as he went up the street. He walked rapidly, a fine, easy figure, swinging his stick in a way that suggested exhilaration. Alice, staring after him through the irregular apertures of a lace curtain, showed no similar buoyancy. Upon the instant she closed the door all sparkle left her: she had become at once the simple and sometimes troubled girl her family knew.

"What's going on out there?" her mother asked, approaching from the dining-room.

"Oh, nothing," Alice said, indifferently, as she turned away. "That Mr. Russell met me down-town and walked up with me."

"Mr. Russell? Oh, the one that's engaged to Mildred?"

"Well—I don't know for certain. He didn't seem so much like an engaged man to me." And she added, in the tone of thoughtful preoccupation: "Anyhow—not so terribly!"

Then she ran upstairs, gave her father his tobacco, filled his pipe for him, and petted him as he lighted it.

CHAPTER XI

AFTER that, she went to her room and sat down before her three-leaved mirror. There was where she nearly always sat when she came into her room, if she had nothing in mind to do. She went to that chair as naturally as a dog goes to his corner.

She leaned forward, observing her profile; gravity seemed to be her mood. But after a long, almost motionless scrutiny, she began to produce dramatic sketches upon that ever-ready stage, her countenance: she showed gaiety, satire, doubt, gentleness, appreciation of a companion and love-in-hiding—all studied in profile first, then repeated for a "three-quarter view." Subsequently she ran through them, facing herself in full.

In this manner she outlined a playful scenario for her next interview with Arthur Russell; but grew solemn again, thinking of the impression she had already sought to give him. She had no twinges for any underminings of her "most intimate friend"—in fact, she felt that her work on a new portrait of Mildred for Mr. Russell had been honest and accurate. But why had it been her instinct to show him an Alice Adams who didn't exist?

Almost everything she had said to him was upon spontaneous impulse, springing to her lips on the instant; yet it all seemed to have been founded upon a careful design, as if some hidden self kept such designs in stock and handed them up to her, ready-made, to be used for its own purpose. What appeared to be the desired result was a false-coloured image in Russell's mind; but if he liked that image he wouldn't be liking Alice Adams; nor would anything he thought about the image be a thought about her. Nevertheless, she knew she would go on with her false, fancy colourings of this nothing as soon as she saw him again; she had just been practising them. "What's the idea?" she wondered. "What makes me tell such lies? Why shouldn't I be just myself?" And then she thought, "But which one is myself?"

Her eyes dwelt on the solemn eyes in the mirror; and her lips, disquieted by a deepening wonder, parted to whisper:

"Who in the world are you?"

The apparition before her had obeyed her like an alert slave, but now, as she subsided to a complete stillness, that aspect changed to the old mockery with which mirrors avenge their wrongs. The nucleus of some queer thing seemed to gather and shape itself behind the nothingness of the reflected eyes until it became almost an actual strange presence. If it could be identified, perhaps the presence was that of the hidden designer who handed up the false, ready-made pictures, and, for unknown purposes, made Alice exhibit them; but whatever it was, she suddenly found it monkey-like and terrifying. In a flutter she jumped up and went to another part of the room.

A moment or two later she was whistling softly as she hung her light coat over a wooden triangle in her closet, and her musing now was quainter than the experience that led to it; for what she thought was this, "I certainly am a queer girl!" She took a little pride in so much originality, believing herself probably the only person in the world to have such thoughts as had been hers since she entered the room, and the first to be disturbed by a strange presence in the mirror. In fact, the effect of the tiny episode became apparent in that look of preoccupied complacency to be seen for a time upon any girl who has found reason to suspect that she is a being without counterpart.

This slight glow, still faintly radiant, was observed across the dinner-table by Walter, but he misinterpreted it. "What *you* lookin' so self-satisfied about?" he inquired, and added in his knowing way, "I saw you, all right, cutie!"

"Where'd you see me?"

"Down-town."

"This afternoon, you mean, Walter?"

"Yes, 'this afternoon, I mean, Walter,'" he returned, burlesquing her voice at least happily enough to please himself; for he laughed applausively. "Oh, you never saw me! I passed you close enough to pull a tooth, but you were awful busy. I never did see anybody as busy as you get, Alice, when you're towin' a barge. My, but you keep your hands goin'! Looked like the air was full of 'em! That's why I'm onto why you look so tickled this evening; I saw you with that big fish."

Mrs. Adams laughed benevolently; she was not displeased with this rallying. "Well, what of it, Walter?" she asked. "If you happen to see your sister on the street when some nice young man is being attentive to her——"

Walter barked and then cackled. "Whoa, Sal!" he said. "You got the parts mixed. It's little Alice that was 'being attentive.' I know the big fish she was attentive to, all right, too."

"Yes," his sister retorted, quietly. "I should think you might have recognized him, Walter."

Walter looked annoyed. "Still harpin' on *that!*" he complained. "The kind of women I like, if they get sore they just hit you somewhere on the face and then they're through. By the way, I heard this Russell was supposed to be your dear, old, sweet friend Mildred's steady. What you doin' walkin' as close to him as all that?"

Mrs. Adams addressed her son in gentle reproof, "Why Walter!"

"Oh, never mind, mama," Alice said. "To the horrid all things are horrid."

"Get out!" Walter protested, carelessly. "I heard all about this Russell down at the shop. Young Joe Lamb's such a talker I wonder he don't ruin his grandfather's business; he keeps all us cheap help standin' round listening to him nine-tenths of our time. Well, Joe told me this Russell's some kin or other to the Palmer family, and he's got some little money of his own, and he's puttin' it into ole Palmer's trust company and Palmer's goin' to make him a vice-president of the company. Sort of a keep-the-money-in-the-family arrangement, Joe Lamb says."

Mrs. Adams looked thoughtful. "I don't see——" she began.

"Why, this Russell's supposed to be tied up to Mildred," her son explained. "When ole Palmer dies this Russell will be his son-in-law, and all he'll haf' to do'll be to barely lift his feet and step into the ole man's shoes. It's certainly a mighty fat hand-me-out for this Russell! You better lay off o' there, Alice. Pick somebody that's got less to lose and you'll make a better showing."

Mrs. Adams's air of thoughtfulness had not departed. "But you say this Mr. Russell is well off on his own account, Walter."

"Oh, Joe Lamb says he's got some little of his own. Didn't know how much."

"Well, then——"

Walter laughed his laugh. "Cut it out," he bade her. "Alice wouldn't run in fourth place."

Alice had been looking at him in a detached way,

as though estimating the value of a specimen in a collection not her own. "Yes," she said, indifferently. "You *really* are vulgar, Walter."

He had finished his meal; and, rising, he came round the table to her and patted her good-naturedly on the shoulder. "Good ole Allie!" he said. "*Honest*, you wouldn't run in fourth place. If I was you I'd never even start in the class. That frozen-face gang will rule you off the track soon as they see your colours."

"Walter!" his mother said again.

"Well, ain't I her brother?" he returned, seeming to be entirely serious and direct, for the moment, at least. "*I* like the ole girl all right. Fact is, sometimes I'm kind of sorry for her."

"But what's it all *about?*" Alice cried. "Simply because you met me down-town with a man I never saw but once before and just barely know! Why all this palaver?"

"'Why?'" he repeated, grinning. "Well, I've seen you start before, you know!" He went to the door, and paused. "I got no date to-night. Take you to the movies, you care to go."

She declined crisply. "No, thanks!"

"Come on," he said, as pleasantly as he knew how.

"Give me a chance to show you a better time than we had up at that frozen-face joint. I'll get you some chop suey afterward."

"No, thanks!"

"All right," he responded and waved a flippant adieu. "As the barber says, 'The better the advice, the worse it's wasted!' Good-*night!*"

Alice shrugged her shoulders; but a moment or two later, as the jar of the carelessly slammed front door went through the house, she shook her head, reconsidering. "Perhaps I ought to have gone with him. It might have kept him away from whatever dreadful people are his friends—at least for one night."

"Oh, I'm sure Walter's a *good* boy," Mrs. Adams said, soothingly; and this was what she almost always said when either her husband or Alice expressed such misgivings. "He's odd, and he's picked up right queer manners; but that's only because we haven't given him advantages like the other young men. But I'm sure he's a *good* boy."

She reverted to the subject a little later, while she washed the dishes and Alice wiped them. "Of course Walter could take his place with the other nice boys of the town even yet," she said. "I mean, if we could afford to help him financially. They all belong to the country clubs and have cars and——"

"Let's don't go into that any more, mama," the daughter begged her. "What's the use?"

"It *could* be of use," Mrs. Adams insisted. "It could if your father——"

"But papa *can't.*"

"Yes, he can."

"But how can he? He told me a man of his age *can't* give up a business he's been in practically all his life, and just go groping about for something that might never turn up at all. I think he's right about it, too, of course!"

Mrs. Adams splashed among the plates with a new vigour heightened by an old bitterness. "Oh, yes," she said. "He talks that way; but he knows better."

"How could he 'know better,' mama?"

"*He* knows how!"

"But what does he know?"

Mrs. Adams tossed her head. "You don't suppose I'm such a fool I'd be urging him to give up something for nothing, do you, Alice? Do you suppose I'd want him to just go 'groping around' like he was telling you? That would be crazy, of course. Little as his work at Lamb's brings in, I wouldn't be so silly as to ask him to give it up just on a *chance* he could find something else. Good gracious, Alice, you must give me credit for a little intelligence once in a while!"

Alice was puzzled. "But what else could there be except a chance? I don't see——"

"Well, *I* do," her mother interrupted, decisively. "That man could make us all well off right now if he wanted to. We could have been rich long ago if he'd ever really felt as he ought to about his family."

"What! Why, how could——"

"You know how as well as I do," Mrs. Adams said, crossly. "I guess you haven't forgotten how he treated me about it the Sunday before he got sick."

She went on with her work, putting into it a sudden violence inspired by the recollection; but Alice, enlightened, gave utterance to a laugh of lugubrious derision. "Oh, the *glue* factory again!" she cried. "How silly!" And she renewed her laughter.

So often do the great projects of parents appear ignominious to their children. Mrs. Adams's conception of a glue factory as a fairy godmother of this family was an absurd old story which Alice had never taken seriously. She remembered that when she was about fifteen her mother began now and then to say something to Adams about a "glue factory," rather timidly, and as a vague suggestion, but never without irritating him. Then, for years, the preposterous subject had not been mentioned; possibly because of some explosion on the part of Adams, when his daughter had not been present. But during the last year Mrs. Adams had quietly gone back to these old hints, reviving them at intervals and also reviving her husband's irritation. Alice's bored impression was that her mother wanted him to found, or buy, or do something, or other, about a glue factory; and that he considered the proposal so impracticable as to be insulting. The parental conversations took place when neither Alice nor Walter was at hand, but sometimes Alice had come in upon the conclusion of one, to find her father in a shouting mood, and shocking the air behind him with profane monosyllables as he departed. Mrs. Adams would be left quiet and troubled; and when Alice, sympathizing with the goaded man, inquired of her mother why these tiresome bickerings had been renewed, she always got the brooding and cryptic answer, "He *could* do it—if he wanted to." Alice failed to comprehend the desirability of a glue factory—to her mind a father engaged in a glue factory lacked impressiveness; had no advantage over a father employed by Lamb and Company; and she supposed that Adams knew better than her mother whether such an enterprise would be profitable or not. Emphatically, he thought it would not, for she had heard him shouting at the end of one of these painful interviews, "You can keep up your dang talk till *you* die and *I* die, but I'll never make one God's cent that way!"

There had been a culmination. Returning from church on the Sunday preceding the collapse with which Adams's illness had begun, Alice found her mother downstairs, weeping and intimidated, while her father's stamping footsteps were loudly audible as he strode up and down his room overhead. So were his endless repetitions of invective loudly audible: "That woman! Oh, that woman! Oh, that danged woman!"

Mrs. Adams admitted to her daughter that it was "the old glue factory" and that her husband's wildness had frightened her into a "solemn promise" never to mention the subject again so long as she had breath. Alice laughed. The "glue factory" idea was not only a bore, but ridiculous, and her mother's evident seriousness about it one of those inexplicable vagaries we sometimes discover in the people we know best. But this Sunday rampage appeared to be the end of it, and when Adams came down to dinner, an hour later, he was unusually cheerful. Alice was glad he had gone wild enough to settle the glue factory once and for all; and she had ceased to think of the episode long before Friday of that week, when Adams was brought home in the middle of the afternoon by his old employer, the "great J. A. Lamb," in the latter's car.

During the long illness the "glue factory" was completely forgotten, by Alice at least; and her laugh was rueful as well as derisive now, in the kitchen, when she realized that her mother's mind again dwelt upon this abandoned nuisance. "I thought you'd got over all that nonsense, mama," she said.

Mrs. Adams smiled, pathetically. "Of course you think it's nonsense, dearie. Young people think everything's nonsense that they don't know anything about."

"Good gracious!" Alice cried. "I should think I used to hear enough about that horrible old glue factory to know something about it!"

"No," her mother returned patiently. "You've never heard anything about it at all."

"I haven't?"

"No. Your father and I didn't discuss it before you children. All you ever heard was when he'd get in such a rage, after we'd been speaking of it, that he couldn't control himself when you came in. Wasn't *I* always quiet? Did *I* ever go on talking about it?"

"No; perhaps not. But you're talking about it now, mama, after you promised never to mention it again."

"I promised not to mention it to your father," said Mrs. Adams, gently. "I haven't mentioned it to him, have I?"

"Ah, but if you mention it to me I'm afraid you *will* mention it to him. You always do speak of things that you have on your mind, and you might get papa all stirred up again about——" Alice paused, a light of divination flickering in her eyes. "Oh!" she cried. "I *see!*"

"What do you see?"

"You *have* been at him about it!"

"Not one single word!"

"No!" Alice cried. "Not a *word*, but that's what you've meant all along! You haven't spoken the words to him, but all this urging him to change, to 'find something better to go into'—it's all been about nothing on earth but your foolish old glue factory that you know upsets him, and you gave your solemn word never to speak to him about again! You didn't say it, but you meant it—and he *knows* that's what you meant! Oh, mama!"

Mrs. Adams, with her hands still automatically at work in the flooded dishpan, turned to face her daughter. "Alice," she said, tremulously, "what do I ask for myself?"

"What?"

"I say, What do I ask for myself? Do you suppose *I* want anything? Don't you know I'd be perfectly content on your father's present income if I were the only person to be considered? What do I care about any pleasure for myself? I'd be willing never to have a maid again; *I* don't mind doing the work. If we didn't have any children I'd be glad to do your father's cooking and the housework and the washing and ironing, too, for the rest of my life. I wouldn't care. I'm a poor cook and a poor housekeeper; I don't do anything well; but it would be good enough for just him and me. I wouldn't ever utter one word of com——"

"Oh, goodness!" Alice lamented. "What *is* it all about?"

"It's about this," said Mrs. Adams, swallowing. "You and Walter are a new generation and you ought to have the same as the rest of the new generation get. Poor Walter—asking you to go to the movies and a Chinese restaurant: the best he had to offer! Don't you suppose *I* see how the poor boy is deteriorating? Don't you suppose I know what *you* have to go through, Alice? And when I think of that man upstairs——" The agitated voice grew louder. "When I think of him and know that nothing in the world but his *stubbornness* keeps my children from having all they want and what they *ought* to have, do you suppose I'm going to hold myself bound to keep to the absolute letter of a silly promise he got from me by behaving like a crazy man? I can't! I can't do it! No mother could sit by and see him lock up a horn of plenty like that in his closet when the children were starving!"

"Oh, goodness, goodness me!" Alice protested. "We aren't precisely 'starving,' are we?"

Mrs. Adams began to weep. "It's just the same. Didn't I see how flushed and pretty you looked, this afternoon, after you'd been walking with this young man that's come here? Do you suppose he'd *look* at a girl like Mildred Palmer if you had what you ought to have? Do you suppose he'd be going into business with her father if *your* father——"

"Good heavens, mama; you're worse than Walter: I just barely know the man! *Don't* be so absurd!"

"Yes, I'm always 'absurd,'" Mrs. Adams moaned. "All I can do is cry, while your father sits upstairs, and his horn of plenty——"

But Alice interrupted with a peal of desperate laughter. "Oh, that 'horn of plenty!' Do come down to earth, mama. How can you call a *glue* factory, that doesn't exist except in your mind, a 'horn of plenty'? Do let's be a little rational!"

"It *could* be a horn of plenty," the tearful Mrs. Adams insisted. "It could! You don't understand a thing about it."

"Well, I'm willing," Alice said, with tired skepticism. "Make me understand, then. Where'd you ever get the idea?"

Mrs. Adams withdrew her hands from the water, dried them on a towel, and then wiped her eyes with a handkerchief. "Your father could make a fortune if he wanted to," she said, quietly. "At least, I don't say a fortune, but anyhow a great deal more than he does make."

"Yes, I've heard that before, mama, and you

think he could make it out of a glue factory. What I'm asking is: How?"

"How? Why, by making glue and selling it. Don't you know how bad most glue is when you try to mend anything? A good glue is one of the rarest things there is; and it would just sell itself, once it got started. Well, your father knows how to make as good a glue as there is in the world."

Alice was not interested. "What of it? I suppose probably anybody could make it if they wanted to."

"I *said* you didn't know anything about it. Nobody else could make it. Your father knows a formula for making it."

"What of that?"

"It's a secret formula. It isn't even down on paper. It's worth any amount of money."

"'Any amount?'" Alice said, remaining incredulous. "Why hasn't papa sold it then?"

"Just because he's too stubborn to do anything with it at all!"

"How did papa get it?"

"He got it before you were born, just after we were married. I didn't think much about it then: it wasn't till you were growing up and I saw how much we needed money that I——"

"Yes, but how did papa get it?" Alice began to feel a little more curious about this possible buried treasure. "Did he invent it?"

"Partly," Mrs. Adams said, looking somewhat preoccupied. "He and another man invented it."

"Then maybe the other man——"

"He's dead."

"Then his family——"

"I don't think he left any family," Mrs. Adams said. "Anyhow, it belongs to your father. At least it belongs to him as much as it does to any one else. He's got an absolutely perfect right to do anything he wants to with it, and it would make us all comfortable if he'd do what I want him to—and he *knows* it would, too!"

Alice shook her head pityingly. "Poor mama!" she said. "Of course he knows it wouldn't do anything of the kind, or else he'd have done it long ago."

"He would, you say?" her mother cried. "That only shows how little you know him!"

"Poor mama!" Alice said again, soothingly. "If papa were like what you say he is, he'd be—why, he'd be crazy!"

Mrs. Adams agreed with a vehemence near passion. "You're right about him for once: that's just what he is! He sits up there in his stubbornness and-lets us slave here in the kitchen when if he wanted to—if he'd so much as lift his little finger——"

"Oh, come, now!" Alice laughed. "You can't build even a glue factory with just one little finger."

Mrs. Adams seemed about to reply that finding fault with a figure of speech was beside the point; but a ringing of the front door bell forestalled the retort. "Now, who do you suppose that is?" she wondered aloud; then her face brightened. "Ah—did Mr. Russell ask if he could——"

"No, he wouldn't be coming this evening," Alice said. "Probably it's the great J. A. Lamb: he usually stops for a minute on Thursdays to ask how papa's getting along. I'll go."

She tossed her apron off, and as she went through the house her expression was thoughtful. She was thinking vaguely about the glue factory and wondering if there might be "something in it" after all. If her mother was right about the rich possibilities of Adams's secret—but that was as far as Alice's speculations upon the matter went at this time: they were checked, partly by the thought that her father probably hadn't enough money for such an enterprise, and partly by the fact that she had arrived at the front door.

CHAPTER XII

THE fine old gentleman revealed when she opened the door was probably the last great merchant in America to wear the chin beard. White as white frost, it was trimmed short with exquisite precision, while his upper lip and the lower expanses of his cheeks were clean and rosy from fresh shaving. With this trim white chin beard, the white waistcoat, the white tie, the suit of fine gray cloth, the broad and brilliantly polished black shoes, and the wide-brimmed gray felt hat, here was a man who had found his style in the seventies of the last century, and thenceforth kept it. Files of old magazines of that period might show him, in woodcut, as, "Type of Boston Merchant"; Nast might have drawn him as an honest statesman. He was eighty, hale and sturdy, not aged; and his quick blue eyes, still unflecked, and as brisk as a boy's, saw everything.

"Well, well, well!" he said, heartily. "You haven't lost any of your good looks since last week,

I see, Miss Alice, so I guess I'm to take it you haven't been worrying over your daddy. The young feller's getting along all right, is he?"

"He's much better; he's sitting up, Mr. Lamb. Won't you come in?"

"Well, I don't know but I might." He turned to call toward twin disks of light at the curb, "Be out in a minute, Billy"; and the silhouette of a chauffeur standing beside a car could be seen to salute in response, as the old gentleman stepped into the hall. "You don't suppose your daddy's receiving callers yet, is he?"

"He's a good deal stronger than he was when you were here last week, but I'm afraid he's not very presentable, though."

"'Presentable?'" The old man echoed her jovially. "Pshaw! I've seen lots of sick folks. *I* know what they look like and how they love to kind of nest in among a pile of old blankets and wrappers. Don't you worry about *that*, Miss Alice, if you think he'd like to see me."

"Of course he would—if——" Alice hesitated; then said quickly, "Of course he'd love to see you and he's quite able to, if you care to come up."

She ran up the stairs ahead of him, and had time to

snatch the crocheted wrap from her father's shoulders. Swathed as usual, he was sitting beside a table, reading the evening paper; but when his employer appeared in the doorway he half rose as if to come forward in greeting.

"Sit still!" the old gentleman shouted. "What do you mean? Don't you know you're weak as a cat? D'you think a man can be sick as long as you have and *not* be weak as a cat? What you trying to do the polite with *me* for?"

Adams gratefully protracted the handshake that accompanied these inquiries. "This is certainly mighty fine of you, Mr. Lamb," he said. "I guess Alice has told you how much our whole family appreciate your coming here so regularly to see how this old bag o' bones was getting along. Haven't you, Alice?"

"Yes, papa," she said; and turned to go out, but Lamb checked her.

"Stay right here, Miss Alice; I'm not even going to sit down. I know how it upsets sick folks when people outside the family come in for the first time."

"*You* don't upset me," Adams said. "I'll feel a lot better for getting a glimpse of you, Mr. Lamb."

The visitor's laugh was husky, but hearty and reassuring, like his voice in speaking. "That's the way all my boys blarney me, Miss Alice," he said. "They think I'll make the work lighter on 'em if they can get me kind of flattered up. You just tell your daddy it's no use; he doesn't get on *my* soft side, pretending he likes to see me even when he's sick."

"Oh, I'm not so sick any more," Adams said. "I expect to be back in my place ten days from now at the longest."

"Well, now, don't hurry it, Virgil; don't hurry it. You take your time; take your time."

This brought to Adams's lips a feeble smile not lacking in a kind of vanity, as feeble. "Why?" he asked. "I suppose you think my department runs itself down there, do you?"

His employer's response was another husky laugh. "Well, well, well!" he cried, and patted Adams's shoulder with a strong pink hand. "Listen to this young feller, Miss Alice, will you! He thinks we can't get along without him a minute! Yes, sir, this daddy of yours believes the whole works 'll just take and run down if he isn't there to keep 'em wound up. I always suspected he thought a good deal of himself, and now I know he does!"

Adams looked troubled. "Well, I don't like to

feel that my salary's going on with me not earning it."

"Listen to him, Miss Alice! Wouldn't you think, now, he'd let me be the one to worry about that? Why, on my word. if your daddy had his way, *I* wouldn't be anywhere. He'd take all my worrying and everything else off my shoulders and shove me right out of Lamb and Company! He *would*!"

"It seems to me I've been soldiering on you a pretty long while, Mr. Lamb," the convalescent said, querulously. "I don't feel right about it; but I'll be back in ten days. You'll see."

The old man took his hand in parting. "All right; we'll see, Virgil. Of course we do need you, seriously speaking; but we don't need you so bad we'll let you come down there before you're fully fit and able." He went to the door. "You hear, Miss Alice? That's what I wanted to make the old feller understand, and what I want you to kind of enforce on him. The old place is there waiting for him, and it'd wait ten years if it took him that long to get good and well. You see that he remembers it, Miss Alice!"

She went down the stairs with him, and he continued to impress this upon her until he had gone out of the front door. And even after that, the husky voice called back from the darkness, as he went to his car, "Don't forget, Miss Alice; let him take his own time. We always want him, but we want him to get good and well first. Good-night, good-night, young lady!"

When she closed the door her mother came from the farther end of the "living-room," where there was no light; and Alice turned to her.

"I can't help liking that old man, mama," she said. "He always sounds so—well, so solid and honest and friendly! I do like him."

But Mrs. Adams failed in sympathy upon this point. "He didn't say anything about raising your father's salary, did he?" she asked, dryly.

"No."

"No. I thought not."

She would have said more, but Alice, indisposed to listen, began to whistle, ran up the stairs, and went to sit with her father. She found him bright-eyed with the excitement a first caller brings into a slow convalescence: his cheeks showed actual hints of colour; and he was smiling tremulously as he filled and lit his pipe. She brought the crocheted scarf and put it about his shoulders again, then took a chair near him.

"I believe seeing Mr. Lamb did do you good, papa," she said. "I sort of thought it might, and that's why I let him come up. You really look a little like your old self again."

Adams exhaled a breathy "Ha!" with the smoke from his pipe as he waved the match to extinguish it. "That's fine," he said. "The smoke I had before dinner didn't taste the way it used to, and I kind of wondered if I'd lost my liking for tobacco, but this one seems to be all right. You bet it did me good to see J. A. Lamb! He's the biggest man that's ever lived in this town or ever will live here; and you can take all the Governors and Senators or anything they've raised here, and put 'em in a pot with him, and they won't come out one-two-three alongside o' him! And to think as big a man as that, with all his interests and everything he's got on his mind—to think he'd never let anything prevent him from coming here once every week to ask how I was getting along, and then walk right upstairs and kind of *call* on me, as it were—well, it makes me sort of feel as if I wasn't so much of a nobody, so to speak, as your mother seems to like to make out sometimes."

"How foolish, papa! Of *course* you're not 'a nobody.'"

Adams chuckled faintly upon his pipe-stem, what vanity he had seeming to be further stimulated by his daughter's applause. "I guess there aren't a whole lot of people in this town that could claim J. A. showed that much interest in 'em," he said. "Of course I don't set up to believe it's all because of merit, or anything like that. He'd do the same for anybody else that'd been with the company as long as I have, but still it *is* something to be with the company that long and have him show he appreciates it."

"Yes, indeed, it is, papa."

"Yes, sir," Adams said, reflectively. "Yes, sir, I guess that's so. And besides, it all goes to show the kind of a man he is. Simon pure, that's what that man is, Alice. Simon pure! There's never been anybody work for him that didn't respect him more than they did any other man in the world, I guess. And when you work for him you know he respects you, too. Right from the start you get the feeling that J. A. puts absolute confidence in you; and that's mighty stimulating: it makes you want to show him he hasn't misplaced it. There's great big moral values to the way a man like him gets you to feeling about your relations with the business: it ain't all just dollars and cents—not by any means!"

He was silent for a time, then returned with increasing enthusiasm to this theme, and Alice was glad to see so much renewal of life in him; he had not spoken with a like cheerful vigour since before his illness. The visit of his idolized great man had indeed been good for him, putting new spirit into him; and liveliness of the body followed that of the spirit. His improvement carried over the night: he slept well and awoke late, declaring that he was "pretty near a well man and ready for business right now." Moreover, having slept again in the afternoon, he dressed and went down to dinner, leaning but lightly on Alice, who conducted him.

"My! but you and your mother have been at it with your scrubbing and dusting!" he said, as they came through the "living-room." "I don't know I ever did see the house so spick and span before!" His glance fell upon a few carnations in a vase, and he chuckled admiringly. "Flowers, too! So *that's* what you coaxed that dollar and a half out o 'me for, this morning!"

Other embellishments brought forth his comment when he had taken his old seat at the head of the small dinner-table. "Why, I declare, Alice!" he exclaimed. "I been so busy looking at all the spick-

and-spanishness after the house-cleaning, and the flowers out in the parlour—'living-room' I suppose you want me to call it, if I just *got* to be fashionable—I been so busy studying over all this so-and-so, I declare I never noticed *you* till this minute! My, but you *are* all dressed up! What's goin' on? What's it about: you so all dressed up, and flowers in the parlour and everything?"

"Don't you see, papa? It's in honour of your coming downstairs again, of course."

"Oh, so that's it," he said. "I never would 'a' thought of that, I guess."

But Walter looked sidelong at his father, and gave forth his sly and knowing laugh. "Neither would I!" he said.

Adams lifted his eyebrows jocosely. "You're jealous, are you, sonny? You don't want the old man to think our young lady'd make so much fuss over him, do you?"

"Go on thinkin' it's over you," Walter retorted, amused. "Go on and think it. It'll do you good."

"Of course I'll think it," Adams said. "It isn't anybody's birthday. Certainly the decorations are on account of me coming downstairs. Didn't you hear Alice say so?"

"Sure, I heard her say so."

"Well, then——"

Walter interrupted him with a little music. Looking shrewdly at Alice, he sang:

"I was walkin' out on Monday with my sweet thing.
She's my neat thing,
My sweet thing:
I'll go round on Tuesday night to see her.
Oh, how we'll spoon——"

"Walter!" his mother cried. "*Where* do you learn such vulgar songs?" However, she seemed not greatly displeased with him, and laughed as she spoke.

"So that's it, Alice!" said Adams. "Playing the hypocrite with your old man, are you? It's some new beau, is it?"

"I only wish it were," she said, calmly. "No. It's just what I said: it's all for you, dear."

"Don't let her con you," Walter advised his father. "She's got expectations. You hang around downstairs a while after dinner and you'll see."

But the prophecy failed, though Adams went to his own room without waiting to test it. No one came.

Alice stayed in the "living-room" until half-past

nine, when she went slowly upstairs. Her mother, almost tearful, met her at the top, and whispered, "You mustn't mind, dearie."

"Mustn't mind what?" Alice asked, and then, as she went on her way, laughed scornfully. "What utter nonsense!" she said.

Next day she cut the stems of the rather scant show of carnations and refreshed them with new water. At dinner, her father, still in high spirits, observed that she had again "dressed up" in honour of his second descent of the stairs; and Walter repeated his fragment of objectionable song; but these jocularities were rendered pointless by the eventless evening that followed; and in the morning the carnations began to appear tarnished and flaccid. Alice gave them a long look, then threw them away; and neither Walter nor her father was inspired to any rallying by her plain costume for that evening. Mrs. Adams was visibly depressed.

When Alice finished helping her mother with the dishes, she went outdoors and sat upon the steps of the little front veranda. The night, gentle with warm air from the south, surrounded her pleasantly, and the perpetual smoke was thinner. Now that the furnaces of dwelling-houses were no longer fired, life in that city had begun to be less like life in a railway tunnel; people were aware of summer in the air, and in the thickened foliage of the shade-trees, and in the sky. Stars were unveiled by the passing of the denser smoke fogs, and to-night they could be seen clearly; they looked warm and near. Other girls sat upon verandas and stoops in Alice's street, cheerful as young fishermen along the banks of a stream.

Alice could hear them from time to time; thin sopranos persistent in laughter that fell dismally upon her ears. She had set no lines or nets herself, and what she had of "expectations," as Walter called them, were vanished. For Alice was experienced; and one of the conclusions she drew from her experience was that when a man says, "I'd take you for anything you wanted me to," he may mean it or he may not; but, if he does, he will not postpone the first opportunity to say something more. Little affairs, once begun, must be warmed quickly; for if they cool they are dead.

But Alice was not thinking of Arthur Russell. When she tossed away the carnations she likewise tossed away her thoughts of that young man. She had been like a boy who sees upon the street, some distance before him, a bit of something round and glittering, a possible dime. He hopes it is a dime, and, until he comes near enough to make sure, he plays that it is a dime. In his mind he has an adventure with it: he buys something delightful. If he picks it up, discovering only some tin-foil which has happened upon a round shape, he feels a sinking. A dulness falls upon him.

So Alice was dull with the loss of an adventure; and when the laughter of other girls reached her, intermittently, she had not sprightliness enough left in her to be envious of their gaiety. Besides, these neighbours were ineligible even for her envy, being of another caste; they could never know a dance at the Palmers', except remotely, through a newspaper. Their laughter was for the encouragement of snappy young men of the stores and offices down-town, clerks, bookkeepers, what not—some of them probably graduates of Frincke's Business College.

Then, as she recalled that dark portal, with its dusty stairway mounting between close walls to disappear in the upper shadows, her mind drew back as from a doorway to Purgatory. Nevertheless, it was a picture often in her reverie; and sometimes it came suddenly, without sequence, into the midst of her other thoughts, as if it leaped up among them from a lower darkness; and when it arrived it wanted to stay. So a traveller, still roaming the world afar, sometimes broods without apparent reason upon his family burial lot: "I wonder if I shall end there."

The foreboding passed abruptly, with a jerk of her breath, as the street-lamp revealed a tall and easy figure approaching from the north, swinging a stick in time to its stride. She had given Russell up—and he came.

"What luck for me!" he exclaimed. "To find you alone!"

Alice gave him her hand for an instant, not otherwise moving. "I'm glad it happened so," she said. "Let's stay out here, shall we? Do you think it's too provincial to sit on a girl's front steps with her?"

"'Provincial?' Why, it's the very best of our institutions," he returned, taking his place beside her. "At least, I think so to-night."

"Thanks! Is that practise for other nights somewhere else?"

"No," he laughed. "The practising all led up to this. Did I come too soon?"

"No," she replied, gravely. "Just in time!"

"I'm glad to be so accurate; I've spent two evenings wanting to come, Miss Adams, instead of doing what I was doing."

"What was that?"

"Dinners. Large and long dinners. Your fellow-citizens are immensely hospitable to a newcomer."

"Oh, no," Alice said. "We don't do it for everybody. Didn't you find yourself charmed?"

"One was a men's dinner," he explained. "Mr. Palmer seemed to think I ought to be shown to the principal business men."

"What was the other dinner?"

"My cousin Mildred gave it."

"Oh, *did* she!" Alice said, sharply, but she recovered herself in the same instant, and laughed. "She wanted to show you to the principal business women, I suppose."

"I don't know. At all events, I shouldn't give myself out to be so much fêted by your 'fellow-citizens,' after all, seeing these were both done by my relatives, the Palmers. However, there are others to follow, I'm afraid. I was wondering—I hoped maybe you'd be coming to some of them. Aren't you?"

"I rather doubt it," Alice said, slowly. "Mildred's

dance was almost the only evening I've gone out since my father's illness began. He seemed better that day; so I went. He was better the other day when he wanted those cigars. He's very much up and down." She paused. "I'd almost forgotten that Mildred is your cousin."

"Not a very near one," he explained. "Mr. Palmer's father was my great-uncle."

"Still, of course you are related."

"Yes; that distantly."

Alice said placidly, "It's quite an advantage."

He agreed. "Yes. It is."

"No," she said, in the same placid tone. "I mean for Mildred."

"I don't see——"

She laughed. "No. You wouldn't. I mean it's an advantage over the rest of us who might like to compete for some of your time; and the worst of it is we can't accuse her of being unfair about it. We can't prove she showed any trickiness in having you for a cousin. Whatever else she might plan to do with you, she didn't plan that. So the rest of us must just bear it!"

"The 'rest of you!'" he laughed. "It's going to mean a great deal of suffering!"

Alice resumed her placid tone. "You're staying at the Palmers', aren't you?"

"No, not now. I've taken an apartment. I'm going to live here; I'm permanent. Didn't I tell you?"

"I think I'd heard somewhere that you were," she said. "Do you think you'll like living here?"

"How can one tell?"

"If I were in your place I think I should be able to tell, Mr. Russell."

"How?"

"Why, good gracious!" she cried. "Haven't you got the most perfect creature in town for your—your cousin? *She* expects to make you like living here, doesn't she? How could you keep from liking it, even if you tried not to, under the circumstances?"

"Well, you see, there's such a lot of circumstances," he explained; "I'm not sure I'll like getting back into a business again. I suppose most of the men of my age in the country have been going through the same experience: the War left us with a considerable restlessness of spirit."

"You were in the War?" she asked, quickly, and as quickly answered herself, "Of course you were!'

"I was a left-over; they only let me out about four

months ago," he said. "It's quite a shake-up trying to settle down again."

"You were in France, then?"

"Oh, yes; but I didn't get up to the front much—only two or three times, and then just for a day or so I was in the transportation service."

"You were an officer, of course."

"Yes," he said. "They let me play I was a major."

"I guessed a major," she said. "You'd always be pretty grand, of course."

Russell was amused. "Well, you see," he informed her, "as it happened, we had at least several other majors in our army. Why would I always be something 'pretty grand?'"

"You're related to the Palmers. Don't you notice they always affect the pretty grand?"

"Then you think I'm only one of their affectations, I take it."

"Yes, you seem to be the most successful one they've got!" Alice said, lightly. "You certainly do belong to them." And she laughed as if at something hidden from him. "Don't you?"

"But you've just excused me for that," he protested. "You said nobody could be blamed for my being their third cousin. What a contradictory girl you are!"

Alice shook her head. "Let's keep away from the kind of girl I am."

"No," he said. "That's just what I came here to talk about."

She shook her head again. "Let's keep first to the kind of man you are. I'm glad you were in the War."

"Why?"

"Oh, I don't know." She was quiet a moment, for she was thinking that here she spoke the truth: his service put about him a little glamour that helped to please her with him. She had been pleased with him during their walk; pleased with him on his own account; and now that pleasure was growing keener. She looked at him, and though the light in which she saw him was little more than starlight, she saw that he was looking steadily at her with a kindly and smiling seriousness. All at once it seemed to her that the night air was sweeter to breathe, as if a distant fragrance of new blossoms had been blown to her. She smiled back to him, and said, "Well, what kind of man are you?"

"I don't know; I've often wondered," he replied. "What kind of girl are you?"

"Don't you remember? I told you the other day. I'm just me!"

"But who is that?"

"You forget everything," said Alice. "You told me what kind of a girl I am. You seemed to think you'd taken quite a fancy to me from the very first."

"So I did," he agreed, heartily.

"But how quickly you forgot it!"

"Oh, no. I only want *you* to say what kind of a girl you are."

She mocked him. "'I don't know; I've often wondered!' What kind of a girl does Mildred tell you I am? What has she said about me since she told you I was 'a Miss Adams?'"

"I don't know; I haven't asked her."

"Then *don't* ask her," Alice said, quickly.

"Why?"

"Because she's such a perfect creature and I'm such an imperfect one. Perfect creatures have the most perfect way of ruining the imperfect ones."

"But then they wouldn't be perfect. Not if they——"

"Oh, yes, they remain perfectly perfect," she assured him. "That's because they never go into details. They're not so vulgar as to come right out and *tell* that you've been in jail for stealing chickens. They just look absent-minded and say in a low voice, 'Oh, very; but I scarcely think you'd like her particularly'; and then begin to talk of something else right away."

His smile had disappeared. "Yes," he said, somewhat ruefully. "That does sound like Mildred. You certainly do seem to know her! Do you know everybody as well as that?"

"Not myself," Alice said. "I don't know myself at all. I got to wondering about that—about who I was—the other day after you walked home with me."

He uttered an exclamation, and added, explaining it, "You do give a man a chance to be fatuous, though! As if it were walking home with me that made you wonder about yourself!"

"It was," Alice informed him, coolly. "I was wondering what I wanted to make you think of me, in case I should ever happen to see you again."

This audacity appeared to take his breath. "By George!" he cried.

"You mustn't be astonished," she said. "What I decided then was that I would probably never dare to be just myself with you—not if I cared to have you want to see me again—and yet here I am, just being myself after all!"

"You *are* the cheeriest series of shocks," Russell exclaimed, whereupon Alice added to the series.

"Tell me: Is it a good policy for me to follow with you?" she asked, and he found the mockery in her voice delightful. "Would you advise me to offer you shocks as a sort of vacation from suavity?"

"Suavity" was yet another sketch of Mildred; a recognizable one, or it would not have been humorous. In Alice's hands, so dexterous in this work, her statuesque friend was becoming as ridiculous as a fine figure of wax left to the mercies of a satirist.

But the lively young sculptress knew better than to overdo: what she did must appear to spring all from mirth; so she laughed as if unwillingly, and said, "I *mustn't* laugh at Mildred! In the first place, she's your—your cousin. And in the second place, she's not meant to be funny; it isn't right to laugh at really splendid people who take themselves seriously. In the third place, you won't come again if I do."

"Don't be sure of that," Russell said, "whatever you do."

"'Whatever I do?'" she echoed. "That sounds as if you thought I *could* be terrific! Be careful; there's one thing I could do that would keep you away."

"What's that?"

"I could tell you not to come," she said. "I wonder if I ought to."

"Why do you wonder if you 'ought to?'"

"Don't you guess?"

"No."

"Then let's both be mysteries to each other," she suggested. "I mystify you because I wonder, and you mystify me because you don't guess why I wonder. We'll let it go at that, shall we?"

"Very well; so long as it's certain that you *don't* tell me not to come again."

"I'll not tell you that—yet," she said. "In fact——" She paused, reflecting, with her head to one side. "In fact, I won't tell you not to come, probably, until I see that's what you want me to tell you. I'll let you out easily—and I'll be sure to see it. Even before you do, perhaps."

"That arrangement suits me," Russell returned, and his voice held no trace of jocularity: he had become serious. "It suits me better if you're enough in earnest to mean that I can come—oh, not whenever I want to; I don't expect so much!—but if you mean that I can see you pretty often."

"Of course I'm in earnest," she said. "But before I say you can come 'pretty often,' I'd like to know how much of my time you'd need if you did come 'whenever you want to'; and of course you wouldn't dare make any answer to that question except one. Wouldn't you let me have Thursdays out?"

"No, no," he protested. "I want to know. Will you let me come pretty often?"

"Lean toward me a little," Alice said. "I want you to understand." And as he obediently bent his head near hers, she inclined toward him as if to whisper; then, in a half-shout, she cried,

"*Yes!*"

He clapped his hands. "By George!" he said. "What a girl you are!"

"Why?"

"Well, for the first reason, because you have such gaieties as that one. I should think your father would actually like being ill, just to be in the house with you all the time."

"You mean by that," Alice inquired, "I keep my family cheerful with my amusing little ways?"

"Yes. Don't you?"

"There were only boys in your family, weren't there, Mr. Russell?"

"I was an only child, unfortunately."

"Yes," she said. "I see you hadn't any sisters."

For a moment he puzzled over her meaning, then saw it, and was more delighted with her than ever. "I can answer a question of yours, now, that I couldn't a while ago."

"Yes, I know," she returned, quietly.

"But how could you know?"

"It's the question I asked you about whether you were going to like living here," she said. "You're about to tell me that now you know you *will* like it."

"More telepathy!" he exclaimed. "Yes, that was it, precisely. I suppose the same thing's been said to you so many times that you——"

"No, it hasn't," Alice said, a little confused for the moment. "Not at all. I meant——" She paused, then asked in a gentle voice, "Would you really like to know?"

"Yes."

"Well, then, I was only afraid you didn't mean it."

"See here," he said. "I did mean it. I told you it was being pretty difficult for me to settle down to things again. Well, it's more difficult than you know, but I think I can pull through in fair spirits if I can see a girl like you 'pretty often.'"

"All right," she said, in a business-like tone. "I've told you that you can if you want to."

"I do want to," he assured her. "I do, indeed!"

"How often is 'pretty often,' Mr. Russell?"

"Would you walk with me sometimes? To-morrow?"

"Sometimes. Not to-morrow. The day after."

"That's splendid!" he said. "You'll walk with me day after to-morrow, and the night after that I'll see you at Miss Lamb's dance, won't I?"

But this fell rather chillingly upon Alice. "Miss Lamb's dance? Which Miss Lamb?" she asked.

"I don't know—it's the one that's just coming out of mourning."

"Oh, Henrietta—yes. Is her dance so soon? I'd forgotten."

"You'll be there, won't you?" he asked. "Please say you're going."

Alice did not respond at once, and he urged her again: "Please do promise you'll be there."

"No, I can't promise anything," she said, slowly. "You see, for one thing, papa might not be well enough."

"But if he is?" said Russell. "If he is you'll surely come, won't you? Or, perhaps——" He hesitated, then went on quickly, "I don't know the rules in this place yet, and different places have different rules;

but do you have to have a chaperone, or don't girls just go to dances with the men sometimes? If they do, would you—would you let me take you?"

Alice was startled. "Good gracious!"

"What's the matter?"

"Don't you think your relatives—— Aren't you expected to go with Mildred—and Mrs. Palmer?"

"Not necessarily. It doesn't matter what I might be expected to do," he said. "Will you go with me?"

"I—— No; I couldn't."

"Why not?"

"I can't. I'm not going."

"But why?"

"Papa's not really any better," Alice said, huskily. "I'm too worried about him to go to a dance." Her voice sounded emotional, genuinely enough; there was something almost like a sob in it. "Let's talk of other things, please."

He acquiesced gently; but Mrs. Adams, who had been listening to the conversation at the open window, just overhead, did not hear him. She had correctly interpreted the sob in Alice's voice, and, trembling with sudden anger, she rose from her knees, and went fiercely to her husband's room.

CHAPTER XIII

HE HAD not undressed, and he sat beside the table, smoking his pipe and reading his newspaper. Upon his forehead the lines in that old pattern, the historical map of his troubles, had grown a little vaguer lately; relaxed by the complacency of a man who not only finds his health restored, but sees the days before him promising once more a familiar routine that he has always liked to follow.

As his wife came in, closing the door behind her, he looked up cheerfully, "Well, mother," he said, "what's the news downstairs?"

"That's what I came to tell you," she informed him, grimly.

Adams lowered his newspaper to his knee and peered over his spectacles at her. She had remained by the door, standing, and the great greenish shadow of the small lamp-shade upon his table revealed her but dubiously. "Isn't everything all right?" he asked. "What's the matter?"

"Don't worry: I'm going to tell you," she said, her grimness not relaxed. "There's matter enough, Virgil Adams. Matter enough to make me sick of being alive!"

With that, the markings on his brows began to emerge again in all their sharpness; the old pattern reappeared. "Oh, my, my!" he lamented. "I thought maybe we were all going to settle down to a little peace for a while. What's it about now?"

"It's about Alice. Did you think it was about *me* or anything for *myself?*"

Like some ready old machine, always in order, his irritability responded immediately and automatically to her emotion. "How in thunder could I think what it's about, or who it's for? *Say* it, and get it over!"

"Oh, I'll 'say' it," she promised, ominously. "What I've come to ask you is, How much longer do you expect me to put up with that old man and his doings?"

"Whose doings? What old man?"

She came at him, fiercely accusing. "You know well enough what old man, Virgil Adams! That old man who was here the other night."

"Mr. Lamb?"

"Yes; 'Mister Lamb!'" She mocked his voice. "What other old man would I be likely to mean, except J. A. Lamb?"

"What's he been doing now?" her husband inquired, satirically. "Where'd you get something new against him since the last time you——"

"Just this!" she cried. "The other night when that man was here, if I'd known how he was going to make my child suffer, I'd never have let him set his foot in my house."

Adams leaned back in his chair as though her absurdity had eased his mind. "Oh, I see," he said. "You've just gone plain crazy. That's the only explanation of such talk, and it suits the case."

"Hasn't that man made us all suffer every day of our lives?" she demanded. "I'd like to know why it is that my life and my children's lives have to be sacrificed to him?"

"How are they 'sacrificed' to him?"

"Because you keep on working for him! Because you keep on letting him hand out whatever miserable little pittance he chooses to give you; that's why! It's as if he were some horrible old Juggernaut and I had to see my children's own father throwing them under the wheels to keep him satisfied."

"I won't hear any more such stuff!" Lifting his paper, Adams affected to read.

"You'd better listen to me," she admonished him. "You might be sorry you didn't, in case he ever tried to set foot in my house again! I might tell him to his face what I think of him."

At this, Adams slapped the newspaper down upon his knee. "Oh, the devil! What's it matter what you think of him?"

"It had better matter to you!" she cried. "Do you suppose I'm going to submit forever to him and his family and what they're doing to my child?"

"What are he and his family doing to 'your child?'"

Mrs. Adams came out with it. "That snippy little Henrietta Lamb has always snubbed Alice every time she's ever had the chance. She's followed the lead of the other girls; they've always all of 'em been jealous of Alice because she dared to try and be happy, and because she's showier and better-looking than they are, even though you do give her only about thirty-five cents a year to do it on! They've all done everything on earth they could to drive the young men away from her and belittle her to 'em; and this mean little Henrietta Lamb's been the worst of the whole crowd to Alice, every time she could see a chance."

"What for?" Adams asked, incredulously. "Why should she or anybody else pick on Alice?"

"'Why?' 'What for?'" his wife repeated with a greater vehemence. "Do *you* ask me such a thing as that? Do *you* really want to know?"

"Yes; I'd want to know—I would if I believed it."

"Then I'll tell you," she said in a cold fury. "It's on account of *you*, Virgil, and nothing else in the world."

He hooted at her. "Oh, yes! These girls don't like *me*, so they pick on Alice."

"Quit your palavering and evading," she said. "A crowd of girls like that, when they get a pretty girl like Alice among them, they act just like wild beasts. They'll tear her to pieces, or else they'll chase her and run her out, because they know if she had half a chance she'd outshine 'em. They can't do that to a girl like Mildred Palmer because she's got money and family to back her. Now you listen to me, Virgil Adams: the way the world is now, money *is* family. Alice would have just as much 'family' as any of 'em—every single bit—if you hadn't fallen behind in the race."

"How did I——"

"Yes, you did!" she cried. "Twenty-five years ago when we were starting and this town was smaller, you and I could have gone with any of 'em if we'd tried hard enough. Look at the people we knew then that do hold their heads up alongside of anybody in this town! *Why* can they? Because the men of those families made money and gave their children everything that makes life worth living! Why can't we hold *our* heads up? Because those men passed you in the race. They went up the ladder, and you—you're still a clerk down at that old hole!"

"You leave that out, please," he said. "I thought you were going to tell me something Henrietta Lamb had done to our Alice."

"You *bet* I'm going to tell you," she assured him, vehemently. "But first I'm telling *why* she does it. It's because you've never given Alice any backing nor any background, and they all know they can do anything they like to her with perfect impunity. If she had the hundredth part of what *they* have to fall back on she'd have made 'em sing a mighty different song long ago!"

"How would she?"

"Oh, my heavens, but you're slow!" Mrs. Adams

moaned. "Look here! You remember how practically all the nicest boys in this town used to come here a few years ago. Why, they were all crazy over her; and the girls *had* to be nice to her then. Look at the difference now! There'll be a whole month go by and not a young man come to call on her, let alone send her candy or flowers, or ever think of *taking* her any place—and yet she's prettier and brighter than she was when they used to come. It isn't the child's fault she couldn't hold 'em, is it? Poor thing, *she* tried hard enough! I suppose you'd say it was her fault, though."

"No; I wouldn't."

"Then whose fault is it?"

"Oh, mine, mine," he said, wearily. "I drove the young men away, of course."

"You might as well have driven 'em, Virgil. It amounts to just the same thing."

"How does it?"

"Because as they got older a good many of 'em began to think more about money; that's one thing. Money's at the bottom of it all, for that matter. Look at these country clubs and all such things: the other girls' families belong and we don't, and Alice don't; and she can't go unless somebody takes her, and nobody does any more. Look at the other girls' houses, and then look at our house, so shabby and old-fashioned she'd be pretty near ashamed to ask anybody to come in and sit down nowadays! Look at her clothes—oh, yes; you think you shelled out a lot for that little coat of hers and the hat and skirt she got last March; but it's nothing. Some of these girls nowadays spend more than your whole salary on their clothes. And what jewellery has she got? A plated watch and two or three little pins and rings of the kind people's maids wouldn't wear now. Good Lord, Virgil Adams, wake up! Don't sit there and tell me you don't know things like this mean *suffering* for the child!"

He had begun to rub his hands wretchedly back and forth over his bony knees, as if in that way he somewhat alleviated the tedium caused by her racking voice. "Oh, my, my!" he muttered. "*Oh*, my, my!"

"Yes, I should think you *would* say 'Oh, my, my!'" she took him up, loudly. "That doesn't help things much! If you ever wanted to *do* anything about it, the poor child might see some gleam of hope in her life. You don't *care* for her, that's the trouble; you don't care a single thing about her."

"I don't?"

"No; you don't. Why, even with your miserable little salary you could have given her more than you have. You're the closest man I ever knew: it's like pulling teeth to get a dollar out of you for her, now and then, and yet you hide some away, every month or so, in some wretched little investment or other. You——"

"Look here, now," he interrupted, angrily. "You look here! If I didn't put a little by whenever I could, in a bond or something, where would you be if anything happened to me? The insurance doctors never passed me; *you* know that. Haven't we got to have *something* to fall back on?"

"Yes, we have!" she cried. "We ought to have something to go on with right now, too, when we need it. Do you suppose these snippets would treat Alice the way they do if she could afford to *entertain?* They leave her out of their dinners and dances simply because they know she can't give any dinners and dances to leave them out of! They know she can't get *even*, and that's the whole story! That's why Henrietta Lamb's done this thing to her now."

Adams had gone back to his rubbing of his knees. "Oh, my, my!" he said. "*What* thing?"

She told him. "Your dear, grand, old Mister Lamb's Henrietta has sent out invitations for a large party—a *large* one. Everybody that is anybody in this town is asked, you can be sure. There's a very fine young man, a Mr. Russell, has just come to town, and he's interested in Alice, and he's asked her to go to this dance with him. Well, Alice can't accept. She can't go with him, though she'd give anything in the world to do it. Do you understand? The reason she can't is because Henrietta Lamb hasn't invited her. Do you want to know why Henrietta hasn't invited her? It's because she knows Alice can't get even, and because she thinks Alice ought to be snubbed like this on account of only being the daughter of one of her grandfather's clerks. I *hope* you understand!"

"Oh, my, my!" he said. "*Oh*, my, my!"

"That's your sweet old employer," his wife cried, tauntingly. "That's your dear, kind, grand old Mister Lamb! Alice has been left out of a good many smaller things, like big dinners and little dances, but this is just the same as serving her notice that she's out of everything! And it's all done by your dear, grand old——"

"Look here!" Adams exclaimed. "I don't want

to hear any more of that! You can't hold him responsible for everything his grandchildren do, I guess! He probably doesn't know a thing about it. You don't suppose he's troubling *his* head over——"

But she burst out at him passionately. "Suppose *you* trouble *your* head about it! You'd better, Virgil Adams! You'd better, unless you want to see your child just dry up into a miserable old maid! She's still young and she has a chance for happiness, if she had a father that didn't bring a millstone to hang around her neck, instead of what he ought to give her! You just wait till you die and God asks you what you had in your breast instead of a heart!"

"Oh, my, my!" he groaned. "What's my heart got to do with it?"

"Nothing! You haven't got one or you'd give her what she needed. Am I asking anything you *can't* do? You know better; you know I'm not!"

At this he sat suddenly rigid, his troubled hands ceasing to rub his knees; and he looked at her fixedly. "Now, tell me," he said, slowly. "Just what *are* you asking?"

"You know!" she sobbed.

"You mean you've broken your word never to speak of *that* to me again?"

"What do *I* care for my word?" she cried, and, sinking to the floor at his feet, rocked herself back and forth there. "Do you suppose I'll let my 'word' keep me from struggling for a little happiness for my children? It won't, I tell you; it won't! I'll struggle for that till I die! I will, till I die—till I die!"

He rubbed his head now instead of his knees, and, shaking all over, he got up and began with uncertain steps to pace the floor. "Hell, hell, hell!" he said. "I've got to go through *that* again!"

"Yes, you have!" she sobbed. "Till I die."

"Yes; that's what you been after all the time I was getting well."

"Yes, I have, and I'll keep on till I die!"

"A fine wife for a man," he said. "Beggin' a man to be a dirty dog!"

"No! To be a *man*—and I'll keep on till I die!"

Adams again fell back upon his last solace: he walked, half staggering, up and down the room, swearing in a rhythmic repetition.

His wife had repetitions of her own, and she kept at them in a voice that rose to a higher and higher pitch, like the sound of an old well-pump. "Till I die! Till I die! Till I *die!*"

She ended in a scream; and Alice, coming up the

stairs, thanked heaven that Russell had gone. She ran to her father's door and went in.

Adams looked at her, and gesticulated shakily at the convulsive figure on the floor. "Can you get her out of here?"

Alice helped Mrs. Adams to her feet; and the stricken woman threw her arms passionately about her daughter.

"Get her out!" Adams said, harshly; then cried, "Wait!"

Alice, moving toward the door, halted, and looked at him blankly, over her mother's shoulder. "What is it, papa?"

He stretched out his arm and pointed at her. "She says—she says you have a mean life, Alice."

"No, papa."

Mrs. Adams turned in her daughter's arms. "Do you hear her lie? Couldn't you be as brave as she is, Virgil?"

"Are you lying, Alice?" he asked. "Do you have a mean time?"

"No, papa."

He came toward her. "Look at me!" he said. "Things like this dance now—is that so hard to bear?"

Alice tried to say, "No, papa," again, but she couldn't. Suddenly and in spite of herself she began to cry.

"Do you hear her?" his wife sobbed. "Now do you——"

He waved at them fiercely. "Get out of here!" he said. "Both of you! Get out of here!"

As they went, he dropped in his chair and bent far forward, so that his haggard face was concealed from them. Then, as Alice closed the door, he began to rub his knees again, muttering, "Oh, my, my! *Oh*, my, my!"

CHAPTER XIV

THERE shone a jovial sun overhead on the appointed "day after to-morrow"; a day not cool yet of a temperature friendly to walkers; and the air, powdered with sunshine, had so much life in it that it seemed to sparkle. To Arthur Russell this was a day like a gay companion who pleased him well; but the gay companion at his side pleased him even better. She looked her prettiest, chattered her wittiest, smiled her wistfulest, and delighted him with all together.

"You look so happy it's easy to see your father's taken a good turn," he told her.

"Yes; he has this afternoon, at least," she said. "I might have other reasons for looking cheerful, though."

"For instance?"

"Exactly!" she said, giving him a sweet look just enough mocked by her laughter. "For instance!"

"Well, go on," he begged.

"Isn't it expected?" she asked.

"Of you, you mean?"

"No," she returned. "For you, I mean!"

In this style, which uses a word for any meaning that quick look and colourful gesture care to endow it with, she was an expert; and she carried it merrily on, leaving him at liberty (one of the great values of the style) to choose as he would how much or how little she meant. He was content to supply mere cues, for although he had little coquetry of his own, he had lately begun to find that the only interesting moments in his life were those during which Alice Adams coquetted with him. Happily, these obliging moments extended themselves to cover all the time he spent with her. However serious she might seem, whatever appeared to be her topic, all was thou-and-I.

He planned for more of it, seeing otherwise a dull evening ahead; and reverted, afterwhile, to a forbidden subject. "About that dance at Miss Lamb's —since your father's so much better——"

She flushed a little. "Now, now!" she chided him. "We agreed not to say any more about that."

"Yes, but since he *is* better——"

Alice shook her head. "He won't be better to-morrow. He always has a bad day after a good one—especially after such a good one as this is."

"But if this time it should be different," Russell persisted; "wouldn't you be willing to come—if he's better by to-morrow evening? Why not wait and decide at the last minute?"

She waved her hands airily. "What a pother!" she cried. "What does it matter whether poor little Alice Adams goes to a dance or not?"

"Well, I thought I'd made it clear that it looks fairly bleak to me if you don't go."

"Oh, yes!" she jeered.

"It's the simple truth," he insisted. "I don't care a great deal about dances these days; and if you aren't going to be there——"

"You could stay away," she suggested. "You wouldn't!"

"Unfortunately, I can't. I'm afraid I'm supposed to be the excuse. Miss Lamb, in her capacity as a friend of my relatives——"

"Oh, she's giving it for *you!* I see! On Mildred's account you mean?"

At that his face showed an increase of colour. "I suppose just on account of my being a cousin of Mildred's and of——"

"Of course! You'll have a beautiful time, too. Henrietta'll see that you have somebody to dance with besides Miss Dowling, poor man!"

"But what I want somebody to see is that I dance with you! And perhaps your father——"

"Wait!" she said, frowning as if she debated whether or not to tell him something of import; then, seeming to decide affirmatively, she asked: "Would you really like to know the truth about it?"

"If it isn't too unflattering."

"It hasn't anything to do with you at all," she said. "Of course I'd like to go with you and to dance with you—though you don't seem to realize that you wouldn't be permitted much time with me."

"Oh, yes, I——"

"Never mind!" she laughed. "Of course you wouldn't. But even if papa should be better to-morrow, I doubt if I'd go. In fact, I know I wouldn't. There's another reason besides papa."

"Is there?"

"Yes. The truth is, I don't get on with Henrietta Lamb. As a matter of fact, I dislike her, and of course that means she dislikes me. I should never think of asking her to anything *I* gave, and I really wonder she asks me to things *she* gives." This was a new inspiration; and Alice, beginning to see her way out of a perplexity, wished that she had thought of it earlier: she should have told him from the first that she and Henrietta had a feud, and consequently exchanged no invitations. Moreover, there was another thing to beset her with little anxieties: she might better not have told him from the first, as she had indeed told him by intimation, that she was the pampered daughter of an indulgent father, presumably able to indulge her; for now she must elaborately keep to the part. Veracity is usually simple; and its opposite, to be successful, should be as simple; but practitioners of the opposite are most often impulsive, like Alice; and, like her, they become enmeshed in elaborations.

"It wouldn't be very nice for me to go to her house," Alice went on, "when I wouldn't want her in mine. I've never admired her. I've always thought she was lacking in some things most people are supposed to be equipped with—for instance, a certain feeling about the death of a father who was always pretty decent to his daughter. Henrietta's father died just eleven months and twenty-seven days before your cousin's dance, but she couldn't stick out those few last days and make it a year; she was there." Alice stopped, then laughed ruefully, exclaiming, "But this is dreadful of me!"

"Is it?"

"Blackguarding her to you when she's giving a big party for you! Just the way Henrietta would blackguard me to you—heaven knows what she *wouldn't* say if she talked about me to you! It would be fair, of course, but—well, I'd rather she didn't!" And with that, Alice let her pretty hand, in its white glove, rest upon his arm for a moment; and he looked down at it, not unmoved to see it there. "I want to be unfair about just this," she said, letting a troubled laughter tremble through her appealing voice as she spoke. "I won't take advantage of her with anybody, except just—you! I'd a little rather you didn't hear anybody blackguard me, and, if you don't mind—could you promise not to give Henrietta the chance?"

It was charmingly done, with a humorous, faint pathos altogether genuine; and Russell found himself suddenly wanting to shout at her, "Oh, you *dear!*" Nothing else seemed adequate; but he controlled the impulse in favour of something more conservative.

"Imagine any one speaking unkindly of you—not praising you!"

"Who *has* praised me to you?" she asked, quickly

"I haven't talked about you with any one; but if I did, I know they'd——"

"No, no!" she cried, and went on, again accompanying her words with little tremulous runs of laughter. "You don't understand this town yet. You'll be surprised when you do; we're different. We talk about one another fearfully! Haven't I just proved it, the way I've been going for Henrietta? Of course I didn't say anything really very terrible about her, but that's only because I don't follow that practise the way most of the others do. They don't stop with the worst of the truth they can find: they make *up* things—yes, they really do! And, oh, I'd *rather* they didn't make up things about me—to you!"

"What difference would it make if they did?" he inquired, cheerfully. "I'd know they weren't true."

"Even if you did know that, they'd make a difference," she said. "Oh, yes, they would! It's too bad, but we don't like anything quite so well that's had specks on it, even if we've wiped the specks off;—it's just that much spoiled, and some things are all spoiled the instant they're the least bit spoiled. What a man thinks about a girl, for instance. Do you want to have what you think about me spoiled, Mr. Russell?"

"Oh, but that's already far beyond reach," he said, lightly.

"But it can't be!" she protested.

"Why not?"

"Because it never can be. Men don't change their minds about one another often: they make it quite an event when they do, and talk about it as if something important had happened. But a girl only has to go down-town with a shoe-string unfastened, and every man who sees her will change his mind about her. Don't you know that's true?"

"Not of myself, I think."

"There!" she cried. "That's precisely what every man in the world would say!"

"So you wouldn't trust me?"

"Well—I'll be awfully worried if you give 'em a chance to tell you that I'm too lazy to tie my shoe-strings!"

He laughed delightedly. "Is that what they do say?" he asked.

"Just about! Whatever they hope will get

results." She shook her head wisely. "Oh, yes; we do that here!"

"But I don't mind loose shoe-strings," he said. "Not if they're yours."

"They'll find out what you do mind."

"But suppose," he said, looking at her whimsically; "suppose I wouldn't mind anything—so long as it's yours?"

She courtesied. "Oh, pretty enough! But a girl who's talked about has a weakness that's often a fatal one."

"What is it?"

"It's this: when she's talked about she isn't *there*. That's how they kill her."

"I'm afraid I don't follow you."

"Don't you see? If Henrietta—or Mildred—or any of 'em—or some of their mothers—oh, we *all* do it! Well, if any of 'em told you I didn't tie my shoe-strings, and if I were there, so that you could see me, you'd know it wasn't true. Even if I were sitting so that you couldn't see my feet, and couldn't tell whether the strings were tied or not just then, still you could look at me, and see that I wasn't the sort of girl to neglect my shoe-strings. But that isn't the way it happens: they'll get at you when

I'm nowhere around and can't remind you of the sort of girl I really am."

"But you don't do that," he complained. "You don't remind me—you don't even tell me—the sort of girl you really are! I'd like to know."

"Let's be serious then," she said, and looked serious enough herself. "Would you honestly like to know?"

"Yes."

"Well, then, you must be careful."

"'Careful?'" The word amused him.

"I mean careful not to get me mixed up," she said. "Careful not to mix up the girl you might hear somebody talking about with the me I honestly try to make you see. If you do get those two mixed up—well, the whole show'll be spoiled!"

"What makes you think so?"

"Because it's——" She checked herself, having begun to speak too impulsively; and she was disturbed, realizing in what tricky stuff she dealt. What had been on her lips to say was, "Because it's happened before!" She changed to, "Because it's so easy to spoil anything—easiest of all to spoil anything that's pleasant."

"That might depend."

"No; it's so. And if you care at all about—about knowing a girl who'd like someone to know her——"

"Just 'someone?' That's disappointing."

"Well—you," she said.

"Tell me how 'careful' you want me to be, then!"

"Well, don't you think it would be nice if you didn't give anybody the chance to talk about me the way—the way I've just been talking about Henrietta Lamb?"

With that they laughed together, and he said, "You may be cutting me off from a great deal of information, you know."

"Yes," Alice admitted. "Somebody might begin to praise me to you, too; so it's dangerous to ask you to change the subject if I ever happen to be mentioned. But after all——" She paused.

"'After all' isn't the end of a thought, is it?"

"Sometimes it is of a girl's thought; I suppose men are neater about their thoughts, and always finish 'em. It isn't the end of the thought I had then, though."

"What is the end of it?"

She looked at him impulsively. "Oh, it's foolish," she said, and she laughed as laughs one who proposes something probably impossible. "But *wouldn't* it be pleasant if two people could ever just keep themselves *to* themselves, so far as they two were concerned? I mean, if they could just manage to be friends without people talking about it, or talking to *them* about it?"

"I suppose that might be rather difficult," he said, more amused than impressed by her idea.

"I don't know: it might be done," she returned, hopefully. "Especially in a town of this size; it's grown so it's quite a huge place these days. People can keep themselves to themselves in a big place better, you know. For instance, nobody knows that you and I are taking a walk together to-day."

"How absurd, when here we are on exhibition!"

"No; we aren't."

"We aren't?"

"Not a bit of it!" she laughed. "We were the other day, when you walked home with me, but anybody could tell that had just happened by chance, on account of your overtaking me; people can always see things like that. But we're not on exhibition now. Look where I've led you!"

Amused and a little bewildered, he looked up and down the street, which was one of gaunt-faced apartment-houses, old, sooty, frame boarding-houses, small groceries and drug-stores, laundries and one-room plumbers' shops, with the sign of a clairvoyant here and there.

"You see?" she said. "I've been leading you without your knowing it. Of course that's because you're new to the town, and you give yourself up to the guidance of an old citizen."

"I'm not so sure, Miss Adams. It might mean that I don't care where I follow so long as I follow you."

"Very well," she said. "I'd like you to keep on following me—at least long enough for me to show you that there's something nicer ahead of us than this dingy street."

"Is that figurative?" he asked.

"Might be!" she returned, gaily. "There's a pretty little park at the end, but it's very proletarian, and nobody you and I know will be more likely to see us there than on this street."

"What an imagination you have!" he exclaimed. "You turn our proper little walk into a Parisian adventure."

She looked at him in what seemed to be a momentary grave puzzlement. "Perhaps you feel that a Parisian adventure mightn't please your—your relatives?"

"Why, no," he returned. "You seem to think of them oftener than I do."

This appeared to amuse Alice, or at least to please her, for she laughed. "Then I can afford to quit thinking of them, I suppose. It's only that I used to be quite a friend of Mildred's—but there! we needn't to go into that. I've never been a friend of Henrietta Lamb's, though, and I almost wish she weren't taking such pains to be a friend of yours."

"Oh, but she's not. It's all on account of——"

"On Mildred's account," Alice finished this for him, coolly. "Yes, of course."

"It's on account of the two families," he was at pains to explain, a little awkwardly. "It's because I'm a relative of the Palmers, and the Palmers and the Lambs seem to be old family friends."

"Something the Adamses certainly are not," Alice said. "Not with either of 'em; particularly not with the Lambs!" And here, scarce aware of what impelled her, she returned to her former elaborations and colourings. "You see, the differences between Henrietta and me aren't entirely personal: I couldn't go to her house even if I liked her. The Lambs and Adamses don't get on with each other, and we've just about come to the breaking-point as it happens."

"I hope it's nothing to bother you."

"Why? A lot of things bother me."

"I'm sorry they do," he said, and seemed simply to mean it.

She nodded gratefully. "That's nice of you, Mr. Russell. It helps. The break between the Adamses and the Lambs is a pretty bothersome thing. It's been coming on a long time." She sighed deeply, and the sigh was half genuine; this half being for her father, but the other half probably belonged to her instinctive rendering of Juliet Capulet, daughter to a warring house. "I hate it all so!" she added.

"Of course you must."

"I suppose most quarrels between families are on account of business," she said. "That's why they're so sordid. Certainly the Lambs seem a sordid lot to me, though of course I'm biased." And with that she began to sketch a history of the commercial antagonism that had risen between the Adamses and the Lambs.

The sketching was spontaneous and dramatic. Mathematics had no part in it; nor was there accurate definition of Mr. Adams's relation to the institution of Lamb and Company. The point was clouded, in fact; though that might easily be set down to the general haziness of young ladies confronted with the mysteries of trade or commerce. Mr. Adams either had been a vague sort of junior member of the firm, it appeared, or else he should have been made some such thing; at all events, he was an old mainstay of the business; and he, as much as any Lamb, had helped to build up the prosperity of the company. But at last, tired of providing so much intelligence and energy for which other people took profit greater than his own, he had decided to leave the company and found a business entirely for himself. The Lambs were going to be enraged when they learned what was afoot.

Such was the impression, a little misted, wrought by Alice's quick narrative. But there was dolorous fact behind it: Adams had succumbed.

His wife, grave and nervous, rather than triumphant, in success, had told their daughter that the great J. A. would be furious and possibly vindictive. Adams was afraid of him, she said.

"But what for, mama?" Alice asked, since this

seemed a turn of affairs out of reason. "What in the world has Mr. Lamb to do with papa's leaving the company to set up for himself? What right has he to be angry about it? If he's such a friend as he claims to be, I should think he'd be glad—that is, if the glue factory turns out well. What will he be angry for?"

Mrs. Adams gave Alice an uneasy glance, hesitated, and then explained that a resignation from Lamb's had always been looked upon, especially by "that old man," as treachery. You were supposed to die in the service, she said bitterly, and her daughter, a little mystified, accepted this explanation. Adams had not spoken to her of his surrender; he seemed not inclined to speak to her at all, or to any one.

Alice was not serious too long, and she began to laugh as she came to the end of her decorative sketch. "After all, the whole thing is perfectly ridiculous," she said. "In fact, it's *funny!* That's on account of what papa's going to throw over the Lamb business *for!* To save your life you couldn't imagine what he's going to do!"

"I won't try, then," Russell assented.

"It takes all the romance out of *me*," she laughed.

"You'll never go for a Parisian walk with me again, after I tell you what I'll be heiress to." They had come to the entrance of the little park; and, as Alice had said, it was a pretty place, especially on a day so radiant. Trees of the oldest forest stood there, hale and serene over the trim, bright grass; and the proletarians had not come from their factories at this hour; only a few mothers and their babies were to be seen, here and there, in the shade. "I think I'll postpone telling you about it till we get nearly home again," Alice said, as they began to saunter down one of the gravelled paths. "There's a bench beside a spring farther on; we can sit there and talk about a lot of things—things not so sticky as my dowry's going to be."

"'Sticky?'" he echoed. "What in the world——"

She laughed despairingly.

"A glue factory!"

Then he laughed, too, as much from friendliness as from amusement; and she remembered to tell him that the project of a glue factory was still "an Adams secret." It would be known soon, however, she added; and the whole Lamb connection would probably begin saying all sorts of things, heaven knew what!

Thus Alice built her walls of flimsy, working always gaily, or with at least the air of gaiety; and even as she rattled on, there was somewhere in her mind a constant little wonder. Everything she said seemed to be necessary to support something else she had said. How had it happened? She found herself telling him that since her father had decided on making so great a change in his ways, she and her mother hoped at last to persuade him to give up that "foolish little house" he had been so obstinate about; and she checked herself abruptly on this declivity just as she was about to slide into a remark concerning her own preference for a "country place." Discretion caught her in time; and something else, in company with discretion, caught her, for she stopped short in her talk and blushed.

They had taken possession of the bench beside the spring, by this time; and Russell, his elbow on the back of the bench and his chin on his hand, the better to look at her, had no guess at the cause of the blush, but was content to find it lovely. At his first sight of Alice she had seemed pretty in the particular way of being pretty that he happened to like best; and, with every moment he spent with her, this prettiness appeared to increase. He felt that he could not look at her enough: his gaze followed the fluttering of the graceful hands in almost continual gesture as she talked; then lifted happily to the vivacious face again. She charmed him.

After her abrupt pause, she sighed, then looked at him with her eyebrows lifted in a comedy appeal. "You haven't said you wouldn't give Henrietta the chance," she said, in the softest voice that can still have a little laugh running in it.

He was puzzled. "Give Henrietta the chance?"

"*You* know! You'll let me keep on being unfair, won't you? Not give the other girls a chance to get even?"

He promised, heartily.

CHAPTER XV

ALICE had said that no one who knew either Russell or herself would be likely to see them in the park or upon the dingy street; but although they returned by that same ungenteel thoroughfare they were seen by a person who knew them both. Also, with some surprise on the part of Russell, and something more poignant than surprise for Alice, they saw this person.

All of the dingy street was ugly, but the greater part of it appeared to be honest. The two pedestrians came upon a block or two, however, where it offered suggestions of a less upright character, like a steady enough workingman with a naughty book sticking out of his pocket. Three or four dim shops, a single story in height, exhibited foul signboards, yet fair enough so far as the wording went; one proclaiming a tobacconist, one a junk-dealer, one a dispenser of "soft drinks and cigars." The most credulous would have doubted these signboards; for the craft of the modern tradesman is exerted to lure indoors the passing glance, since if the glance is pleased the feet may follow; but this alleged tobacconist and his neighbours had long been fond of dust on their windows, evidently, and shades were pulled far down on the glass of their doors. Thus the public eye, small of pupil in the light of the open street, was intentionally not invited to the dusky interiors. Something different from mere lack of enterprise was apparent; and the signboards might have been omitted; they were pains thrown away, since it was plain to the world that the business parts of these shops were the brighter back rooms implied by the dark front rooms; and that the commerce there was in perilous new liquors and in dice and rough girls.

Nothing could have been more innocent than the serenity with which these wicked little places revealed themselves for what they were; and, bound by this final tie of guilelessness, they stood together in a row which ended with a companionable barbershop, much like them. Beyond was a series of soot-harried frame two-story houses, once part of a cheerful neighbourhood when the town was middle-aged and settled, and not old and growing. These houses, all carrying the label, "Rooms," had the worried look of vacancy that houses have when they are too full of everybody without being anybody's home; and there was, too, a surreptitious air about them, as if, like the false little shops, they advertised something by concealing it.

One of them—the one next to the barber-shop—had across its front an ample, jig-sawed veranda, where aforetime, no doubt, the father of a family had fanned himself with a palm-leaf fan on Sunday afternoons, watching the surreys go by, and where his daughter listened to mandolins and badinage on starlit evenings; but, although youth still held the veranda, both the youth and the veranda were in decay. The four or five young men who lounged there this afternoon were of a type known to shady pool-parlours. Hats found no favour with them; all of them wore caps; and their tight clothes, apparently from a common source, showed a vivacious fancy for oblique pockets, false belts, and Easter-egg colourings. Another thing common to the group was the expression of eye and mouth; and Alice, in the midst of her other thoughts, had a distasteful thought about this.

The veranda was within a dozen feet of the sidewalk, and as she and her escort came nearer, she

"She had seemed pretty in the particular way he liked best; and with every moment he spent with her, this prettiness appeared to increase."

took note of the young men, her face hardening a little, even before she suspected there might be a resemblance between them and any one she knew. Then she observed that each of these loungers wore not for the occasion, but as of habit, a look of furtively amused contempt; the mouth smiled to one side as if not to dislodge a cigarette, while the eyes kept languidly superior. All at once Alice was reminded of Walter; and the slight frown caused by this idea had just begun to darken her forehead when Walter himself stepped out of the open door of the house and appeared upon the veranda. Upon his head was a new straw hat, and in his hand was a Malacca stick with an ivory top, for Alice had finally decided against it for herself and had given it to him. His mood was lively: he twirled the stick through his fingers like a drum-major's baton, and whistled loudly.

Moreover, he was indeed accompanied. With him was a thin girl who had made a violent black-and-white poster of herself: black dress, black flimsy boa, black stockings, white slippers, great black hat down upon the black eyes; and beneath the hat a curve of cheek and chin made white as whitewash, and in strong bilateral motion with gum.

The loungers on the veranda were familiars of the pair; hailed them with cacklings; and one began to sing, in a voice all tin:

> "Then my skirt, Sal, and me did go
> Right straight to the moving-pitcher show.
> *Oh,* you bashful vamp!"

The girl laughed airily. "God, but you guys are wise!" she said. "Come on, Wallie."

Walter stared at his sister; then grinned faintly, and nodded at Russell as the latter lifted his hat in salutation. Alice uttered an incoherent syllable of exclamation, and, as she began to walk faster, she bit her lip hard, not in order to look wistful, this time, but to help her keep tears of anger from her eyes.

Russell laughed cheerfully. "Your brother certainly seems to have found the place for 'colour' to-day," he said. "That girl's talk must be full of it."

But Alice had forgotten the colour she herself had used in accounting for Walter's peculiarities, and she did not understand. "What?" she said, huskily.

"Don't you remember telling me about him? How he was going to write, probably, and would go anywhere to pick up types and get them to talk?"

She kept her eyes ahead, and said sharply, "I think his literary tastes scarcely cover *this* case!"

"Don't be too sure. He didn't look at all disconcerted. He didn't seem to mind your seeing him."

"That's all the worse, isn't it?"

"Why, no," her friend said, genially. "It means he didn't consider that he was engaged in anything out of the way. You can't expect to understand everything boys do at his age; they do all sorts of queer things, and outgrow them. Your brother evidently has a taste for queer people, and very likely he's been at least half sincere when he's made you believe he had a literary motive behind it. We all go through——"

"Thanks, Mr. Russell," she interrupted. "Let's don't say any more."

He looked at her flushed face and enlarged eyes; and he liked her all the better for her indignation: this was how good sisters ought to feel, he thought, failing to understand that most of what she felt was not about Walter. He ventured only a word more. "Try not to mind it so much; it really doesn't amount to anything."

She shook her head, and they went on in silence; she did not look at him again until they stopped before her own house. Then she gave him only one glimpse of her eyes before she looked down. "It's spoiled, isn't it?" she said, in a low voice.

"What's 'spoiled?'"

"Our walk—well, everything. Somehow it always—is."

"'Always is' what?" he asked.

"Spoiled," she said.

He laughed at that; but without looking at him she suddenly offered him her hand, and, as he took it, he felt a hurried, violent pressure upon his fingers, as if she meant to thank him almost passionately for being kind. She was gone before he could speak to her again.

In her room, with the door locked, she did not go to her mirror, but to her bed, flinging herself face down, not caring how far the pillows put her hat awry. Sheer grief had followed her anger; grief for the calamitous end of her bright afternoon, grief for the "end of everything," as she thought then. Nevertheless, she gradually grew more composed, and, when her mother tapped on the door presently, let her in. Mrs. Adams looked at her with quick apprehension.

"Oh, poor child! Wasn't he——"

Alice told her. "You see how it—how it made me look, mama," she quavered, having concluded her narrative. "I'd tried to cover up Walter's awfulness at the dance with that story about his being 'literary,' but no story was big enough to cover this up—and oh! it must make him think I tell stories about other things!"

"No, no, no!" Mrs. Adams protested. "Don't you see? At the worst, all *he* could think is that Walter told stories to you about why he likes to be with such dreadful people, and you believed them. That's all *he'd* think; don't you see?"

Alice's wet eyes began to show a little hopefulness. "You honestly think it might be that way, mama?"

"Why, from what you've told me he said, I *know* it's that way. Didn't he say he wanted to come again?"

"N-no," Alice said, uncertainly. "But I think he will. At least I begin to think so now. He——" She stopped.

"From all you tell me, he seems to be a very desirable young man," Mrs. Adams said, primly.

Her daughter was silent for several moments; then new tears gathered upon her downcast lashes. "He's just—dear!" she faltered.

Mrs. Adams nodded. "He's told you he isn't engaged, hasn't he?"

"No. But I know he isn't. Maybe when he first came here he was near it, but I know he's not."

"I guess Mildred Palmer would *like* him to be, all right!" Mrs. Adams was frank enough to say, rather triumphantly; and Alice, with a lowered head, murmured:

"Anybody—would."

The words were all but inaudible.

"Don't you worry," her mother said, and patted her on the shoulder. "Everything will come out all right; don't you fear, Alice. Can't you see that beside any other girl in town you're just a perfect *queen?* Do you think any young man that wasn't prejudiced, or something, would need more than just one look to——"

But Alice moved away from the caressing hand. "Never mind, mama. I wonder he looks at me at all. And if he does again, after seeing my brother with those horrible people——"

"Now, now!" Mrs. Adams interrupted, expostulating mournfully. "I'm sure Walter's a *good* boy——"

"You are?" Alice cried, with a sudden vigour. "You *are?*"

"I'm sure he's *good*, yes—and if he isn't, it's not his fault. It's mine."

"What nonsense!"

"No, it's true," Mrs. Adams lamented. "I tried to bring him up to be good, God knows; and when he was little he was the best boy I ever saw. When he came from Sunday-school he'd always run to me and we'd go over the lesson together; and he let me come in his room at night to hear his prayers almost until he was sixteen. Most boys won't do that with their mothers—not nearly that long. I tried so hard to bring him up right—but if anything's gone wrong it's my fault."

"How could it be? You've just said——"

"It's because I didn't make your father take this—this new step earlier. Then Walter might have had all the advantages that other——"

"Oh, mama, *please!*" Alice begged her. "Let's don't go over all that again. Isn't it more important to think what's to be done about him? Is he going to be allowed to go on disgracing us as he does?"

Mrs. Adams sighed profoundly. "I don't know

what to do," she confessed, unhappily. "Your father's so upset about—about this new step he's taking—I don't feel as if we ought to——"

"No, no!" Alice cried. "Papa mustn't be distressed with this, on top of everything else. But *something's* got to be done about Walter."

"What can be?" her mother asked, helplessly. "What can be?"

Alice admitted that she didn't know.

At dinner, an hour later, Walter's habitually veiled glance lifted, now and then, to touch her furtively;—he was waiting, as he would have said, for her to "spring it"; and he had prepared a brief and sincere defense to the effect that he made his own living, and would like to inquire whose business it was to offer intrusive comment upon his private conduct. But she said nothing, while his father and mother were as silent as she. Walter concluded that there was to be no attack, but changed his mind when his father, who ate only a little, and broodingly at that, rose to leave the table and spoke to him.

"Walter," he said, "when you've finished I wish you'd come up to my room. I got something I want to say to you."

Walter shot a hard look at his apathetic sister, then turned to his father. "Make it to-morrow," he said. "This is Satad'y night and I got a date."

"No," Adams said, frowning. "You come up before you go out. It's important."

"All right; I've had all I want to eat," Walter returned. "I got a few minutes. Make it quick."

He followed his father upstairs, and when they were in the room together Adams shut the door, sat down, and began to rub his knees.

"Rheumatism?" the boy inquired, slyly. "That what you want to talk to me about?"

"No." But Adams did not go on; he seemed to be in difficulties for words, and Walter decided to help him.

"Hop ahead and spring it," he said. "Get it off your mind: I'll tell the world *I* should worry! You aren't goin' to bother *me* any, so why bother yourself? Alice hopped home and told you she saw me playin' around with some pretty gay-lookin' berries and you——"

"Alice?" his father said, obviously surprised. "It's nothing about Alice."

"Didn't she tell you——"

"I haven't talked with her all day."

"Oh, I see," Walter said. "She told mother and mother told you."

"No, neither of 'em have told me anything. What was there to tell?"

Walter laughed. "Oh, it's nothin'," he said. "I was just startin' out to buy a girl friend o' mine a rhinestone buckle I lost to her on a bet, this afternoon, and Alice came along with that big Russell fish; and I thought she looked sore. She expects me to like the kind she likes, and I don't like 'em. I thought she'd prob'ly got you all stirred up about it."

"No, no," his father said, peevishly. "I don't know anything about it, and I don't care to know anything about it. I want to talk to you about something important."

Then, as he was again silent, Walter said, "Well, *talk* about it; I'm listening."

"It's this," Adams began, heavily. "It's about me going into this glue business. Your mother's told you, hasn't she?"

"She said you were goin' to leave the old place down-town and start a glue factory. That's all I know about it; I got my own affairs to 'tend to."

"Well, this is your affair," his father said, frowning. "You can't stay with Lamb and Company."

Walter looked a little startled. "What you mean, I can't? Why not?"

"You've got to help me," Adams explained slowly; and he frowned more deeply, as if the interview were growing increasingly laborious for him. "It's going to be a big pull to get this business on its feet."

"Yes!" Walter exclaimed with a sharp skepticism. "I should say it was!" He stared at his father incredulously. "Look here; aren't you just a little bit sudden, the way you're goin' about things? You've let mother shove you a little too fast, haven't you? Do you know anything about what it means to set up a new business these days?"

"Yes, I know all about it," Adams said. "About this business, I do."

"How do you?"

"Because I made a long study of it. I'm not afraid of going about it the wrong way; but it's a hard job and you'll have to put in all whatever sense and strength you've got."

Walter began to breathe quickly, and his lips were agitated; then he set them obstinately. "Oh, I will," he said.

"Yes, you will," Adams returned, not noticing that his son's inflection was satiric. "It's going to take every bit of energy in your body, and all the energy I got left in mine, and every cent of the little I've saved, besides something I'll have to raise on this house. I'm going right at it, now I've got to; and you'll have to quit Lamb's by the end of next week."

"Oh, I will?" Walter's voice grew louder, and there was a shrillness in it. "I got to quit Lamb's the end of next week, have I?" He stepped forward, angrily. "Listen!" he said. "I'm not walkin' out o' Lamb's, see? I'm not quittin' down there: I stay with 'em, see?"

Adams looked up at him, astonished. "You'll leave there next Saturday," he said. "I've got to have you."

"You don't anything o' the kind," Walter told him, sharply. "Do you expect to pay me anything?"

"I'd pay you about what you been getting down there."

"Then pay somebody else; *I* don't know anything about glue. You get somebody else."

"No. You've got to——"

Walter cut him off with the utmost vehemence. "Don't tell me what I got to do! *I* know what I got to do better'n you, I guess! I stay at Lamb's, see?"

Adams rose angrily. "You'll do what I tell you. You can't stay down there."

"Why can't I?"

"Because I won't let you."

"Listen! Keep on not lettin' me: I'll be there just the same."

At that his father broke into a sour laughter. "*They* won't let you, Walter! They won't have you down there after they find out I'm going."

"Why won't they? You don't think they're goin' to be all shot to pieces over losin' *you*, do you?"

"I tell you they won't let you stay," his father insisted, loudly.

"Why, what do they care whether you go or not?"

"They'll care enough to fire *you*, my boy!"

"Look here, then; show me why."

"They'll do it!"

"Yes," Walter jeered; "you keep sayin' they will, but when I ask you to show me why, you keep sayin' they will! That makes little headway with *me*, I can tell you!"

Adams groaned, and, rubbing his head, began to

pace the floor. Walter's refusal was something he had not anticipated; and he felt the weakness of his own attempt to meet it: he seemed powerless to do anything but utter angry words, which, as Walter said, made little headway. "Oh, my, my!" he muttered, "*Oh*, my, my!"

Walter, usually sallow, had grown pale: he watched his father narrowly, and now took a sudden resolution. "Look here," he said. "When you say Lamb's is likely to fire me because you're goin' to quit, you talk like the people that have to be locked up. I don't know where you get such things in your head; Lamb and Company won't know you're gone. Listen: I can stay there long as I want to. But I'll tell you what I'll do: make it worth my while and I'll hook up with your old glue factory, after all."

Adams stopped his pacing abruptly, and stared at him. "'Make it worth your while?' What you mean?"

"I got a good use for three hundred dollars right now," Walter said. "Let me have it and I'll quit Lamb's to work for you. Don't let me have it and I *swear* I won't!"

"Are you crazy?"

"Is everybody crazy that needs three hundred dollars?"

"Yes," Adams said. "They are if they ask *me* for it, when I got to stretch every cent I can lay my hands on to make it look like a dollar!"

"You won't do it?"

Adams burst out at him. "You little fool! If I had three hundred dollars to throw away, besides the pay I expected to give you, haven't you got sense enough to see I could hire a man worth three hundred dollars more to me than you'd be? It's a *fine* time to ask me for three hundred dollars, isn't it! What *for?* Rhinestone buckles to throw around on your 'girl friends?' Shame on you! Ask me to *bribe* you to help yourself and your own family!"

"I'll give you a last chance," Walter said. "Either you do what I want, or I won't do what you want. Don't ask me again after this, because——"

Adams interrupted him fiercely. "'Ask you again!' Don't worry about that, my boy! All I ask you is to get out o' my room."

"Look here," Walter said, quietly; and his lopsided smile distorted his livid cheek. "Look here: I expect *you* wouldn't give me three hundred dollars to save my life, would you?"

"You make me sick," Adams said, in his bitterness. "Get out of here."

Walter went out, whistling; and Adams drooped into his old chair again as the door closed. "*Oh*, my, my!" he groaned. "Oh, Lordy, Lordy! The way of the transgressor——"

CHAPTER XVI

HE MEANT his own transgression and his own way; for Walter's stubborn refusal appeared to Adams just then as one of the inexplicable but righteous besettings he must encounter in following that way. "Oh, Lordy, Lord!" he groaned, and then, as resentment moved him—"That dang boy! Dang idiot!" Yet he knew himself for a greater idiot because he had not been able to tell Walter the truth. He could not bring himself to do it, nor even to state his case in its best terms; and that was because he felt that even in its best terms the case was a bad one.

Of all his regrets the greatest was that in a moment of vanity and tenderness, twenty-five years ago, he had told his young wife a business secret. He had wanted to show how important her husband was becoming, and how much the head of the universe, J. A. Lamb, trusted to his integrity and ability. The great man had an idea: he thought of "branching out a little," he told Adams confidentially, and there were possibilities of profit in glue.

What he wanted was a liquid glue to be put into little bottles and sold cheaply. "The kind of thing that sells itself," he said; "the kind of thing that pays its own small way as it goes along, until it has profits enough to begin advertising it right. Everybody has to use glue, and if I make mine convenient and cheap, everybody'll buy mine. But it's got to be glue that'll *stick;* it's got to be the best; and if we find how to make it we've got to keep it a big secret, of course, or anybody can steal it from us. There was a man here last month; he knew a formula he wanted to sell me, 'sight unseen'; but he was in such a hurry I got suspicious, and I found he'd managed to steal it, working for the big packers in their glue-works. We've got to find a better glue than that, anyhow. I'm going to set you and Campbell at it. You're a practical, wide-awake young feller, and Campbell's a mighty good chemist; I guess you two boys ought to make something happen."

His guess was shrewd enough. Working in a shed a little way outside the town, where their cheery employer visited them sometimes to study their malodorous stews, the two young men found what Lamb had set them to find. But Campbell was thoughtful over the discovery. "Look here," he said. "Why ain't this just about yours and mine? After all, it may be Lamb's money that's paid for the stuff we've used, but it hasn't cost much."

"But he pays *us*," Adams remonstrated, horrified by his companion's idea. "He paid us to do it. It belongs absolutely to him."

"Oh, I know he *thinks* it does," Campbell admitted, plaintively. "I suppose we've got to let him take it. It's not patentable, and he'll have to do pretty well by us when he starts his factory, because he's got to depend on us to run the making of the stuff so that the workmen can't get onto the process. You better ask him the same salary I do, and mine's going to be high."

But the high salary, thus pleasantly imagined, was never paid. Campbell died of typhoid fever, that summer, leaving Adams and his employer the only possessors of the formula, an unwritten one; and Adams, pleased to think himself more important to the great man than ever, told his wife that there could be little doubt of his being put in sole charge of the prospective glue-works. Unfortunately, the enterprise remained prospective.

Its projector had already become "inveigled

into another side-line," as he told Adams. One of his sons had persuaded him to take up a "cough-lozenge," to be called the "Jalamb Balm Trochee"; and the lozenge did well enough to amuse Mr. Lamb and occupy his spare time, which was really about all he had asked of the glue project. He had "all the *money* anybody ought to want," he said, when Adams urged him; and he could "start up this little glue side-line" at any time; the formula was safe in their two heads.

At intervals Adams would seek opportunity to speak of "the little glue side-line" to his patron, and to suggest that the years were passing; but Lamb, petting other hobbies, had lost interest. "Oh, I'll start it up some day, maybe. If I don't, I may turn it over to my heirs: it's always an asset, worth something or other, of course. We'll probably take it up some day, though, you and I."

The sun persistently declined to rise on that day, and, as time went on, Adams saw that his rather timid urgings bored his employer, and he ceased to bring up the subject. Lamb apparently forgot all about glue, but Adams discovered that unfortunately there was someone else who remembered it.

"It's really *yours*," she argued, that painful day

when for the first time she suggested his using his knowledge for the benefit of himself and his family. "Mr. Campbell might have had a right to part of it, but he died and didn't leave any kin, so it belongs to you."

"Suppose J. A. Lamb hired me to saw some wood," Adams said. "Would the sticks belong to me?"

"He hasn't got any right to take your invention and bury it," she protested. "What good is it doing him if he doesn't *do* anything with it? What good is it doing *anybody?* None in the world! And what harm would it do him if you went ahead and did this for yourself and for your children? None in the world! And what could he do to you if he *was* old pig enough to get angry with you for doing it? He couldn't do a single thing, and you've admitted he couldn't, yourself. So what's your reason for depriving your children and your wife of the benefits you know you could give 'em?"

"Nothing but decency," he answered; and she had her reply ready for that. It seemed to him that, strive as he would, he could not reach her mind with even the plainest language; while everything that she said to him, with such vehemence, sounded like so much obstinate gibberish. Over and over he pressed her with the same illustration, on the point of ownership, though he thought he was varying it.

"Suppose he hired me to build him a house: would that be *my* house?"

"He didn't hire you to build him a house. You and Campbell invented——"

"Look here: suppose you give a cook a soup-bone and some vegetables, and pay her to make you a soup: has she got a right to take and sell it? You know better!"

"I know *one* thing: if that old man tried to keep your own invention from you he's no better than a robber!"

They never found any point of contact in all their passionate discussions of this ethical question; and the question was no more settled between them, now that Adams had succumbed, than it had ever been. But at least the wrangling about it was over: they were grave together, almost silent, and an uneasiness prevailed with her as much as with him.

He had already been out of the house, to walk about the small green yard; and on Monday afternoon he sent for a taxicab and went down-town, but kept a long way from the "wholesale section," where stood the formidable old oblong pile of Lamb and Company. He arranged for the sale of the bonds he had laid away, and for placing a mortgage upon his house; and on his way home, after five o'clock, he went to see an old friend, a man whose term of service with Lamb and Company was even a little longer than his own.

This veteran, returned from the day's work, was sitting in front of the apartment house where he lived, but when the cab stopped at the curb he rose and came forward, offering a jocular greeting. "Well, well, Virgil Adams! I always thought you had a sporty streak in you. Travel in your own hired private automobile nowadays, do you? Pamperin' yourself because you're still layin' off sick, I expect."

"Oh, I'm well enough again, Charley Lohr," Adams said, as he got out and shook hands. Then, telling the driver to wait, he took his friend's arm, walked to the bench with him, and sat down. "I been practically well for some time," he said. "I'm fixin' to get into harness again."

"Bein' sick has certainly produced a change of heart in you," his friend laughed. "You're the last man I ever expected to see blowin' yourself—or anybody else—to a taxicab! For that matter, I never heard of you bein' in *any* kind of a cab, 'less'n it might be when you been pall-bearer for somebody. What's come over you?"

"Well, I got to turn over a new leaf, and that's a fact," Adams said. "I got a lot to do, and the only way to accomplish it, it's got to be done soon, or I won't have anything to live on while I'm doing it."

"What you talkin' about? What you got to do except to get strong enough to come back to the old place?"

"Well——" Adams paused, then coughed, and said slowly, "Fact is, Charley Lohr, I been thinking likely I wouldn't come back."

"What! What you talkin' about?"

"No," said Adams. "I been thinking I might likely kind of branch out on my own account."

"Well, I'll be doggoned!" Old Charley Lohr was amazed; he ruffled up his gray moustache with thumb and forefinger, leaving his mouth open beneath, like a dark cave under a tangled wintry thicket. "Why, that's the doggonedest thing I ever heard!" he said. "I already am the oldest inhabitant down there, but if you go, there won't be anybody else of the old generation at all. What on earth you thinkin' of goin' into?"

"Well," said Adams, "I rather you didn't mention it till I get started—of course anybody'll know what it is by then—but I *have* been kind of planning to put a liquid glue on the market."

His friend, still ruffling the gray moustache upward, stared at him in frowning perplexity. "Glue?" he said. "*Glue!*"

"Yes. I been sort of milling over the idea of taking up something like that."

"Handlin' it for some firm, you mean?"

"No. Making it. Sort of a glue-works likely."

Lohr continued to frown. "Let me think," he said. "Didn't the ole man have some such idea once, himself?"

Adams leaned forward, rubbing his knees; and he coughed again before he spoke. "Well, yes. Fact is, he did. That is to say, a mighty long while ago he did."

"I remember," said Lohr. "He never said anything about it that I know of; but seems to me I recollect we had sort of a rumour around the place how you and that man—le's see, wasn't his name Campbell, that died of typhoid fever? Yes, that was it, Campbell. Didn't the ole man have you and Campbell workin' sort of private on some glue proposition or other?"

"Yes, he did." Adams nodded. "I found out a good deal about glue then, too."

"Been workin' on it since, I suppose?"

"Yes. Kept it in my mind and studied out new things about it."

Lohr looked serious. "Well, but see here," he said. "I hope it ain't anything the ole man'll think might infringe on whatever he had you doin' for *him.* You know how he is: broad-minded, liberal, free-handed man as walks this earth, and if he thought he owed you a cent he'd sell his right hand for a pork-chop to pay it, if that was the only way; but if he got the idea anybody was tryin' to get the better cf him, he'd sell *both* his hands, if he had to, to keep 'em from doin' it. Yes, at eighty, he would! Not that I mean I think you might be tryin' to get the better of him, Virg. You're a mighty close ole codger, but such a thing ain't in you. What I mean: I hope there ain't any chance for the ole man to *think* you might be——"

"Oh, no," Adams interrupted. "As a matter of fact, I don't believe he'll ever think about it at all, and if he did he wouldn't have any real right to feel offended at me: the process I'm going to use is one I expect to change and improve a lot different from the one Campbell and I worked on for him."

"Well, that's good," said Lohr. "Of course you know what you're up to: you're old enough, God knows!" He laughed ruefully. "My, but it will seem funny to me—down there with you gone! I expect you and I both been gettin' to be pretty much dead-wood in the place, the way the young fellows look at it, and the only one that'd miss either of us would be the other one! Have you told the ole man yet?"

"Well——" Adams spoke laboriously. "No. No, I haven't. I thought—well, that's what I wanted to see you about."

"What can I do?"

"I thought I'd write him a letter and get you to hand it to him for me."

"My soul!" his friend exclaimed. "Why on earth don't you just go down there and tell him?"

Adams became pitiably embarrassed. He stammered, coughed, stammered again, wrinkling his face so deeply he seemed about to weep; but finally he contrived to utter an apologetic laugh. "I ought to do that, of course; but in some way or other I just don't seem to be able to—to manage it."

"Why in the world not?" the mystified Lohr inquired.

"I could hardly tell you—'less'n it is to say that when you been with one boss all your life it's so—so kind of embarrassing—to quit him, I just can't make up my mind to go and speak to him about it. No; I got it in my head a letter's the only satisfactory way to do it, and I thought I'd ask you to hand it to him."

"Well, of course I don't mind doin' that for you," Lohr said, mildly. "But why in the world don't you just mail it to him?"

"Well, I'll tell you," Adams returned. "You know, like that, it'd have to go through a clerk and that secretary of his, and I don't know who all. There's a couple of kind of delicate points I want to put in it: for instance, I want to explain to him how much improvement and so on I'm going to introduce on the old process I helped to work out with Campbell when we were working for him, so't he'll understand it's a different article and no infringement at all. Then there's another thing: you see all during while I was sick he had my salary paid to me—it amounts to considerable, I was on my back so long. Under the circumstances, because I'm quitting, I don't feel as if I ought to accept it, and so I'll have a check for him in the letter to cover it, and I want to be sure he knows it, and gets it personally. If it had to go through a lot of other people, the way it would if I put it in the mail, why, you can't tell. So what I thought: if you'd hand it to him for me, and maybe if he happened to read it right then, or anything, it might be you'd notice whatever he'd happen to say about it—and you could tell me afterward."

"All right," Lohr said. "Certainly if you'd rather do it that way, I'll hand it to him and tell you what he says; that is, if he says anything and I hear him. Got it written?"

"No; I'll send it around to you last of the week." Adams moved toward his taxicab. "Don't say anything to anybody about it, Charley, especially till after that."

"All right."

"And, Charley, I'll be mighty obliged to you," Adams said, and came back to shake hands in farewell. "There's one thing more you might do—if you'd ever happen to feel like it." He kept his eyes rather vaguely fixed on a point above his friend's head as he spoke, and his voice was not well controlled. "I been—I been down there a good many years and I may not 'a' been so much use lately as I was at first, but I always *tried* to do my best for the old firm. If anything turned out so's they *did* kind of take offense with me, down there, why, just say a good word for me—if you'd happen to feel like it, maybe."

Old Charley Lohr assured him that he would speak a good word if opportunity became available; then, after the cab had driven away, he went up to his small apartment on the third floor and muttered ruminatively until his wife inquired what he was talking to himself about.

"Ole Virg Adams," he told her. "He's out again after his long spell of sickness, and the way it looks to me he'd better stayed in bed."

"You mean he still looks too bad to be out?"

"Oh, I expect he's gettin' his *health* back," Lohr said, frowning.

"Then what's the matter with him? You mean he's lost his mind?"

"My goodness, but women do jump at conclusions!" he exclaimed.

"Well," said Mrs. Lohr, "what other conclusion did you leave me to jump at?"

Her husband explained with a little heat: "People can have a sickness that *affects* their mind, can't they? Their mind can get some affected without bein' *lost*, can't it?"

"Then you mean the poor man's mind does seem affected?"

"Why, no; I'd scarcely go as far as that," Lohr said, inconsistently, and declined to be more definite.

Adams devoted the latter part of that evening to the composition of his letter—a disquieting task not completed when, at eleven o'clock, he heard his daughter coming up the stairs. She was singing to herself in a low, sweet voice, and Adams paused to listen incredulously, with his pen lifted and his mouth open, as if he heard the strangest sound in the world. Then he set down the pen upon a blotter, went to his door, and opened it, looking out at her as she came.

"Well, dearie, you seem to be feeling pretty good," he said. "What you been doing?"

"Just sitting out on the front steps, papa."

"All alone, I suppose."

"No. Mr. Russell called."

"Oh, he did?" Adams pretended to be surprised. "What all could you and he find to talk about till this hour o' the night?"

She laughed gaily. "You don't know me, papa!"

"How's that?"

"You've never found out that I always do all the talking."

"Didn't you let him get a word in all evening?"

"Oh, yes; every now and then."

Adams took her hand and petted it. "Well, what did he say?"

Alice gave him a radiant look and kissed him. "Not what you think!" she laughed; then slapped his cheek with saucy affection, pirouetted across the narrow hall and into her own room, and curtsied to him as she closed her door.

Adams went back to his writing with a lighter heart; for since Alice was born she had been to him the apple of his eye, his own phrase in thinking of her; and what he was doing now was for her. He smiled as he picked up his pen to begin a new draft of the painful letter; but presently he looked puzzled. After all, she could be happy just as things were, it seemed. Then why had he taken what his wife called "this new step," which he had so long resisted?

He could only sigh and wonder. "Life works out pretty peculiarly," he thought; for he couldn't go back now, though the reason he couldn't was not clearly apparent. He had to go ahead.

CHAPTER XVII

HE WAS out in his taxicab again the next morning, and by noon he had secured what he wanted.

It was curiously significant that he worked so quickly. All the years during which his wife had pressed him toward his present shift he had sworn to himself, as well as to her, that he would never yield; and yet when he did yield he had no plans to make, because he found them already prepared and worked out in detail in his mind; as if he had long contemplated the "step" he believed himself incapable of taking.

Sometimes he had thought of improving his income by exchanging his little collection of bonds for a "small rental property," if he could find "a good buy"; and he had spent many of his spare hours rambling over the enormously spreading city and its purlieus, looking for the ideal "buy." It remained unattainable, so far as he was concerned; but he found other things.

Not twice a crow's mile from his own house there was a dismal and slummish quarter, a decayed "industrial district" of earlier days. Most of the industries were small; some of them died, perishing of bankruptcy or fire; and a few had moved, leaving their shells. Of the relics, the best was a brick building which had been the largest and most important factory in the quarter: it had been injured by a long vacancy almost as serious as a fire, in effect, and Adams had often guessed at the sum needed to put it in repair.

When he passed it, he would look at it with an interest which he supposed detached and idly speculative. "That'd be just the thing," he thought. "If a fellow had money enough, and took a notion to set up some new business on a big scale, this would be a pretty good place—to make glue, for instance, if that wasn't out of the question, of course. It would take a lot of money, though; a great deal too much for *me* to expect to handle—even if I'd ever dream of doing such a thing."

Opposite the dismantled factory was a muddy, open lot of two acres or so, and near the middle of the lot, a long brick shed stood in a desolate abandonment, not happily decorated by old coatings of theatrical and medicinal advertisements. But the brick shed had two wooden ells, and, though both shed and ells were of a single story, here was empty space enough for a modest enterprise—"space enough for almost anything, to start with," Adams thought, as he walked through the low buildings, one day, when he was prospecting in that section. "Yes, I suppose I *could* swing this," he thought. "If the process belonged to me, say, instead of being out of the question because it isn't my property—or if I was the kind of man to do such a thing anyhow, here would be something I could probably get hold of pretty cheap. They'd want a lot of money for a lease on that big building over the way—but this, why, I should think it'd be practically nothing at all."

Then, by chance, meeting an agent he knew, he made inquiries—merely to satisfy a casual curiosity, he thought—and he found matters much as he had supposed, except that the owners of the big building did not wish to let, but to sell it, and this at a price so exorbitant that Adams laughed. But the long brick shed in the great muddy lot was for sale or to let, or "pretty near to be given away," he learned, if anybody would take it.

Adams took it now, though without seeing that he

had been destined to take it, and that some dreary wizard in the back of his head had foreseen all along that he would take it, and planned to be ready. He drove in his taxicab to look the place over again, then down-town to arrange for a lease; and came home to lunch with his wife and daughter. Things were "moving," he told them.

He boasted a little of having acted so decisively, and said that since the dang thing had to be done, it was "going to be done *right!*" He was almost cheerful, in a feverish way, and when the cab came for him again, soon after lunch, he explained that he intended not only to get things done right, but also to "get 'em done quick!" Alice, following him to the front door, looked at him anxiously and asked if she couldn't help. He laughed at her grimly.

"Then let me go along with you in the cab," she begged. "You don't look able to start in so hard, papa, just when you're barely beginning to get your strength back. Do let me go with you and see if I can't help—or at least take care of you if you should get to feeling badly."

He declined, but upon pressure let her put a tiny bottle of spirits of ammonia in his pocket, and promised to make use of it if he "felt faint or anything." Then he was off again; and the next morning had men at work in his sheds, though the wages he had to pay frightened him.

He directed the workmen in every detail, hurrying them by example and exhortations, and receiving, in consequence, several declarations of independence, as well as one resignation, which took effect immediately. "Yous capitalusts seem to think a man's got nothin' to do but break his back p'doosin' wealth fer yous to squander," the resigning person loudly complained. "You look out: the toiler's day is a-comin', and it ain't so fur off, neither!" But the capitalist was already out of hearing, gone to find a man to take this orator's place.

By the end of the week, Adams felt that he had moved satisfactorily forward in his preparations for the simple equipment he needed; but he hated the pause of Sunday. He didn't *want* any rest, he told Alice impatiently, when she suggested that the idle day might be good for him.

Late that afternoon he walked over to the apartment house where old Charley Lohr lived, and gave his friend the letter he wanted the head of Lamb and Company to receive "personally." "I'll take it as a mighty great favour in you to hand it to him personally, Charley," he said, in parting. "And you won't forget, in case he says anything about it—and remember if you ever do get a chance to put in a good word for me later, you know——"

Old Charley promised to remember, and, when Mrs. Lohr came out of the "kitchenette," after the door closed, he said thoughtfully, "Just skin and bones."

"You mean Mr. Adams is?" Mrs. Lohr inquired.

"Who'd you think I meant?" he returned. "One o' these partridges in the wall-paper?"

"Did he look so badly?"

"Looked kind of distracted to *me*," her husband replied. "These little thin fellers can stand a heap sometimes, though. He'll be over here again Monday."

"Did he say he would?"

"No," said Lohr. "But he will. You'll see. He'll be over to find out what the big boss says when I give him this letter. Expect I'd be kind of anxious, myself, if I was him."

"Why would you? What's Mr. Adams doing to be so anxious about?"

Lohr's expression became one of reserve, the look of a man who has found that when he speaks his inner thoughts his wife jumps too far to conclusions. "Oh, nothing," he said. "Of course any man starting up a new business is bound to be pretty nervous a while. He'll be over here to-morrow evening, all right; you'll see."

The prediction was fulfilled: Adams arrived just after Mrs. Lohr had removed the dinner dishes to her "kitchenette"; but Lohr had little information to give his caller.

"He didn't say a word, Virgil; nary a word. I took it into his office and handed it to him, and he just sat and read it; that's all. I kind of stood around as long as I could, but he was sittin' at his desk with his side to me, and he never turned around full toward me, as it were, so I couldn't hardly even tell anything. All I know: he just read it."

"Well, but see here," Adams began, nervously. "Well——"

"Well what, Virg?"

"Well, but what did he say when he *did* speak?"

"He didn't speak. Not so long I was in there, anyhow. He just sat there and read it. Read kind of slow. Then, when he came to the end, he turned back and started to read it all over again. By that time there was three or four other men standin' around in the office waitin' to speak to him, and I had to go."

Adams sighed, and stared at the floor, irresolute. "Well, I'll be getting along back home then, I guess, Charley. So you're sure you couldn't tell anything what he might have thought about it, then?"

"Not a thing in the world. I've told you all I know, Virg."

"I guess so, I guess so," Adams said, mournfully. "I feel mighty obliged to you, Charley Lohr; mighty obliged. Good-night to you." And he departed, sighing in perplexity.

On his way home, preoccupied with many thoughts, he walked so slowly that once or twice he stopped and stood motionless for a few moments, without being aware of it; and when he reached the juncture of the sidewalk with the short brick path that led to his own front door, he stopped again, and stood for more than a minute. "Ah, I wish I knew," he whispered, plaintively. "I do wish I knew what he thought about it."

He was roused by a laugh that came lightly from the little veranda near by. "Papa!" Alice called gaily. "What *are* you standing there muttering to yourself about?"

"Oh, are you there, dearie?" he said, and came up the path. A tall figure rose from a chair on the veranda.

"Papa, this is Mr. Russell."

The two men shook hands, Adams saying, "Pleased to make your acquaintance," as they looked at each other in the faint light diffused through the opaque glass in the upper part cf the door. Adams's impression was cf a strong and tall young man, fashionable but gentle; and Russell's was cf a dried, little old business man with a grizzled moustache, worried bright eyes, shapeless dark clothes, and a homely manner.

"Nice evening," Adams said further, as their hands parted. "Nice time o' year it is, but we don't always have as good weather as this; that's the trouble of it. Well——" He went to the door. "Well—I bid you good evening," he said, and retired within the house.

Alice laughed. "He's the old-fashionedest man in town, I suppose—and frightfully impressed with *you*, I could see!"

"What nonsense!" said Russell. "How could anybody be impressed with me?"

"Why not? Because you're quiet? Good gracious! Don't you know that you're the *most* impressive sort? We chatterers spend all our time playing to you quiet people."

"Yes; we're only the audience."

"'Only!'" she echoed. "Why, we live for you, and we can't live without you."

"I wish you couldn't," said Russell. "That would be a new experience for both of us, wouldn't it?"

"It might be a rather bleak one for me," she answered, lightly. "I'm afraid I'll miss these summer evenings with you when they're over. I'll miss them enough, thanks!"

"Do they have to be over some time?" he asked.

"Oh, everything's over *some* time, isn't it?"

Russell laughed at her. "Don't let's look so far ahead as that," he said. "We don't need to be already thinking of the cemetery, do we?"

"I didn't," she said, shaking her head. "Our summer evenings will be over before then, Mr. Russell."

"Why?" he asked.

"Good heavens!" she said. "*There's* laconic eloquence: almost a proposal in a single word! Never mind, I shan't hold you to it. But to answer you:

well, I'm always looking ahead, and somehow I usually see about how things are coming out."

"Yes," he said. "I suppose most of us do; at least it seems as if we did, because we so seldom feel surprised by the way they do come out. But maybe that's only because life isn't like a play in a theatre, and most things come about so gradually we get used to them."

"No, I'm sure I can see quite a long way ahead," she insisted, gravely. "And it doesn't seem to me as if our summer evenings could last very long. Something'll interfere—somebody will, I mean—they'll *say* something——"

"What if they do?"

She moved her shoulders in a little apprehensive shiver. "It'll change you," she said. "I'm just sure something spiteful's going to happen to me. You'll feel differently about—things."

"Now, isn't that an idea!" he exclaimed.

"It will," she insisted. "I know something spiteful's going to happen!"

"You seem possessed by a notion not a bit flattering to me," he remarked.

"Oh, but isn't it? That's just what it is! Why isn't it?"

"Because it implies that I'm made of such soft material the slightest breeze will mess me all up. I'm not so like that as I evidently appear; and if it's true that we're afraid other people will do the things we'd be most likely to do ourselves, it seems to me that I ought to be the one to be afraid. I ought to be afraid that somebody may say something about me to you that will make you believe I'm a professional forger."

"No. We both know they won't," she said. "We both know you're the sort of person everybody in the world says nice things about." She lifted her hand to silence him as he laughed at this. "Oh, of course you are! I think perhaps you're a little flirtatious—most quiet men have that one sly way with 'em—oh, yes, they do! But you happen to be the kind of man everybody loves to praise. And if you weren't, *I* shouldn't hear anything terrible about you. I told you I was unpopular: I don't see anybody at all any more. The only man except you who's been to see me in a month is that fearful little fat Frank Dowling, and I sent word to *him* I wasn't home. Nobody'd tell me of your wickedness, you see."

"Then let me break some news to you," Russell

said. "Nobody would tell me of yours, either. Nobody's even mentioned you to me."

She burlesqued a cry of anguish. "That *is* obscurity! I suppose I'm too apt to forget that they say the population's about half a million nowadays. There *are* other people to talk about, you feel, then?"

"None that I want to," he said. "But I should think the size of the place might relieve your mind of what seems to insist on burdening it. Besides, I'd rather you thought me a better man than you do."

"What kind of a man do I think you are?"

"The kind affected by what's said about people instead of by what they do themselves."

"Aren't you?"

"No, I'm not," he said. "If you want our summer evenings to be over you'll have to drive me away yourself."

"Nobody else could?"

"No."

She was silent, leaning forward, with her elbows on her knees and her clasped hands against her lips. Then, not moving, she said softly:

'Well—I won't!"

She was silent again, and he said nothing, but

looked at her, seeming to be content with looking. Her attitude was one only a graceful person should assume, but she was graceful; and, in the wan light, which made a prettily shaped mist of her, she had beauty. Perhaps it was beauty of the hour, and of the love scene almost made into form by what they had both just said, but she had it; and though beauty of the hour passes, he who sees it will long remember it and the hour when it came.

"What are you thinking of?" he asked.

She leaned back in her chair and did not answer at once. Then she said:

"I don't know; I doubt if I was thinking of anything. It seems to me I wasn't. I think I was just being sort of sadly happy just then."

"Were you? Was it 'sadly,' too?"

"Don't you know?" she said. "It seems to me that only little children can be just happily happy. I think when we get older our happiest moments are like the one I had just then: it's as if we heard strains of minor music running through them—oh, so sweet, but oh, so sad!"

"But what makes it sad for *you?*"

"I don't know," she said, in a lighter tone. "Perhaps it's a kind of useless foreboding I seem to have pretty often. It may be that—or it may be poor papa."

"You *are* a funny, delightful girl, though!" Russell laughed. "When your father's so well again that he goes out walking in the evenings!"

"He does too much walking," Alice said. "Too much altogether, over at his new plant. But there isn't any stopping him." She laughed and shook her head. "When a man gets an ambition to be a multi-millionaire his family don't appear to have much weight with him. He'll walk all he wants to, in spite of them."

"I suppose so," Russell said, absently; then he leaned forward. "I wish I could understand better why you were 'sadly' happy."

Meanwhile, as Alice shed what further light she could on this point, the man ambitious to be a "multi-millionaire" was indeed walking too much for his own good. He had gone to bed, hoping to sleep well and rise early for a long day's work, but he could not rest, and now, in his nightgown and slippers, he was pacing the floor of his room.

"I wish I *did* know," he thought, over and over. "I *do* wish I knew how he feels about it."

CHAPTER XVIII

THAT was a thought almost continuously in his mind, even when he was hardest at work; and, as the days went on and he could not free himself, he became querulous about it. "I guess I'm the biggest dang fool alive," he told his wife as they sat together one evening. "I got plenty else to bother me, without worrying my head off about what *he* thinks. I can't help what he thinks; it's too late for that. So why should I keep pestering myself about it?"

"It'll wear off, Virgil," Mrs. Adams said, reassuringly. She was gentle and sympathetic with him, and for the first time in many years he would come to sit with her and talk, when he had finished his day's work. He had told her, evading her eye, "Oh, I don't blame you. You didn't get after me to do this on your own account; you couldn't help it."

"Yes; but it don't wear off," he complained. "This afternoon I was showing the men how I wanted my vats to go, and I caught my fool self standing there saying to my fool self, 'It's funny I don't hear how he feels about it from *some*body.' I was saying it aloud, almost—and it *is* funny I don't hear anything!"

"Well, you see what it means, don't you, Virgil? It only means he hasn't said anything to anybody about it. Don't you think you're getting kind of morbid over it?"

"Maybe, maybe," he muttered.

"Why, yes," she said, briskly. "You don't realize what a little bit of a thing all this is to him. It's been a long, long while since the last time you even mentioned glue to him, and he's probably forgotten everything about it."

"You're off your base; it isn't like him to forget things," Adams returned, peevishly. "He may seem to forget 'em, but he don't."

"But he's not thinking about this, or you'd have heard from him before now."

Her husband shook his head. "Ah, that's just it!" he said. "Why *haven't* I heard from him?"

"It's all your morbidness, Virgil. Look at Walter: if Mr. Lamb held this up against you, would he still let Walter stay there? Wouldn't he have discharged Walter if he felt angry with you?"

"That dang boy!" Adams said. "If he *wanted* to come with me now, I wouldn't hardly let him. What do you suppose makes him so bull-headed?"

"But hasn't he a right to choose for himself?" she asked. "I suppose he feels he ought to stick to what he thinks is sure pay. As soon as he sees that you're going to succeed with the glue-works he'll want to be with you quick enough."

"Well, he better get a little sense in his head," Adams returned, crossly. "He wanted me to pay him a three-hundred-dollar bonus in advance, when anybody with a grain of common sense knows I need every penny I can lay my hands on!"

"Never mind," she said. "He'll come around later and be glad of the chance."

"He'll have to beg for it then! *I* won't ask him again."

"Oh, Walter will come out all right; you needn't worry. And don't you see that Mr. Lamb's not discharging him means there's no hard feeling against you, Virgil?"

"I can't make it out at all," he said, frowning. "The only thing I can *think* it means is that J. A. Lamb is so fair-minded—and of course he *is* one of the fair-mindedest men alive—I suppose that's the reason he hasn't fired Walter. He may know," Adams concluded, morosely—"he may know that's just another thing to make me feel all the meaner: keeping my boy there on a salary after I've done him an injury."

"Now, now!" she said, trying to comfort him. "You couldn't do anybody an injury to save your life, and everybody knows it."

"Well, anybody ought to know I wouldn't *want* to do an injury, but this world isn't built so't we can do just what we want." He paused, reflecting. "Of course there may be one explanation of why Walter's still there: J. A. maybe hasn't noticed that he *is* there. There's so many I expect he hardly knows him by sight."

"Well, just do quit thinking about it," she urged him. "It only bothers you without doing any good. Don't you know that?"

"Don't I, though!" he laughed, feebly. "I know it better'n anybody! How funny that is: when you know thinking about a thing only pesters you without helping anything at all, and yet you keep right on pestering yourself with it!"

"But *why?*" she said. "What's the use when you know you haven't done anything wrong, Virgil?

You said yourself you were going to improve the process so much it would be different from the old one, and you'd *really* have a right to it."

Adams had persuaded himself of this when he yielded; he had found it necessary to persuade himself of it—though there was a part of him, of course, that remained unpersuaded; and this discomfiting part of him was what made his present trouble. "Yes, I know," he said. "That's true, but I can't quite seem to get away from the fact that the principle of the process is a good deal the same—well, it's more'n that; it's just *about* the same as the one he hired Campbell and me to work out for him. Truth is, nobody could tell the difference, and I don't know as there *is* any difference except in these improvements I'm making. Of course, the improvements do give me pretty near a perfect right to it, as a person might say; and that's one of the things I thought of putting in my letter to him; but I was afraid he'd just think I was trying to make up excuses, so I left it out. I kind of worried all the time I was writing that letter, because if he thought I *was* just making up excuses, why, it might set him just so much more against me."

Ever since Mrs. Adams had found that she was to

have her way, the depths of her eyes had been troubled by a continuous uneasiness; and, although she knew it was there, and sometimes veiled it by keeping the revealing eyes averted from her husband and children, she could not always cover it under that assumption of absent-mindedness. The uneasy look became vivid, and her voice was slightly tremulous now, as she said, "But what if he *should* be against you—although I don't believe he is, of course—you told me he couldn't *do* anything to you, Virgil."

"No," he said, slowly. "I can't see how he could do anything. It was just a secret, not a patent; the thing ain't patentable. I've tried to think what he could do—supposing he was to want to—but I can't figure out anything at all that would be any harm to me. There isn't any way in the world it could be made a question of law. Only thing he could do'd be to *tell* people his side of it, and set 'em against me. I been kind of waiting for that to happen, all along."

She looked somewhat relieved. "So did I expect it," she said. "I was dreading it most on Alice's account: it might have—well, young men are so easily influenced and all. But so far as the business is concerned, what if Mr. Lamb did talk? That wouldn't amount to much. It wouldn't affect the business; not to hurt. And, besides, he isn't even doing that."

"No; anyhow not yet, it seems." And Adams sighed again, wistfully. "But I *would* give a good deal to know what he thinks!"

Before his surrender he had always supposed that if he did such an unthinkable thing as to seize upon the glue process for himself, what he would feel must be an overpowering shame. But shame is the rarest thing in the world: what he felt was this unremittent curiosity about his old employer's thoughts. It was an obsession, yet he did not want to hear what Lamb "thought" from Lamb himself, for Adams had a second obsession, and this was his dread of meeting the old man face to face. Such an encounter could happen only by chance and unexpectedly; since Adams would have avoided any deliberate meeting, so long as his legs had strength to carry him, even if Lamb came to the house to see him. But people do meet unexpectedly; and when Adams had to be down-town he kept away from the "wholesale district." One day he did see Lamb, as the latter went by in his car, impassive, going home to lunch; and Adams, in the crowd at a corner, knew that the old man had not seen him. Nevertheless, in a street car, on the way back to his sheds, an hour later, he was still subject to little shivering seizures of horror.

He worked unceasingly, seeming to keep at it even in his sleep, for he always woke in the midst of a planning and estimating that must have been going on in his mind before consciousness of himself returned. Moreover, the work, thus urged, went rapidly, in spite of the high wages he had to pay his labourers for their short hours. "It eats money," he complained, and, in fact, by the time his vats and boilers were in place it had eaten almost all he could supply; but in addition to his equipment he now owned a stock of "raw material," raw indeed; and when operations should be a little further along he was confident his banker would be willing to "carry" him.

Six weeks from the day he had obtained his lease he began his glue-making. The terrible smells came out of the sheds and went writhing like snakes all through that quarter of the town. A smiling man, strolling and breathing the air with satisfaction, would turn a corner and smile no more, but hurry. However, coloured people had almost all the dwellings of this old section to themselves; and although even they were troubled, there was recompense for them. Being philosophic about what appeared to them as in the order of nature, they sought neither escape nor redress, and soon learned to bear what the wind brought them. They even made use of it to enrich those figures of speech with which the native impulses of coloured people decorate their communications: they flavoured metaphor, simile, and invective with it; and thus may be said to have enjoyed it. But the man who produced it took a hot bath as soon as he reached his home the evening of that first day when his manufacturing began. Then he put on fresh clothes; but after dinner he seemed to be haunted, and asked his wife if she "noticed anything."

She laughed and inquired what he meant.

"Seems to me as if that glue-works smell hadn't quit hanging to me," he explained. "Don't you notice it?"

"No! What an idea!"

He laughed, too, but uneasily; and told her he was sure "the dang glue smell" was somehow sticking to him. Later, he went outdoors and walked up and down the small yard in the dusk; but now and then he stood still, with his head lifted, and sniffed the air suspiciously. "Can *you* smell it?" he called to Alice, who sat upon the veranda, prettily dressed and waiting in a reverie.

"Smell what, papa?"

"That dang glue-works."

She did the same thing her mother had done: laughed, and said, "No! How foolish! Why, papa, it's over two miles from here!"

"You don't get it at all?" he insisted.

"The idea! The air is lovely to-night, papa."

The air did not seem lovely to him, for he was positive that he detected the taint. He wondered how far it carried, and if J. A. Lamb would smell it, too, out on his own lawn a mile to the north; and if he did, would he guess what it was? Then Adams laughed at himself for such nonsense; but could not rid his nostrils of their disgust. To him the whole town seemed to smell of his glue-works.

Nevertheless, the glue was making, and his sheds were busy. "Guess we're stirrin' up this ole neighbourhood with more than the smell," his foreman remarked one morning.

"How's that?" Adams inquired.

"That great big, enormous ole dead butterine factory across the street from our lot," the man said. "Nothin' like settin' an example to bring real estate to life. That place is full o' carpenters startin' in to make a regular buildin' of it again. Guess you ought to have the credit of it, because you was the first man in ten years to see any possibilities in this neighbourhood."

Adams was pleased, and, going out to see for himself, heard a great hammering and sawing from within the building; while carpenters were just emerging gingerly upon the dangerous roof. He walked out over the dried mud of his deep lot, crossed the street, and spoke genially to a workman who was removing the broken glass of a window on the ground floor.

"Here! What's all this howdy-do over here?"

"Goin' to fix her all up, I guess," the workman said. "Big job it is, too."

"Sh' think it would be."

"Yes, sir; a pretty big job—a pretty big job. Got men at it on all four floors and on the roof. They're doin' it *right*."

"Who's doing it?"

"Lord! I d' know. Some o' these here big manufacturing corporations, I guess."

"What's it going to be?"

"They tell *me*," the workman answered—"they tell *me* she's goin' to be a butterine factory again.

Anyways, I hope she won't be anything to smell like that glue-works you got over there—not while *I'm* workin' around her, anyways!"

"That smell's all right," Adams said. "You soon get used to it."

"You do?" The man appeared incredulous. "Listen! I was over in France: it's a good thing them Dutchmen never thought of it; we'd of had to quit!"

Adams laughed, and went back to his sheds. "I guess my foreman was right," he told his wife, that evening, with a little satisfaction. "As soon as one man shows enterprise enough to found an industry in a broken-down neighbourhood, somebody else is sure to follow. I kind of like the look of it: it'll help make our place seem sort of more busy and prosperous when it comes to getting a loan from the bank—and I got to get one mighty soon, too. I did think some that if things go as well as there's every reason to think they *ought* to, I might want to spread out and maybe get hold of that old factory myself; but I hardly expected to be able to handle a proposition of that size before two or three years from now, and anyhow there's room enough on the lot I got, if we need more buildings some day. Things are going about as fine as I could ask: I hired some girls to-day to do the bottling—coloured girls along about sixteen to twenty years old. Afterwhile, I expect to get a machine to put the stuff in the little bottles, when we begin to get good returns; but half a dozen of these coloured girls can do it all right now, by hand. We're getting to have really quite a little plant over there: yes, sir, quite a regular little plant!"

He chuckled, and at this cheerful sound, of a kind his wife had almost forgotten he was capable of producing, she ventured to put her hand upon his arm. They had gone outdoors, after dinner, taking two chairs with them, and were sitting through the late twilight together, keeping well away from the "front porch," which was not yet occupied, however. Alice was in her room changing her dress.

"Well, honey," Mrs. Adams said, taking confidence not only to put her hand upon his arm, but to revive this disused endearment;—"it's grand to have you so optimistic. Maybe some time you'll admit I was right, after all. Everything's going so well, it seems a pity you didn't take this—this step—long ago. Don't you think maybe so, Virgil?"

"Well—if I was ever going to, I don't know but I might as well of. I got to admit the proposition begins to look pretty good: I know the stuff'll sell, and I can't see a thing in the world to stop it. It does look good, and if—if——" He paused.

"If what?" she said, suddenly anxious.

He laughed plaintively, as if confessing a superstition. "It's funny—well, it's mighty funny about that smell. I've got so used to it at the plant I never seem to notice it at all over there. It's only when I get away. Honestly, can't you notice——?"

"Virgil!" She lifted her hand to strike his arm chidingly. "Do quit harping on that nonsense!"

"Oh, of course it don't amount to anything," he said. "A person can stand a good deal of just smell. It don't *worry* me any."

"I should think not—especially as there isn't any."

"Well," he said, "I feel pretty fair over the whole thing—a lot better'n I ever expected to, anyhow. I don't know as there's any reason I shouldn't tell you so."

She was deeply pleased with this acknowledgment, and her voice had tenderness in it as she responded: "There, honey! Didn't I always say you'd be glad if you did it?"

Embarrassed, he coughed loudly, then filled his pipe and lit it. "Well," he said, slowly, "it's a puzzle. Yes, sir, it's a puzzle."

"What is?"

"Pretty much everything, I guess."

As he spoke, a song came to them from a lighted window over their heads. Then the window darkened abruptly, but the song continued as Alice went down through the house to wait on the little veranda. "*Mi chiamo Mimi,*" she sang, and in her voice throbbed something almost startling in its sweetness. Her father and mother listened, not speaking until the song stopped with the click of the wire screen at the front door as Alice came out.

"My!" said her father. "How sweet she does sing! I don't know as I ever heard her voice sound nicer than it did just then."

"There's something that makes it sound that way," his wife told him.

"I suppose so," he said, sighing. "I suppose so. You think——"

"She's just terribly in love with him!"

"I expect that's the way it ought to be," he said, then drew upon his pipe for reflection, and became murmurous with the symptoms of melancholy laughter. "It don't make things less of a puzzle, though, does it?"

"In what way, Virgil?"

"Why, here," he said—"here we go through all this muck and moil to help fix things nicer for her at home, and what's it all amount to? Seems like she's just gone ahead the way she'd 'a' gone anyhow; and *now,* I suppose, getting ready to up and leave us! Ain't that a puzzle to you? It is to me."

"Oh, but things haven't gone that far yet."

"Why, you just said——"

She gave a little cry of protest. "Oh, they aren't *engaged* yet. Of course they *will* be; he's just as much interested in her as she is in him, but——"

"Well, what's the trouble then?"

"You *are* a simple old fellow!" his wife exclaimed, and then rose from her chair. "That reminds me," she said.

"What of?" he asked. "What's my being simple remind you of?"

"Nothing!" she laughed. "It wasn't you that reminded me. It was just something that's been on my mind. I don't believe he's actually ever been inside our house!"

"Hasn't he?"

"I actually don't believe he ever has," she said. "Of course we must——" She paused, debating.

"We must what?"

"I guess I better talk to Alice about it right now," she said. "He don't usually come for about half an hour yet; I guess I've got time." And with that she walked away, leaving him to his puzzles.

CHAPTER XIX

ALICE was softly crooning to herself as her mother turned the corner of the house and approached through the dusk.

"Isn't it the most *beautiful* evening!" the daughter said. "*Why* can't summer last all year? Did you ever know a lovelier twilight than this, mama?"

Mrs. Adams laughed, and answered, "Not since I was your age, I expect."

Alice was wistful at once. "Don't they stay beautiful after my age?"

"Well, it's not the same thing."

"Isn't it? Not—ever?"

"You may have a different kind from mine," the mother said, a little sadly. "I think you will, Alice. You deserve——"

"No, I don't. I don't deserve anything, and I know it. But I'm getting a great deal these days—more than I ever dreamed *could* come to me. I'm—I'm pretty happy, mama!"

"Dearie!" Her mother would have kissed her, but Alice drew away.

"Oh, I don't mean——" She laughed nervously. "I wasn't meaning to tell you I'm *engaged*, mama. We're not. I mean—oh! things seem pretty beautiful in spite of all I've done to spoil 'em."

"You?" Mrs. Adams cried, incredulously. "What have you done to spoil anything?"

"Little things," Alice said. "A thousand little silly—oh, what's the use? He's so honestly what he is —just simple and good and intelligent—I feel a tricky mess beside him! I don't see why he likes me; and sometimes I'm afraid he wouldn't if he knew me."

"He'd just worship you," said the fond mother. "And the more he knew you, the more he'd worship you."

Alice shook her head. "He's not the worshiping kind. Not like that at all. He's more——"

But Mrs. Adams was not interested in this analysis, and she interrupted briskly, "Of course it's time your father and I showed some interest in him. I was just saying I actually don't believe he's ever been inside the house."

"No," Alice said, musingly; "that's true: I don't believe he has. Except when we've walked in the evening we've always sat out here, even those two times when it was drizzly. It's so much nicer."

"We'll have to do *something* or other, of course," her mother said.

"What like?"

"I was thinking——" Mrs. Adams paused. "Well, of course we could hardly put off asking him to dinner, or something, much longer."

Alice was not enthusiastic; so far from it, indeed, that there was a melancholy alarm in her voice. "Oh, mama, must we? Do you think so?"

"Yes, I do. I really do."

"Couldn't we—well, couldn't we wait?"

"It looks queer," Mrs. Adams said. "It isn't the thing at all for a young man to come as much as he does, and never more than just barely meet your father and mother. No. We ought to do something."

"But a dinner!" Alice objected. "In the first place, there isn't anybody I want to ask. There isn't anybody I *would* ask."

"I didn't mean trying to give a big dinner," her mother explained. "I just mean having him to dinner. That mulatto woman, Malena Burns, goes out by the day, and she could bring a waitress. We can get some flowers for the table and some to put in the living-room. We might just as well go ahead and do it to-morrow as any other time; because your father's in a fine mood, and I saw Malena this afternoon and told her I might want her soon. She said she didn't have any engagements this week, and I can let her know to-night. Suppose when he comes you ask him for to-morrow, Alice. Everything'll be very nice, I'm sure. Don't worry about it."

"Well—but——" Alice was uncertain.

"But don't you see, it looks so queer, not to do *something?*" her mother urged. "It looks so kind of poverty-stricken. We really oughtn't to wait any longer."

Alice assented, though not with a good heart. "Very well, I'll ask him, if you think we've got to."

"That matter's settled then," Mrs. Adams said. "I'll go telephone Malena, and then I'll tell your father about it."

But when she went back to her husband, she found him in an excited state of mind, and Walter standing before him in the darkness. Adams was almost shouting, so great was his vehemence.

"Hush, hush!" his wife implored, as she came near them. "They'll hear you out on the front porch!"

"I don't care who hears me," Adams said, harshly, though he tempered his loudness. "Do you want to know what this boy's asking me for? I thought he'd maybe come to tell me he'd got a little sense in his head at last, and a little decency about what's due his family! I thought he was going to ask me to take him into my plant. No, ma'am; *that's* not what he wants!"

"No, it isn't," Walter said. In the darkness his face could not be seen; he stood motionless, in what seemed an apathetic attitude; and he spoke quietly, "No," he repeated. "That isn't what I want."

"You stay down at that place," Adams went on, hotly, "instead of trying to be a little use to your family; and the only reason you're *allowed* to stay there is because Mr. Lamb's never happened to notice you *are* still there! You just wait——"

"You're off," Walter said, in the same quiet way. "He knows I'm there. He spoke to me yesterday: he asked me how I was getting along with my work."

"He did?" Adams said, seeming not to believe him.

"Yes. He did."

"What else did he say, Walter?" Mrs. Adams asked quickly.

"Nothin'. Just walked on."

"I don't believe he knew who you were," Adams declared.

"Think not? He called me 'Walter Adams.'"

At this Adams was silent; and Walter, after waiting a moment, said:

"Well, are you going to do anything about me? About what I told you I got to have?"

"What is it, Walter?" his mother asked, since Adams did not speak.

Walter cleared his throat, and replied in a tone as quiet as that he had used before, though with a slight huskiness, "I got to have three hundred and fifty dollars. You better get him to give it to me if you can."

Adams found his voice. "Yes," he said, bitterly. "That's all he asks! He won't do anything I ask *him* to, and in return he asks me for three hundred and fifty dollars! That's all!"

"What in the world!" Mrs. Adams exclaimed. "What *for*, Walter?"

"I got to have it," Walter said.

"But what *for?*"

His quiet huskiness did not alter. "I got to have it."

"But can't you tell us——"

"I got to have it."

"That's all you can get out of him," Adams said. "He seems to think it'll bring him in three hundred and fifty dollars!"

A faint tremulousness became evident in the husky voice. "Haven't you got it?"

"*No*, I haven't got it!" his father answered. "And I've got to go to a bank for more than my pay-roll next week. Do you think I'm a mint?"

"I don't understand what you mean, Walter," Mrs. Adams interposed, perplexed and distressed. "If your father had the money, of course he'd need every cent of it, especially just now, and, anyhow, you could scarcely expect him to give it to you, unless you told us what you want with it. But he hasn't got it."

"All right," Walter said; and after standing a moment more, in silence, he added, impersonally, "I don't see as you ever did anything much for me, anyhow—either of you."

Then, as if this were his valedictory, he turned his back upon them, walked away quickly, and was at once lost to their sight in the darkness.

"There's a fine boy to've had the trouble of raising!" Adams grumbled. "Just crazy, that's all."

"What in the world do you suppose he wants all that money for?" his wife said, wonderingly. "I can't imagine what he could *do* with it. I wonder——" She paused. "I wonder if he——"

"If he what?" Adams prompted her irritably.

"If he *could* have bad—associates."

"God knows!" said Adams. "*I* don't! It just looks to me like he had something in him I don't understand. You can't keep your eye on a boy all the time in a city this size, not a boy Walter's age. You got a girl pretty much in the house, but a boy'll follow his nature. *I* don't know what to do with him!"

Mrs. Adams brightened a little. "He'll come *out* all right," she said. "I'm sure he will. I'm sure he'd never be anything really bad: and he'll come around all right about the glue-works, too; you'll see. Of course every young man wants money—it doesn't prove he's doing anything wrong just because he asks you for it."

"No. All it proves to me is that he hasn't got good sense—asking me for three hundred and fifty dollars, when he knows as well as you do the position I'm in! If I wanted to, I couldn't hardly let him have three hundred and fifty cents, let alone dollars!"

"I'm afraid you'll have to let *me* have that much—and maybe a little more," she ventured, timidly; and she told him of her plans for the morrow. He objected vehemently.

"Oh, but Alice has probably asked him by this time," Mrs. Adams said. "It really must be done, Virgil: you don't want him to think she's ashamed of us, do you?"

"Well, go ahead, but just let me stay away," he begged. "Of course I expect to undergo a kind of talk with him, when he gets ready to say something to us about Alice, but I do hate to have to sit through a fashionable dinner."

"Why, it isn't going to bother you," she said; "just one young man as a guest."

"Yes, I know; but you want to have all this fancy cookin'; and I see well enough you're going to get that old dress suit out of the cedar chest in the attic, and try to make me put it on me."

"I do think you better, Virgil."

"I hope the moths have got in it," he said. "Last time I wore it was to the banquet, and it was pretty old then. Of course I didn't mind wearing it to the banquet so much, because that was what you might call quite an occasion." He spoke with some reminiscent complacency; "the banquet," an affair now five years past, having provided the one time in his life when he had been so distinguished among his fellow-citizens as to receive an invitation to be present, with some seven hundred others, at the annual eating and speech-making of the city's Chamber of Commerce. "Anyhow, as you say, I think it would look foolish of me to wear a dress suit for just one young man," he went on protesting, feebly. "What's the use of all so much howdy-do, anyway? You don't expect him to believe we put on all that style every night, do you? Is that what you're after?"

"Well, we want him to think we live nicely," she admitted.

"So that's it!" he said, querulously. "You want him to think that's our regular gait, do you? Well, he'll know better about me, no matter how you fix me up, because he saw me in my regular suit the evening she introduced me to him, and he could tell anyway I'm not one of these moving-picture sporting-men that's always got a dress suit on. Besides, you and Alice certainly have some idea he'll come *again*, haven't you? If they get things settled between 'em he'll be around the house and to meals most any time, won't he? You don't hardly expect to put on style all the time, I guess. Well, he'll see then that this kind of thing was all show-off and bluff, won't he? What about it?"

"Oh, well, by *that* time——" She left the sentence unfinished, as if absently. "You could let us have a little money for to-morrow, couldn't you, honey?"

"Oh, I reckon, I reckon," he mumbled. "A girl like Alice is some comfort: she don't come around acting as if she'd commit suicide if she didn't get three hundred and fifty dollars in the next five minutes. I expect I can spare five or six dollars for your show-off if I got to."

However, she finally obtained fifteen before his bedtime; and the next morning "went to market" after breakfast, leaving Alice to make the beds. Walter had not yet come downstairs. "You had better call him," Mrs. Adams said, as she departed with a big basket on her arm. "I expect he's pretty sleepy; he was out so late last night I didn't hear him come in, though I kept awake till after midnight, listening for him. Tell him he'll be late to work if he doesn't hurry; and see that he drinks his coffee, even if he hasn't time for anything else. And when Malena comes, get her started in the kitchen: show her where everything is." She waved her hand, as she set out for a corner where the cars stopped. "Everything'll be lovely. Don't forget about Walter."

Nevertheless, Alice forgot about Walter for a few minutes. She closed the door, went into the "living-room" absently, and stared vaguely at one of the old brown-plush rocking-chairs there. Upon her forehead were the little shadows of an apprehensive reverie, and her thoughts overlapped one another in a fretful jumble. "What will he think? These old chairs—they're hideous. I'll scrub those soot-streaks on the columns: it won't do any good, though. That long crack in the column—nothing can help it. What will he think of papa? I hope mama won't talk too much. When he thinks of Mildred's house, or of Henrietta's, or any of 'em, beside this—— She said she'd buy plenty of roses; that ought to help some. Nothing could be done about these horrible chairs: can't take 'em up in the attic—a room's got to have chairs! Might have rented some. No; if he ever comes again he'd see they weren't here. 'If he ever comes again'—oh, it won't be *that* bad! But it won't be what he expects. I'm responsible for what he expects: he expects just what the airs I've put on have made him expect. What did I want to pose so to him for—as if papa were a wealthy man and all that? What *will* he think? The photograph of the Colosseum's a rather good thing, though. It helps some—as if we'd bought it in Rome perhaps. I hope he'll think so; he believes I've been abroad, of course. The other night he said, 'You remember the feeling you get in the Sainte-Chapelle'—There's another lie of mine, not saying I didn't remember because I'd never been there. What makes me do it? Papa *must* wear his evening clothes. But Walter——"

With that she recalled her mother's admonition, and went upstairs to Walter's door. She tapped upon it with her fingers.

"Time to get up, Walter. The rest of us had breakfast over half an hour ago, and it's nearly eight o'clock. You'll be late. Hurry down and I'll have some coffee and toast ready for you." There came no sound from within the room, so she rapped louder.

"Wake up, Walter!"

She called and rapped again, without getting any response, and then, finding that the door yielded to her, opened it and went in. Walter was not there.

He had been there, however; had slept upon the bed, though not inside the covers; and Alice supposed he must have come home so late that he had been too sleepy to take off his clothes. Near the foot of the bed was a shallow closet where he kept his "other suit" and his evening clothes; and the door stood open, showing a bare wall. Nothing whatever was in the closet, and Alice was rather surprised at this for a moment. "That's queer," she murmured; and then she decided that when he woke he found the clothes he had slept in "so mussy" he had put on his "other suit," and had gone out before breakfast with the mussed clothes to have them pressed, taking his evening things with them. Satisfied with this explanation, and failing to observe that it did not account for the absence of shoes from the closet floor, she nodded absently, "Yes, that must be it"; and, when her mother returned, told her that Walter had probably breakfasted down-town. They did not delay over this; the coloured woman had arrived, and the basket's disclosures were important.

"I stopped at Worlig's on the way back," said Mrs. Adams, flushed with hurry and excitement. "I bought a can of caviar there. I thought we'd have little sandwiches brought into the 'living-room' before dinner, the way you said they did when you went to that dinner at the——"

"But I think that was to go with cocktails, mama, and of course we haven't——"

"No," Mrs. Adams said. "Still, I think it would be nice. We can make them look very dainty, on a tray, and the waitress can bring them in. I thought we'd have the soup already on the table; and we can walk right out as soon as we have the sandwiches, so it won't get cold. Then, after the soup, Malena says she can make sweetbread patés with mushrooms: and for the meat course we'll have larded fillet. Malena's really a fancy cook, you know, and she says she can do anything like that to perfection. We'll have peas with the fillet, and potato balls and Brussels sprouts. Brussels sprouts are fashionable now, they told me at market. Then will come the chicken salad, and after that the ice-cream—she's going to make an angel-food cake to go with it—and then coffee and crackers and a new kind of cheese I got at Worlig's, he says is very fine."

Alice was alarmed. "Don't you think perhaps it's too much, mama?"

"It's better to have too much than too little," her mother said, cheerfully. "We don't want him to think we're the kind that skimp. Lord knows we have to enough, though, most of the time! Get the flowers in water, child. I bought 'em at market because they're so much cheaper there, but they'll keep fresh and nice. You fix 'em any way you want. Hurry! It's got to be a busy day."

She had bought three dozen little roses. Alice took them and began to arrange them in vases, keeping the stems separated as far as possible so that the clumps would look larger. She put half a dozen in each of three vases in the "living-room," placing one vase on the table in the center of the room, and one at each end of the mantelpiece. Then she took the rest of the roses to the dining-room; but she postponed the arrangement of them until the table should be set, just before dinner. She was thoughtful; planning to dry the stems and lay them on the tablecloth like a vine of roses running in a delicate design, if she found that the dozen and a half she had left were enough for that. If they weren't she would arrange them in a vase.

She looked a long time at the little roses in the basin of water, where she had put them; then she sighed, and went away to heavier tasks, while her mother worked in the kitchen with Malena. Alice dusted the "living-room" and the dining-room vigorously, though all the time with a look that grew more and more pensive; and having dusted everything, she wiped the furniture; rubbed it hard. After that, she washed the floors and the woodwork.

Emerging from the kitchen at noon, Mrs. Adams found her daughter on hands and knees, scrubbing the bases of the columns between the hall and the "living-room."

"Now, dearie," she said, "you mustn't tire yourself out, and you'd better come and eat something. Your father said he'd get a bite down-town to-day—he was going down to the bank—and Walter eats down-town all the time lately, so I thought we wouldn't bother to set the table for lunch. Come on and we'll have something in the kitchen."

"No," Alice said, dully, as she went on with he work. "I don't want anything."

Her mother came closer to her. "Why, what's the matter?" she asked, briskly. "You seem kind of pale, to me; and you don't look—you don't look *happy*."

"Well——" Alice began, uncertainly, but said no more.

"See here!" Mrs. Adams exclaimed. "This is all just for you! You ought to be *enjoying* it. Why, it's the first time we've—we've entertained in I don't know how long! I guess it's almost since we had that little party when you were eighteen. What's the matter with you?"

"Nothing. I don't know."

"But, dearie, aren't you looking *forward* to this evening?"

The girl looked up, showing a pallid and solemn face. "Oh, yes, of course," she said, and tried to smile. "Of course we had to do it—I do think it'll be nice. Of course I'm looking forward to it."

CHAPTER XX

SHE was indeed "looking forward" to that evening, but in a cloud of apprehension; and, although she could never have guessed it, this was the simultaneous condition of another person —none other than the guest for whose pleasure so much cooking and scrubbing seemed to be necessary. Moreover, Mr. Arthur Russell's premonitions were no product of mere coincidence; neither had any magical sympathy produced them. His state of mind was rather the result of rougher undercurrents which had all the time been running beneath the surface of a romantic friendship.

Never shrewder than when she analyzed the gentlemen, Alice did not libel him when she said he was one of those quiet men who are a bit flirtatious, by which she meant that he was a bit "susceptible," the same thing—and he had proved himself susceptible to Alice upon his first sight of her. "There!" he said to himself. "Who's that?" And in the crowd of girls at his cousin's dance, all strangers to him, she was the one he wanted to know.

Since then, his summer evenings with her had been as secluded as if, for three hours after the falling of dusk, they two had drawn apart from the world to some dear bower of their own. The little veranda was that glamorous nook, with a faint golden light falling through the glass of the closed door upon Alice, and darkness elsewhere, except for the one round globe of the street lamp at the corner. The people who passed along the sidewalk, now and then, were only shadows with voices, moving vaguely under the maple trees that loomed in obscure contours against the stars. So, as the two sat together, the back of the world was the wall and closed door behind them; and Russell, when he was away from Alice, always thought of her as sitting there before the closed door. A glamour was about her thus, and a spell upon him; but he had a formless anxiety never put into words: all the pictures of her in his mind stopped at the closed door.

He had another anxiety; and, for the greater part, this was of her own creating. She had too often asked him (no matter how gaily) what he heard about her; too often begged him not to hear anything.

Then, hoping to forestall whatever he might hear, she had been at too great pains to account for it, to discredit and mock it; and, though he laughed at her for this, telling her truthfully he did not even hear her mentioned, the everlasting irony that deals with all such human forefendings prevailed.

Lately, he had half confessed to her what a nervousness she had produced. "You make me dread the day when I'll hear somebody speaking of you. You're getting me so upset about it that if I ever hear anybody so much as say the name 'Alice Adams,' I'll run!" The confession was but half of one because he laughed; and she took it for an assurance of loyalty in the form of burlesque. She misunderstood: he laughed, but his nervousness was genuine.

After any stroke of events, whether a happy one or a catastrophe, we see that the materials for it were a long time gathering, and the only marvel is that the stroke was not prophesied. What bore the air of fatal coincidence may remain fatal indeed, to this later view; but, with the haphazard aspect dispelled, there is left for scrutiny the same ancient hint from the Infinite to the effect that since events have never yet failed to be law-abiding, perhaps it were well for us to deduce that they will continue to be so until further notice.

. . . On the day that was to open the closed door in the background of his pictures of Alice, Russell lunched with his relatives. There were but the four people, Russell and Mildred and her mother and father, in the great, cool dining-room. Arched French windows, shaded by awnings, admitted a mellow light and looked out upon a green lawn ending in a long conservatory, which revealed through its glass panes a carnival of plants in luxuriant blossom. From his seat at the table, Russell glanced out at this pretty display, and informed his cousins that he was surprised. "You have such a glorious spread of flowers all over the house," he said, "I didn't suppose you'd have any left out yonder. In fact, I didn't know there were so many splendid flowers in the world."

Mrs. Palmer, large, calm, fair, like her daughter, responded with a mild reproach: "That's because you haven't been cousinly enough to get used to them, Arthur. You've almost taught us to forget what you look like."

In defense Russell waved a hand toward her husband. "You see, he's begun to keep me so hard at work——"

But Mr. Palmer declined the responsibility. "Up to four or five in the afternoon, perhaps," he said. "After that, the young gentleman is as much a stranger to me as he is to my family. I've been wondering who she could be."

"When a man's preoccupied there must be a lady then?" Russell inquired.

"That seems to be the view of your sex," Mrs. Palmer suggested. "It was my husband who said it, not Mildred or I."

Mildred smiled faintly. "Papa may be singular in his ideas; they may come entirely from his own experience, and have nothing to do with Arthur."

"Thank you, Mildred," her cousin said, bowing to her gratefully. "You seem to understand my character—and your father's quite as well!"

However, Mildred remained grave in the face of this customary pleasantry, not because the old jest, worn round, like what preceded it, rolled in an old groove, but because of some preoccupation of her own. Her faint smile had disappeared, and, as her cousin's glance met hers, she looked down; yet not before he had seen in her eyes the flicker of something like a question—a question both poignant and dismayed. He may have understood it; for his own smile vanished at once in favour of a reciprocal solemnity.

"You see, Arthur," Mrs. Palmer said, "Mildred is always a good cousin. She and I stand by you, even if you do stay away from us for weeks and weeks." Then, observing that he appeared to be so occupied with a bunch of iced grapes upon his plate that he had not heard her, she began to talk to her husband, asking him what was "going on down-town."

Arthur continued to eat his grapes, but he ventured to look again at Mildred after a few moments. She, also, appeared to be occupied with a bunch of grapes though she ate none, and only pulled them from their stems. She sat straight, her features as composed and pure as those of a new marble saint in a cathedral niche; yet her downcast eyes seemed to conceal many thoughts; and her cousin, against his will, was more aware of what these thoughts might be than of the leisurely conversation between her father and mother. All at once, however, he heard something that startled him, and he listened—and here was the effect of all Alice's forefendings; he listened from the first with a sinking heart.

Mr. Palmer, mildly amused by what he was telling his wife, had just spoken the words, "this Virgil Adams." What he had said was, "this Virgil Adams —that's the man's name. Queer case."

"Who told you?" Mrs. Palmer inquired, not much interested.

"Alfred Lamb," her husband answered. "He was laughing about his father, at the club. You see the old gentleman takes a great pride in his judgment of men, and always boasted to his sons that he'd never in his life made a mistake in trusting the wrong man. Now Alfred and James Albert, Junior, think they have a great joke on him; and they've twitted him so much about it he'll scarcely speak to them. From the first, Alfred says, the old chap's only repartee was, 'You wait and you'll see!' And they've asked him so often to show them what they're going to see that he won't say anything at all!"

"He's a funny old fellow," Mrs. Palmer observed. "But he's so shrewd I can't imagine his being deceived for such a long time. Twenty years, you said?"

"Yes, longer than that, I understand. It appears when this man—this Adams—was a young clerk, the old gentleman trusted him with one of his business secrets, a glue process that Mr. Lamb had spent some money to get hold of. The old chap thought this Adams was going to have quite a future with the Lamb concern, and of course never dreamed he was dishonest. Alfred says this Adams hasn't been of any real use for years, and they should have let him go as dead wood, but the old gentleman wouldn't hear of it, and insisted on his being kept on the pay-roll; so they just decided to look on it as a sort of pension. Well, one morning last March the man had an attack of some sort down there, and Mr. Lamb got his own car out and went home with him, himself, and worried about him and went to see him no end, all the time he was ill."

"He would," Mrs. Palmer said, approvingly. "He's a kind-hearted creature, that old man."

Her husband laughed. "Alfred says he thinks his kind-heartedness is about cured! It seems that as soon as the man got well again he deliberately walked off with the old gentleman's glue secret. Just calmly stole it! Alfred says he believes that if he had a stroke in the office now, himself, his father wouldn't lift a finger to help him!"

Mrs. Palmer repeated the name to herself thoughtfully. "'Adams'—'Virgil Adams.' You said his name was Virgil Adams?"

"Yes."

She looked at her daughter. "Why, you know who that is, Mildred," she said, casually. "It's that Alice Adams's father, isn't it? Wasn't his name Virgil Adams?"

"I think it is," Mildred said.

Mrs. Palmer turned toward her husband. "You've seen this Alice Adams here. Mr. Lamb's pet swindler must be her father."

Mr. Palmer passed a smooth hand over his neat gray hair, which was not disturbed by this effort to stimulate recollection. "Oh, yes," he said. "Of course—certainly. Quite a good-looking girl—one of Mildred's friends. How queer!"

Mildred looked up, as if in a little alarm, but did not speak. Her mother set matters straight. "Fathers *are* amusing," she said smilingly to Russell, who was looking at her, though how fixedly she did not notice; for she turned from him at once to enlighten her husband. "Every girl who meets Mildred, and tries to push the acquaintance by coming here until the poor child has to hide, isn't a *friend* of hers, my dear!"

Mildred's eyes were downcast again, and a faint colour rose in her cheeks. "Oh, I shouldn't put it quite that way about Alice Adams," she said, in a low voice. "I saw something of her for a time. She's not unattractive—in a way."

Mrs. Palmer settled the whole case of Alice carelessly. "A pushing sort of girl," she said. "A very pushing little person."

"I——" Mildred began; and, after hesitating, concluded, "I rather dropped her."

"Fortunate you've done so," her father remarked, cheerfully. "Especially since various members of the Lamb connection are here frequently. They mightn't think you'd show great tact in having her about the place." He laughed, and turned to his cousin. "All this isn't very interesting to poor Arthur. How terrible people are with a newcomer in a town; they talk as if he knew all about everybody!"

"But we don't know anything about these queer people, ourselves," said Mrs. Palmer. "We know something about the girl, of course—she used to be a bit *too* conspicuous, in fact! However, as you say, we might find a subject more interesting for Arthur." She smiled whimsically upon the young man. "Tell the truth," she said. "Don't you fairly detest going into business with that tyrant yonder?"

"What? Yes—I beg your pardon!" he stammered.

"You were right," Mrs. Palmer said to her husband. "You've bored him so, talking about thievish clerks, he can't even answer an honest question."

But Russell was beginning to recover his outward composure. "Try me again," he said. "I'm afraid I was thinking of something else."

This was the best he found to say. There was a part of him that wanted to protest and deny, but he had not heat enough, in the chill that had come upon him. Here was the first "mention" of Alice, and with it the reason why it was the first: Mr. Palmer had difficulty in recalling her, and she happened to be spoken of, only because her father's betrayal of a benefactor's trust had been so peculiarly atrocious that, in the view of the benefactor's family, it contained enough of the element of humour to warrant a mild laugh at a club. There was the deadliness of the story: its lack of malice, even of resentment. Deadlier still were Mrs. Palmer's phrases: "a pushing sort of girl," "a very pushing little person," and "used to be a bit *too* conspicuous, in fact." But she spoke placidly and by chance; being as obviously without unkindly motive as Mr. Palmer was when he related the cause of Alfred

Lamb's amusement. Her opinion of the obscure young lady momentarily her topic had been expressed, moreover, to her husband, and at her own table. She sat there, large, kind, serene—a protest might astonish but could not change her; and Russell, crumpling in his strained fingers the lace-edged little web of a napkin on his knee, found heart enough to grow red, but not enough to challenge her.

She noticed his colour, and attributed it to the embarrassment of a scrupulously gallant gentleman caught in a lapse of attention to a lady. "Don't be disturbed," she said, benevolently. "People aren't expected to listen all the time to their relatives. A high colour's very becoming to you, Arthur; but it really isn't necessary between cousins. You can always be informal enough with us to listen only when you care to."

His complexion continued to be ruddier than usual, however, throughout the meal, and was still somewhat tinted when Mrs. Palmer rose. "The man's bringing you cigarettes here," she said, nodding to the two gentlemen. "We'll give you a chance to do the sordid kind of talking we know you really like. Afterwhile, Mildred will show you what's in bloom in the hothouse, if you wish, Arthur."

Mildred followed her, and, when they were alone in another of the spacious rooms, went to a window and looked out, while her mother seated herself near the center of the room in a gilt armchair, mellowed with old Aubusson tapestry. Mrs. Palmer looked thoughtfully at her daughter's back, but did not speak to her until coffee had been brought for them.

"Thanks," Mildred said, not turning, "I don't care for any coffee, I believe."

"No?" Mrs. Palmer said, gently. "I'm afraid our good-looking cousin won't think you're very talkative, Mildred. You spoke only about twice at lunch. I shouldn't care for him to get the idea you're piqued because he's come here so little lately, should you?"

"No, I shouldn't," Mildred answered in a low voice, and with that she turned quickly, and came to sit near her mother. "But it's what I am afraid of! Mama, did you notice how red he got?"

"You mean when he was caught not listening to a question of mine? Yes; it's very becoming to him."

"Mama, I don't think that was the reason. I don't think it was because he wasn't listening, I mean."

"No?"

"I think his colour and his not listening came from the same reason," Mildred said, and although she had come to sit near her mother, she did not look at her. "I think it happened because you and papa——" She stopped.

"Yes?" Mrs. Palmer said, good-naturedly, to prompt her. "Your father and I did something embarrassing?"

"Mama, it was because of those things that came out about Alice Adams."

"How could that bother Arthur? Does he know her?"

"Don't you remember?" the daughter asked. "The day after my dance I mentioned how odd I thought it was in him—I was a little disappointed in him. I'd been seeing that he met everybody, of course, but she was the only girl *he* asked to meet; and he did it as soon as he noticed her. I hadn't meant to have him meet her—in fact, I was rather sorry I'd felt I had to ask her, because she—oh, well, she's the sort that 'tries for the new man,' if she has half a chance; and sometimes they seem quite fascinated—for a time, that is. I thought Arthur was above all that; or at the very least I gave him credit for being too sophisticated."

"I see," Mrs. Palmer said, thoughtfully. "I remember now that you spoke of it. You said it seemed a little peculiar, but of course it really wasn't: a 'new man' has nothing to go by, except his own first impressions. You can't blame poor Arthur—she's quite a piquant looking little person. You think he's seen something of her since then?"

Mildred nodded slowly. "I never dreamed such a thing till yesterday, and even then I rather doubted it—till he got so red, just now! I was surprised when he asked to meet her, but he just danced with her once and didn't mention her afterward; I forgot all about it—in fact, I virtually forgot all about *her*. I'd seen quite a little of her——"

"Yes," said Mrs. Palmer. "She did keep coming here!"

"But I'd just about decided that it really wouldn't do," Mildred went on. "She isn't—well, I didn't admire her."

"No," her mother assented, and evidently followed a direct connection of thought in a speech apparently irrelevant. "I understand the young Malone wants to marry Henrietta. I hope she won't; he seems rather a gross type of person."

"Oh, he's just one," Mildred said. "I don't know

that he and Alice Adams were ever engaged—she never told me so. She may not have been engaged to any of them; she was just enough among the other girls to get talked about—and one of the reasons I felt a little inclined to be nice to her was that they seemed to be rather edging her out of the circle. It wasn't long before I saw they were right, though. I happened to mention I was going to give a dance and she pretended to take it as a matter of course that I meant to invite her brother—at least, I thought she pretended; she may have really believed it. At any rate, I had to send him a card; but I didn't intend to be let in for that sort of thing again, of course. She's what you said, 'pushing'; though I'm awfully sorry you said it."

"Why shouldn't I have said it, my dear?"

"Of course I didn't say 'shouldn't.'" Mildred explained, gravely. "I meant only that I'm sorry it happened."

"Yes; but why?"

"Mama"— Mildred turned to her, leaning forward and speaking in a lowered voice—"Mama, at first the change was so little it seemed as if Arthur hardly knew it himself. He'd been lovely to me always, and he was still lovely to me—but—oh, well, you've understood—after my dance it was more as if it was just his nature and his training to be lovely to me, as he would be to everyone—a kind of politeness. He'd never said he *cared* for me, but after that I could see he didn't. It was clear—after that. I didn't know what had happened; I couldn't think of anything I'd done. Mama—it was Alice Adams."

Mrs. Palmer set her little coffee-cup upon the table beside her, calmly following her own motion with her eyes, and not seeming to realize with what serious entreaty her daughter's gaze was fixed upon her. Mildred repeated the last sentence of her revelation, and introduced a stress of insistence.

"Mama, it *was* Alice Adams!"

But Mrs. Palmer declined to be greatly impressed, so far as her appearance went, at least; and to emphasize her refusal, she smiled indulgently. "What makes you think so?"

"Henrietta told me yesterday."

At this Mrs. Palmer permitted herself to laugh softly aloud. "Good heavens! Is Henrietta a soothsayer? Or is she Arthur's particular *confidante?*"

"No. Ella Dowling told her."

Mrs. Palmer's laughter continued. "Now we have it!" she exclaimed. "It's a game of gossip:

Arthur tells Ella, Ella tells Henrietta, and Henrietta tells——"

"Don't laugh, please, mama," Mildred begged. "Of course Arthur didn't tell anybody. It's roundabout enough, but it's true. I know it! I hadn't quite believed it, but I knew it was true when he got so red. He looked—oh, for a second or so he looked —stricken! He thought I didn't notice it. Mama, he's been to see her almost every evening lately. They take long walks together. That's why he hasn't been here."

Of Mrs. Palmer's laughter there was left only her indulgent smile, which she had not allowed to vanish. "Well, what of it?" she said.

"Mama!"

"Yes," said Mrs. Palmer. "What of it?"

"But don't you see?" Mildred's well-tutored voice, though modulated and repressed even in her present emotion, nevertheless had a tendency to quaver. "It's true. Frank Dowling was going to see her one evening and he saw Arthur sitting on the stoop with her, and didn't go in. And Ella used to go to school with a girl who lives across the street from here. She told Ella——"

"Oh, I understand," Mrs. Palmer interrupted.

"Suppose he does go there. My dear, I said, 'What of it?'"

"I don't see what you mean, mama. I'm so afraid he might think we knew about it, and that you and papa said those things about her and her father on that account—as if we abused them because he goes there instead of coming here."

"Nonsense!" Mrs. Palmer rose, went to a window, and, turning there, stood with her back to it, facing her daughter and looking at her cheerfully. "Nonsense, my dear! It was perfectly clear that she was mentioned by accident, and so was her father. What an extraordinary man! If Arthur makes friends with people like that, he certainly knows better than to expect to hear favourable opinions of them. Besides, it's only a little passing thing with him."

"Mama! When he goes there almost every——"

"Yes," Mrs. Palmer said, dryly. "It seems to me I've heard somewhere that other young men have gone there 'almost every!' She doesn't last, apparently. Arthur's gallant, and he's impressionable—but he's fastidious, and fastidiousness is always the check on impressionableness. A girl belongs to her family, too—and this one does especially, it strikes me! Arthur's very sensible; he sees more than you'd think."

Mildred looked at her hopefully. "Then you don't believe he's likely to imagine we said those things of her in any meaning way?"

At this, Mrs. Palmer laughed again. "There's one thing you seem not to have noticed, Mildred."

"What's that?"

"It seems to have escaped your attention that he never said a word."

"Mightn't that mean——?" Mildred began, but she stopped.

"No, it mightn't," her mother replied, comprehending easily. "On the contrary, it might mean that instead of his feeling it too deeply to speak, he was getting a little illumination."

Mildred rose and came to her. "*Why* do you suppose he never told us he went there? Do you think he's—do you think he's pleased with her, and yet ashamed of it? *Why* do you suppose he's never spoken of it?"

"Ah, that," Mrs. Palmer said;—"that might possibly be her own doing. If it is, she's well paid by what your father and I said, because we wouldn't have said it if we'd known that Arthur——" She checked herself quickly. Looking over her daughter's shoulder, she saw the two gentlemen coming from the corridor toward the wide doorway of the room; and she greeted them cheerfully. "If you've finished with each other for a while," she added, "Arthur may find it a relief to put his thoughts on something prettier than a trust company—and more fragrant."

Arthur came to Mildred.

"Your mother said at lunch that perhaps you'd——"

"I didn't say 'perhaps,' Arthur," Mrs. Palmer interrupted, to correct him. "I said she would. If you care to see and smell those lovely things out yonder, she'll show them to you. Run along, children!"

Half an hour later, glancing from a window, she saw them come from the hothouses and slowly cross the lawn. Arthur had a fine rose in his buttonhole and looked profoundly thoughtful.

CHAPTER XXI

THAT morning and noon had been warm, though the stirrings of a feeble breeze made weather not flagrantly intemperate; but at about three o'clock in the afternoon there came out of the southwest a heat like an affliction sent upon an accursed people, and the air was soon dead of it. Dripping negro ditch-diggers whooped with satires praising hell and hot weather, as the tossing shovels flickered up to the street level, where sluggish male pedestrians carried coats upon hot arms, and fanned themselves with straw hats, or, remaining covered, wore soaked handkerchiefs between scalp and straw. Clerks drooped in silent, big department stores; stenographers in offices kept as close to electric fans as the intervening bulk of their employers would let them; guests in hotels left the lobbies and went to lie unclad upon their beds; while in hospitals the patients murmured querulously against the heat, and perhaps against some noisy motorist who strove to feel the air by splitting it, not troubled by any foreboding that he, too, that hour next week, might need quiet near a hospital. The "hot spell" was a true spell, one upon men's spirits; for it was so hot that, in suburban outskirts, golfers crept slowly back over the low undulations of their club lands, abandoning their matches and returning to shelter.

Even on such a day, sizzling work had to be done, as in winter. There were glowing furnaces to be stoked, liquid metals to be poured; but such tasks found seasoned men standing to them; and in all the city probably no brave soul challenged the heat more gamely than Mrs. Adams did, when, in a corner of her small and fiery kitchen, where all day long her hired African immune cocked fiercely, she pressed her husband's evening clothes with a hot iron. No doubt she risked her life, but she risked it cheerfully in so good and necessary a service for him. She would have given her life for him at any time, and both his and her own for her children.

Unconscious of her own heroism, she was surprised to find herself rather faint when she finished her ironing. However, she took heart to believe that the clothes looked better, in spite of one or two scorched places; and she carried them upstairs to her husband's room before increasing blindness forced her to grope for the nearest chair. Then, trying to rise and walk, without having sufficiently recovered, she had to sit down again; but after a little while she was able to get upon her feet; and, keeping her hand against the wall, moved successfully to the door of her own room. Here she wavered; might have gone down, had she not been stimulated by the thought of how much depended upon her;—she made a final great effort, and floundered across the room to her bureau, where she kept some simple restoratives. They served her need, or her faith in them did; and she returned to her work.

She went down the stairs, keeping a still tremulous hand upon the rail; but she smiled brightly when Alice looked up from below, where the woodwork was again being tormented with superfluous attentions.

"Alice, *don't!*" her mother said, commiseratingly. "You did all that this morning and it looks lovely. What's the use of wearing yourself out on it? You ought to be lying down, so's to look fresh for tonight."

"Hadn't you better lie down yourself?" the daughter returned. "Are you ill, mama?"

"Certainly not. What in the world makes you think so?"

"You look pretty pale," Alice said, and sighed heavily. "It makes me ashamed, having you work so hard—for me."

"How foolish! I think it's fun, getting ready to entertain a little again, like this. I only wish it hadn't turned so hot: I'm afraid your poor father'll suffer—his things are pretty heavy, I noticed. Well, it'll do him good to bear something for style's sake this once, anyhow!" She laughed, and coming to Alice, bent down and kissed her. "Dearie," she said, tenderly, "wouldn't you please slip upstairs now and take just a little teeny nap to please your mother?"

But Alice responded only by moving her head slowly, in token of refusal.

"Do!" Mrs. Adams urged. "You don't want to look worn out, do you?"

"I'll *look* all right," Alice said, huskily. "Do you like the way I've arranged the furniture now? I've tried all the different ways it'll go."

"It's lovely," her mother said, admiringly. "I thought the last way you had it was pretty, too. But you know best; I never knew anybody with so much taste. If you'd only just quit now, and take a little rest——"

"There'd hardly be time, even if I wanted to; it's after five—but I couldn't; really, I couldn't. How do you think we can manage about Walter—to see that he wears his evening things, I mean?"

Mrs. Adams pondered. "I'm afraid he'll make a lot of objections, on account of the weather and everything. I wish we'd had a chance to tell him last night or this morning. I'd have telephoned to him this afternoon except—well, I scarcely like to call him up at that place, since your father——"

"No, of course not, mama."

"If Walter gets home late," Mrs. Adams went on, "I'll just slip out and speak to him, in case Mr. Russell's here before he comes. I'll just tell him he's *got* to hurry and get his things on."

"Maybe he won't come home to dinner," Alice suggested, rather hopefully. "Sometimes he doesn't."

"No; I think he'll be here. When he doesn't come he usually telephones by this time to say not to wait for him; he's very thoughtful about that. Well, it really is getting late: I must go and tell her she ought to be preparing her fillet. Dearie, *do* rest a little."

"You'd much better do that yourself," Alice called after her, but Mrs. Adams shook her head cheerily, not pausing on her way to the fiery kitchen.

Alice continued her useless labours for a time; then carried her bucket to the head of the cellar stairway, where she left it upon the top step; and, closing the door, returned to the "living-room." Again she changed the positions of the old plush rocking-chairs, moving them into the corners where she thought they might be least noticeable; and while thus engaged she was startled by a loud ringing of the door-bell. For a moment her face was panic-stricken, and she stood staring; then she realized that Russell would not arrive for another hour, at the earliest, and recovering her equipoise, went to the door.

Waiting there, in a languid attitude, was a young coloured woman, with a small bundle under her arm and something malleable in her mouth. "Listen," she said. "You folks expectin' a coloured lady?"

"No," said Alice. "Especially not at the front door."

"Listen," the coloured woman said again. "Listen. Say, listen. Ain't they another coloured lady awready here by the day? Listen. Ain't Miz Malena Burns here by the day this evenin'? Say, listen. This the number house she give *me*."

"Are you the waitress?" Alice asked, dismally.

"Yes'm, if Malena here."

"Malena is here," Alice said, and hesitated; but she decided not to send the waitress to the back door; it might be a risk. She let her in. "What's your name?"

"Me? I'm name' Gertrude. Miss Gertrude Collamus."

"Did you bring a cap and apron?"

Gertrude took the little bundle from under her arm. "Yes'm. I'm all fix'."

"I've already set the table," Alice said. "I'll show you what we want done."

She led the way to the dining-room, and, after offering some instruction there, received by Gertrude with languor and a slowly moving jaw, she took her into the kitchen, where the cap and apron were put on. The effect was not fortunate; Gertrude's eyes were noticeably bloodshot, an affliction made more apparent by the white cap; and Alice drew her mother apart, whispering anxiously,

"Do you suppose it's too late to get someone else?"

"I'm afraid it is," Mrs. Adams said. "Malena says it was hard enough to get *her!* You have to pay them so much that they only work when they feel like it."

"Mama, could you ask her to wear her cap straighter? Every time she moves her head she gets it on one side, and her skirt's too long behind and too short in front—and oh, I've *never* seen such *feet!*" Alice laughed desolately. "And she *must* quit that terrible chewing!"

"Never mind; I'll get to work with her. I'll straighten her out all I can, dearie; don't worry." Mrs. Adams patted her daughter's shoulder encouragingly. "Now *you* can't do another thing, and if you don't run and begin dressing you won't be ready. It'll only take me a minute to dress, myself, and I'll be down long before you will. Run, darling! I'll look after everything."

Alice nodded vaguely, went up to her room, and, after only a moment with her mirror, brought from her closet the dress of white organdie she had worn the night when she met Russell for the first time. She laid it carefully upon her bed, and began to make ready to put it on. Her mother came in, half an hour later, to "fasten" her.

"*I'm* all dressed," Mrs. Adams said, briskly. "Of course it doesn't matter. He won't know what the rest of us even look like: How could he? I know I'm an old *sight*, but all I want is to look respectable. Do I?"

"You look like the best woman in the world; that's all!" Alice said, with a little gulp.

Her mother laughed and gave her a final scrutiny. "You might use just a tiny bit more colour, dearie—I'm afraid the excitement's made you a little pale. And you *must* brighten up! There's sort of a look in your eyes as if you'd got in a trance and couldn't get out. You've had it all day. I must run: your father wants me to help him with his studs. Walter hasn't come yet, but I'll look after him; don't worry, And you better *hurry*, dearie, if you're going to take any time fixing the flowers on the table."

She departed, while Alice sat at the mirror again, to follow her advice concerning a "tiny bit more colour." Before she had finished, her father knocked at the door, and, when she responded, came in. He was dressed in the clothes his wife had pressed; but he had lost substantially in weight since they were made for him; no one would have thought that they had been pressed. They hung from him voluminously, seeming to be the clothes of a larger man.

"Your mother's gone downstairs," he said, in a voice of distress. "One of the buttonholes in my shirt is too large and I can't keep the dang thing fastened. *I* don't know what to do about it! I only got one other white shirt, and it's kind of ruined: I tried it before I did this one. Do you s'pose you could do anything?"

"I'll see," she said.

"My collar's got a frayed edge," he complained, as she examined his troublesome shirt. "It's a good deal like wearing a saw; but I expect it'll wilt down flat pretty soon, and not bother me long. I'm liable to wilt down flat, myself, I expect; I don't know as I remember any such hot night in the last ten or twelve years." He lifted his head and sniffed the flaccid air, which was laden with a heavy odour. "My, but that smell is pretty strong!" he said.

"Stand still, please, papa," Alice begged him. "I can't see what's the matter if you move around. How absurd you are about your old glue smell, papa! There isn't a vestige of it, of course."

"I didn't mean glue," he informed her. "I mean cabbage. Is that fashionable now, to have cabbage when there's company for dinner?"

"That isn't cabbage, papa. It's Brussels sprouts."

"Oh, is it? I don't mind it much, because it keeps that glue smell off me, but it's fairly strong. I expect you don't notice it so much because you been in the house with it all along, and got used to it while it was growing."

"It is pretty dreadful," Alice said. "Are all the windows open downstairs?"

"I'll go down and see, if you'll just fix that hole up for me."

"I'm afraid I can't," she said. "Not unless you take your shirt off and bring it to me. I'll have to sew the hole smaller."

"Oh, well, I'll go ask your mother to——"

"No," said Alice. "She's got everything on her hands. Run and take it off. Hurry, papa; I've got to arrange the flowers on the table before he comes."

He went away, and came back presently, half undressed, bringing the shirt. "There's *one* comfort," he remarked, pensively, as she worked. "I've got that collar off—for a while, anyway. I wish I could go to table like this; I could stand it a good deal better. Do you seem to be making any headway with the dang thing?"

"I think probably I can——"

Downstairs the door-bell rang, and Alice's arms jerked with the shock.

"Golly!" her father said. "Did you stick your finger with that fool needle?"

She gave him a blank stare. "He's come!"

She was not mistaken, for, upon the little veranda, Russell stood facing the closed door at last. However, it remained closed for a considerable time after he rang. Inside the house the warning summons of the bell was immediately followed by another sound, audible to Alice and her father as a crash preceding a series of muffled falls. Then came a distant voice, bitter in complaint.

"Oh, Lord!" said Adams. "What's that?"

Alice went to the top of the front stairs, and her mother appeared in the hall below.

"Mama!"

Mrs. Adams looked up. "It's all right," she said, in a loud whisper. "Gertrude fell down the cellar stairs. Somebody left a bucket there, and——" She was interrupted by a gasp from Alice, and hastened to reassure her. "Don't worry, dearie. She may limp a little, but——"

Adams leaned over the banisters. "Did she break anything?" he asked.

"Hush!" his wife whispered. "No. She seems upset and angry about it, more than anything else; but she's rubbing herself, and she'll be all right in time to bring in the little sandwiches. Alice! Those flowers!"

"I know, mama. But——"

"Hurry!" Mrs. Adams warned her. "Both of you hurry! I *must* let him in!"

She turned to the door, smiling cordially, even before she opened it. "Do come right in, Mr. Russell," she said, loudly, lifting her voice for additional warning to those above. "I'm *so* glad to receive you informally, this way, in our own little home. There's a hat-rack here under the stairway," she continued, as Russell, murmuring some response, came into the hall. "I'm afraid you'll think it's almost *too* informal, my coming to the door, but unfortunately our housemaid's just had a little accident—oh, nothing to mention! I just thought we better not keep you waiting any longer. Will you step into our living-room, please?"

She led the way between the two small columns, and seated herself in one of the plush rocking-chairs, selecting it because Alice had once pointed out that the chairs, themselves, were less noticeable when they had people sitting in them. "Do sit down, Mr. Russell; it's so very warm it's really quite a trial just to stand up!"

"Thank you," he said, as he took a seat. "Yes. It is quite warm." And this seemed to be the extent of his responsiveness for the moment. He was grave, rather pale; and Mrs. Adams's impression of him, as she formed it then, was of "a distinguished-looking young man, really elegant in the best sense of the word, but timid and formal when he first meets you." She beamed upon him, and used with everything she said a continuous accompaniment of laughter, meaningless except that it was meant to convey cordiality. "Of course we *do* have a great deal of warm weather," she informed him. "I'm glad it's so much cooler in the house than it is outdoors."

"Yes," he said. "It is pleasanter indoors." And, stopping with this single untruth, he permitted himself the briefest glance about the room; then his eyes returned to his smiling hostess.

"Most people make a great fuss about hot weather," she said. "The only person I know who doesn't mind the heat the way other people do is Alice. She always seems as cool as if we had a breeze blowing, no matter how hot it is. But then she's so amiable she never minds anything. It's just her character. She's always been that way since she was a little child; always the same to everybody, high and low. I think character's the most important thing in the world, after all, don't you, Mr. Russell?"

"Yes," he said, solemnly; and touched his bedewed white forehead with a handkerchief.

"Indeed it is," she agreed with herself, never failing to continue her murmur of laughter. "That's what I've always told Alice; but she never sees anything good in herself, and she just laughs at me when I praise her. She sees good in everybody *else* in the world, no matter how unworthy they are, or how they behave toward *her;* but she always underestimates herself. From the time she was a little child she was always that way. When some other little girl would behave selfishly or meanly toward her, do you think she'd come and tell me? Never a word to anybody! The little thing was too proud! She was the same way about school. The teachers had to tell me when she took a prize; she'd bring it home and keep it in her room without a word about it to her father and mother. Now, Walter was just the other way. Walter would——" But here Mrs. Adams checked herself, though she increased the volume of her laughter. "How silly of me!" she exclaimed. "I expect you know how mothers *are*, though, Mr. Russell. Give us a chance and we'll talk about our children forever! Alice would feel terribly if she knew how I've been going on about her to you."

In this Mrs. Adams was right, though she did not herself suspect it, and upon an almost inaudible word or two from him she went on with her topic. "Of course my excuse is that few mothers have a daughter like Alice. I suppose we all think the same way about our children, but *some* of us must be right when we feel we've got the best. Don't you think so?"

"Yes. Yes, indeed."

"I'm sure *I* am!" she laughed. "I'll let the others speak for themselves." She paused reflectively. "No; I think a mother knows when she's got a treasure in her family. If she *hasn't* got one, she'll pretend she has, maybe; but if she has, she knows it. I certainly know *I* have. She's always been what people call 'the joy of the household'—always cheerful, no matter what went wrong, and always ready to smooth things over with some bright, witty saying. You must be sure not to *tell* we've had this little chat about her—she'd just be furious with me—but she *is* such a dear child! You won't tell her, will you?"

"No," he said, and again applied the handkerchief to his forehead for an instant. "No, I'll——" He paused, and finished lamely: "I'll—not tell her."

Thus reassured, Mrs. Adams set before him some details of her daughter's popularity at sixteen, dwelling upon Alice's impartiality among her young suitors: "She never could *bear* to hurt their feelings, and always treated all of them just alike. About half a dozen of them were just *bound* to marry her! Naturally, her father and I considered any such idea ridiculous; she was too young, of course."

Thus the mother went on with her biographical sketches, while the pale young man sat facing her under the hard overhead light of a white globe, set to the ceiling; and listened without interrupting. She was glad to have the chance to tell him a few things about Alice he might not have guessed for himself, and, indeed, she had planned to find such an opportunity, if she could; but this was getting to be altogether too much of one, she felt. As time passed, she was like an actor who must improvise to keep the audience from perceiving that his fellow-players have missed their cues; but her anxiety was not betrayed to the still listener; she had a valiant soul.

Alice, meanwhile, had arranged her little roses on the table in as many ways, probably, as there were blossoms; and she was still at it when her father arrived in the dining-room by way of the back stairs and the kitchen.

"It's pulled out again," he said. "But I guess there's no help for it now; it's too late, and anyway it lets some air into me when it bulges. I can sit so's it won't be noticed much, I expect. Isn't it time you quit bothering about the looks of the table? Your mother's been talking to him about half an hour now, and I had the idea he came on your account, not hers. Hadn't you better go and——"

"Just a minute." Alice said, piteously. "Do *you* think it looks all right?"

"The flowers? Fine! Hadn't you better leave 'em the way they are, though?"

"Just a minute," she begged again. "Just *one* minute, papa!" And she exchanged a rose in front of Russell's plate for one that seemed to her a little larger.

"You better come on," Adams said, moving to the door.

"Just *one* more second, papa." She shook her head, lamenting. "Oh, I wish we'd rented some silver!"

"Why?"

"Because so much of the plating has rubbed off a lot of it. *Just* a second, papa." And as she spoke she hastily went round the table, gathering the knives and forks and spoons that she thought had their plating best preserved, and exchanging them for more damaged pieces at Russell's place. "There!" she sighed, finally. "Now I'll come." But at the door she paused to look back dubiously, over her shoulder.

"What's the matter now?"

"The roses. I believe after all I shouldn't have tried that vine effect; I ought to have kept them in water, in the vase. It's so hot, they already begin to look a little wilted, out on the dry tablecloth like that. I believe I'll——"

"Why, look here, Alice!" he remonstrated, as she seemed disposed to turn back. "Everything'll burn up on the stove if you keep on——"

"Oh, well," she said, "the vase was terribly ugly; I can't do any better. We'll go in." But with her hand on the door-knob she paused. "No, papa.

We mustn't go in by this door. It might look as if——"

"As if what?"

"Never mind," she said. "Let's go the other way."

"I don't see what difference it makes," he grumbled, but nevertheless followed her through the kitchen, and up the back stairs then through the upper hallway. At the top of the front stairs she paused for a moment, drawing a deep breath; and then, before her father's puzzled eyes, a transformation came upon her. Her shoulders, like her eyelids, had been drooping, but now she threw her head back: the shoulders straightened, and the lashes lifted over sparkling eyes; vivacity came to her whole body in a flash; and she tripped down the steps, with her pretty hands rising in time to the lilting little tune she had begun to hum.

At the foot of the stairs, one of those pretty hands extended itself at full arm's length toward Russell, and continued to be extended until it reached his own hand as he came to meet her. "How terrible of me!" she exclaimed. "To be so late coming down! And papa, too—I think you know each other."

Her father was advancing toward the young man, expecting to shake hands with him, but Alice stood between them, and Russell, a little flushed, bowed to him gravely over her shoulder, without looking at him; whereupon Adams, slightly disconcerted, put his hands in his pockets and turned to his wife.

"I guess dinner's more'n ready," he said. "We better go sit down."

But she shook her head at him fiercely, "Wait!" she whispered.

"What for? For Walter?"

"No; he can't be coming," she returned, hurriedly, and again warned him by a shake of her head. "Be quiet!"

"Oh, well——" he muttered.

"Sit down!"

He was thoroughly mystified, but obeyed her gesture and went to the rocking-chair in the opposite corner, where he sat down, and, with an expression of meek inquiry, awaited events.

Meanwhile, Alice prattled on: "It's really not a fault of mine, being tardy. The shameful truth is I was trying to hurry papa. He's incorrigible: he stays so late at his terrible old factory—terrible *new* factory, I should say. I hope you don't *hate* us for making you dine with us in such fearful weather! I'm nearly dying of the heat, myself, so you have a fellow-sufferer, if that pleases you. Why is it we always bear things better if we think other people have to stand them, too?" And she added, with an excited laugh: "*Silly* of us, don't you think?"

Gertrude had just made her entrance from the dining-room, bearing a tray. She came slowly, with an air of resentment; and her skirt still needed adjusting, while her lower jaw moved at intervals, though not now upon any substance, but reminiscently, of habit. She halted before Adams, facing him.

He looked plaintive. "What you want o' me?" he asked.

For response, she extended the tray toward him with a gesture of indifference; but he still appeared to be puzzled. "What in the world——?" he began, then caught his wife's eye, and had presence of mind enough to take a damp and plastic sandwich from the tray. "Well, I'll *try* one," he said, but a moment later, as he fulfilled this promise, an expression of intense dislike came upon his features, and he would have returned the sandwich to Gertrude. However, as she had crossed the room to Mrs. Adams he checked the gesture, and sat helplessly, with the sandwich in his hand. He made another effort to get rid of it as the waitress passed him, on her way back to the dining-room, but she appeared not to observe him, and he continued to be troubled by it.

Alice was a loyal daughter. "These are delicious, mama," she said; and turning to Russell, "You missed it; you should have taken one. Too bad we couldn't have offered you what ought to go with it, of course, but——"

She was interrupted by the second entrance of Gertrude, who announced, "Dinner serve'," and retired from view.

"Well, well!" Adams said, rising from his chair, with relief. "That's good! Let's go see if we can eat it." And as the little group moved toward the open door of the dining-room he disposed of his sandwich by dropping it in the empty fireplace.

Alice, glancing back over her shoulder, was the only one who saw him, and she shuddered in spite of herself. Then, seeing that he looked at her entreatingly, as if he wanted to explain that he was doing the best he could, she smiled upon him sunnily, and began to chatter to Russell again.

CHAPTER XXII

ALICE kept her sprightly chatter going when they sat down, though the temperature of the room and the sight of hot soup might have discouraged a less determined gayety. Moreover, there were details as unpropitious as the heat: the expiring roses expressed not beauty but pathos, and what faint odour they exhaled was no rival to the lusty emanations of the Brussels sprouts; at the head of the table, Adams, sitting low in his chair, appeared to be unable to flatten the uprising wave of his starched bosom; and Gertrude's manner and expression were of a recognizable hostility during the long period of vain waiting for the cups of soup to be emptied. Only Mrs. Adams made any progress in this direction; the others merely feinting, now and then lifting their spoons as if they intended to do something with them.

Alice's talk was little more than cheerful sound, but, to fill a desolate interval, served its purpose; and her mother supported her with ever-faithful cooings of applausive laughter. "What a funny thing weather is!" the girl ran on. "Yesterday it was cool—angels had charge of it—and to-day they had an engagement somewhere else, so the devil saw his chance and started to move the equator to the North Pole; but by the time he got half-way, he thought of something else he wanted to do, and went off; and left the equator here, right on top of *us!* I wish he'd come back and get it!"

"Why, Alice dear!" her mother cried, fondly. "What an imagination! Not a very pious one, I'm afraid Mr. Russell might think, though!" Here she gave Gertrude a hidden signal to remove the soup; but, as there was no response, she had to make the signal more conspicuous. Gertrude was leaning against the wall, her chin moving like a slow pendulum, her streaked eyes fixed mutinously upon Russell. Mrs. Adams nodded several times, increasing the emphasis of her gesture, while Alice talked briskly; but the brooding waitress continued to brood. A faint snap of the fingers failed to disturb her; nor was a covert hissing whisper of avail, and Mrs. Adams was beginning to show signs of strain when her daughter relieved her.

"Imagine our trying to eat anything so hot as

soup on a night like this!" Alice laughed. "What *could* have been in the cook's mind not to give us something iced and jellied instead? Of course it's because she's equatorial, herself, originally, and only feels at home when Mr. Satan moves it north." She looked round at Gertrude, who stood behind her. "Do take this dreadful soup away!"

Thus directly addressed, Gertrude yielded her attention, though unwillingly, and as if she decided only by a hair's weight not to revolt, instead. However, she finally set herself in slow motion; but overlooked the supposed head of the table, seeming to be unaware of the sweltering little man who sat there. As she disappeared toward the kitchen with but three of the cups upon her tray he turned to look plaintively after her, and ventured an attempt to recall her.

"Here!" he said, in a low voice. "Here, you!"

"What is it, Virgil?" his wife asked.

"What's her name?"

Mrs. Adams gave him a glance of sudden panic, and, seeing that the guest of the evening was not looking at her, but down at the white cloth before him, she frowned hard, and shook her head.

Unfortunately Alice was not observing her mother, and asked, innocently: "What's whose name, papa?"

"Why, this young darky woman," he explained. "She left mine."

"Never mind," Alice laughed. "There's hope for you, papa. She hasn't gone forever!"

"I don't know about that," he said, not content with this impulsive assurance. "She *looked* like she is." And his remark, considered as a prediction, had begun to seem warranted before Gertrude's return with china preliminary to the next stage of the banquet.

Alice proved herself equal to the long gap, and rattled on through it with a spirit richly justifying her mother's praise of her as "always ready to smooth things over"; for here was more than long delay to be smoothed over. She smoothed over her father and mother for Russell; and she smoothed over him for them, though he did not know it, and remained unaware of what he owed her. With all this, throughout her prattlings, the girl's bright eyes kept seeking his with an eager gayety, which but little veiled both interrogation and entreaty—as if she asked: "Is it too much for you? Can't you bear it? Won't you *please* bear it? I would for you. Won't you give me a sign that it's all right?"

He looked at her but fleetingly, and seemed to

suffer from the heat, in spite of every manly effort not to wipe his brow too often. His colour, after rising when he greeted Alice and her father, had departed, leaving him again moistly pallid; a condition arising from discomfort, no doubt, but, considered as a decoration, almost poetically becoming to him. Not less becoming was the faint, kindly smile, which showed his wish to express amusement and approval; and yet it was a smile rather strained and plaintive, as if he, like Adams, could only do the best he could.

He pleased Adams, who thought him a fine young man, and decidedly the quietest that Alice had ever shown to her family. In her father's opinion this was no small merit; and it was to Russell's credit, too, that he showed embarrassment upon this first intimate presentation; here was an applicant with both reserve and modesty. "So far, he seems to be first rate—a mighty fine young man," Adams thought; and, prompted by no wish to part from Alice but by reminiscences of apparent candidates less pleasing, he added, "At last!"

Alice's liveliness never flagged. Her smoothing over of things was an almost continuous performance, and had to be. Yet, while she chattered through the hot and heavy courses, the questions she asked herself were as continuous as the performance, and as poignant as what her eyes seemed to be asking Russell. Why had she not prevailed over her mother's fear of being "skimpy?" Had she been, indeed, as her mother said she looked, "in a trance?" But above all: What was the matter with *him?* What had happened? For she told herself with painful humour that something even worse than this dinner must be "the matter with him."

The small room, suffocated with the odour of boiled sprouts, grew hotter and hotter as more and more food appeared, slowly borne in, between deathly long waits, by the resentful, loud-breathing Gertrude. And while Alice still sought Russell's glance, and read the look upon his face a dozen different ways, fearing all of them; and while the straggling little flowers died upon the stained cloth, she felt her heart grow as heavy as the food, and wondered that it did not die like the roses.

With the arrival of coffee, the host bestirred himself to make known a hospitable regret, "By George!" he said. "I meant to buy some cigars." He addressed himself apologetically to the guest. "I don't know what I was thinking about, to forget to bring some home with me. I don't use 'em myself—unless somebody hands me one, you might say. I've always been a pipe-smoker, pure and simple, but I ought to remembered for kind of an occasion like this."

"Not at all," Russell said. "I'm not smoking at all lately; but when I do, I'm like you, and smoke a pipe."

Alice started, remembering what she had told him when he overtook her on her way from the tobacconist's; but, after a moment, looking at him, she decided that he must have forgotten it. If he had remembered, she thought, he could not have helped glancing at her. On the contrary, he seemed more at ease, just then, than he had since they sat down, for he was favouring her father with a thoughtful attention as Adams responded to the introduction of a man's topic into the conversation at last. "Well, Mr. Russell, I guess you're right, at that. I don't say but what cigars may be all right for a man that can afford 'em, if he likes 'em better than a pipe, but you take a good old pipe now——"

He continued, and was getting well into the eulogium customarily provoked by this theme, when there came an interruption: the door-bell rang, and he paused inquiringly, rather surprised.

Mrs. Adams spoke to Gertrude in an undertone:

"Just say, 'Not at home.'"

"What?"

"If it's callers, just say we're not at home."

Gertrude spoke out freely: "You mean you astin' me to 'tend you' front do' fer you?"

She seemed both incredulous and affronted, but Mrs. Adams persisted, though somewhat apprehensively. "Yes. Hurry—uh—please. Just say we're not at home—if you please."

Again Gertrude obviously hesitated between compliance and revolt, and again the meeker course fortunately prevailed with her. She gave Mrs. Adams a stare, grimly derisive, then departed. When she came back she said:

"He say he wait."

"But I told you to tell anybody we were not at home," Mrs Adams returned. "Who is it?"

"Say he name Mr. Law."

"We don't know any Mr. Law."

"Yes'm; he know you. Say he anxious to speak Mr. Adams. Say he wait."

"Tell him Mr. Adams is engaged."

"Hold on a minute," Adams intervened. "Law?

No. I don't know any Mr. Law. You sure you got the name right?"

"Say he name Law," Gertrude replied, looking at the ceiling to express her fatigue. "Law. 'S all he tell me; 's all I know."

Adams frowned. "Law," he said. "Wasn't it maybe 'Lohr?'"

"Law," Gertrude repeated. 'S all he tell me; 's all I know."

"What's he look like?"

"He ain't much," she said. "'Bout you' age; got brustly white moustache, nice eye-glasses."

"It's Charley Lohr!" Adams exclaimed. "I'll go see what he wants."

"But, Virgil," his wife remonstrated, "do finish your coffee; he might stay all evening. Maybe he's come to call."

Adams laughed. "He isn't much of a caller, I expect. Don't worry: I'll take him up to my room." And turning toward Russell, "Ah—if you'll just excuse me," he said; and went out to his visitor.

When he had gone, Mrs. Adams finished her coffee, and, having glanced intelligently from her guest to her daughter, she rose. "I think perhaps I ought to go and shake hands with Mr. Lohr, myself," she said, adding in explanation to Russell, as she reached the door, "He's an old friend of my husband's and it's a very long time since he's been here."

Alice nodded and smiled to her brightly, but upon the closing of the door, the smile vanished; all her liveliness disappeared; and with this change of expression her complexion itself appeared to change, so that her rouge became obvious, for she was pale beneath it. However, Russell did not see the alteration, for he did not look at her; and it was but a momentary lapse—the vacation of a tired girl, who for ten seconds lets herself look as she feels. Then she shot her vivacity back into place as by some powerful spring.

"Penny for your thoughts!" she cried, and tossed one of the wilted roses at him, across the table. "I'll bid more than a penny; I'll bid tuppence—no, a poor little dead rose—a rose for your thoughts, Mr. Arthur Russell! What are they?"

He shook his head. "I'm afraid I haven't any."

"No, of course not," she said. "Who could have thoughts in weather like this? Will you *ever* forgive us?"

"What for?"

"Making you eat such a heavy dinner—I mean

look at such a heavy dinner, because you certainly didn't do more than look at it—on such a night! But the crime draws to a close, and you can begin to cheer up!" She laughed gaily, and, rising, moved to the door. "Let's go in the other room; your fearful duty is almost done, and you can run home as soon as you want to. That's what you're dying to do."

"Not at all," he said in a voice so feeble that she laughed aloud.

"Good gracious!" she cried. "I hadn't realized it was *that* bad!"

For this, though he contrived to laugh, he seemed to have no verbal retort whatever; but followed her into the "living-room," where she stopped and turned, facing him.

"Has it really been so frightful?" she asked.

"Why, of course not. Not at all."

"Of course yes, though, you mean!"

"Not at all. It's been most kind of your mother and father and you."

"Do you know," she said, "you've never once looked at me for more than a second at a time the whole evening? And it seemed to me I looked rather nice to-night, too!"

"You always do," he murmured.

"I don't see how you know," she returned; and then stepping closer to him, spoke with gentle solicitude: "Tell me: you're really feeling wretchedly, aren't you? I know you've got a fearful headache, or something. Tell me!"

"Not at all."

"You are ill—I'm sure of it."

"Not at all."

"On your word?"

"I'm really quite all right."

"But if you are——" she began; and then, looking at him with a desperate sweetness, as if this were her last resource to rouse him, "What's the matter, little boy?" she said with lisping tenderness. "Tell auntie!"

It was a mistake, for he seemed to flinch, and to lean backward, however, slightly. She turned away instantly, with a flippant lift and drop of both hands. "Oh, my dear!" she laughed. "I won't eat you!"

And as the discomfited young man watched her, seeming able to lift his eyes, now that her back was turned, she went to the front door and pushed open the screen. "Let's go out on the porch," she said. "Where we belong!"

Then, when he had followed her out, and they were seated, "Isn't this better?" she asked. "Don't you feel more like yourself out here?"

He began a murmur: "Not at——"

But she cut him off sharply: "Please don't say 'Not at all' again!"

"I'm sorry."

"You do seem sorry about something," she said. "What is it? Isn't it time you were telling me what's the matter?"

"Nothing. Indeed nothing's the matter. Of course one *is* rather affected by such weather as this. It may make one a little quieter than usual, of course."

She sighed, and let the tired muscles of her face rest. Under the hard lights, indoors, they had served her until they ached, and it was a luxury to feel that in the darkness no grimacings need call upon them.

"Of course, if you won't tell me——" she said.

"I can only assure you there's nothing to tell."

"I know what an ugly little house it is," she said. "Maybe it was the furniture—or mama's vases that upset you. Or was it mama herself—or papa?"

"Nothing 'upset' me."

At that she uttered a monosyllable of doubting laughter. "I wonder why you say that."

"Because it's so."

"No. It's because you're too kind, or too conscientious, or too embarrassed—anyhow too something—to tell me." She leaned forward, elbows on knees and chin in hands, in the reflective attitude she knew how to make graceful. "I have a feeling that you're not going to tell me," she said, slowly. "Yes—even that you're never going to tell me. I wonder—I wonder——"

"Yes? What do you wonder?"

"I was just thinking—I wonder if they haven't done it, after all."

"I don't understand."

"I wonder," she went on, still slowly, and in a voice of reflection, "I wonder who *has* been talking about me to you, after all? Isn't that it?"

"Not at——" he began, but checked himself and substituted another form of denial. "Nothing is 'it.'"

"Are you sure?"

"Why, yes."

"How curious!" she said.

"Why?"

"Because all evening you've been so utterly different."

"But in this weather——"

"No. That wouldn't make you afraid to look at me all evening!"

"But I did look at you. Often."

"No. Not really a *look*."

"But I'm looking at you now."

"Yes—in the dark!" she said. "No—the weather might make you even quieter than usual, but it wouldn't strike you so nearly dumb. No—and it wouldn't make you seem to be under such a strain—as if you thought only of escape!"

"But I haven't——"

"You shouldn't," she interrupted, gently. "There's nothing you have to escape from, you know. You aren't committed to—to this friendship."

"I'm sorry you think——" he began, but did not complete the fragment.

She took it up. "You're sorry I think you're so different, you mean to say, don't you? Never mind: that's what you did mean to say, but you couldn't finish it because you're not good at deceiving."

"Oh, no," he protested, feebly. "I'm not deceiving. "I'm——"

"Never mind," she said again. "You're sorry I think you're so different—and all in one day—since last night. Yes, your voice *sounds* sorry, too. It sounds sorrier than it would just because of my thinking something you could change my mind about in a minute—so it means you're sorry you *are* different."

"No—I——"

But disregarding the faint denial, "Never mind," she said. "Do you remember one night when you told me that nothing anybody else could do would ever keep you from coming here? That if you—if you left me—it would be because I drove you away myself?"

"Yes," he said, huskily. "It was true."

"Are you sure?"

"Indeed I am," he answered in a low voice, but with conviction.

"Then——" She paused. "Well—but I haven't driven you away."

"No."

"And yet you've gone," she said, quietly.

"Do I seem so stupid as all that?"

"You know what I mean." She leaned back in her chair again, and her hands, inactive for once, lay motionless in her lap. When she spoke it was in a rueful whisper:

"I wonder if I *have* driven you away?"

"You've done nothing—nothing at all," he said.

"I wonder——" she said once more, but she stopped. In her mind she was going back over their time together since the first meeting—fragments of talk, moments of silence, little things of no importance, little things that might be important; moonshine, sunshine, starlight; and her thoughts zigzagged among the jumbling memories; but, as if she made for herself a picture of all these fragments, throwing them upon the canvas haphazard, she saw them all just touched with the one tainting quality that gave them coherence, the faint, false haze she had put over this friendship by her own pretendings. And, if this terrible dinner, or anything, or everything, had shown that saffron tint in its true colour to the man at her side, last night almost a lover, then she had indeed of herself driven him away, and might well feel that she was lost.

"Do you know?" she said, suddenly, in a clear, loud voice. "I have the strangest feeling. I feel as if I were going to be with you only about five minutes more in all the rest of my life!"

"Why, no," he said. "Of course I'm coming to see you—often. I——"

"No," she interrupted. "I've never had a feeling like this before. It's—it's just *so;* that's all! You're *going*—why, you're never coming here again!" She stood up, abruptly, beginning to tremble all over. "Why, it's *finished,* isn't it?" she said, and her trembling was manifest now in her voice. "Why, it's all *over,* isn't it? Why, yes!"

He had risen as she did. "I'm afraid you're awfully tired and nervous," he said. "I really ought to be going."

"Yes, of *course* you ought," she cried, despairingly. "There's nothing else for you to do. When anything's spoiled, people *can't* do anything but run away from it. So good-bye!"

"At least," he returned, huskily, "we'll only—only say good-night."

Then, as moving to go, he stumbled upon the veranda steps, "Your *hat!*" she cried. "I'd like to keep it for a souvenir, but I'm afraid you need it!"

She ran into the hall and brought his straw hat from the chair where he had left it. "You poor thing!" she said, with quavering laughter. "Don't you know you can't go without your hat?"

Then, as they faced each other for the short moment which both of them knew would be the last of all their veranda moments, Alice's broken laughter grew louder. "What a thing to say!" she cried. "What a romantic parting—talking about *hats!*"

Her laughter continued as he turned away, but other sounds came from within the house, clearly audible with the opening of a door upstairs—a long and wailing cry of lamentation in the voice of Mrs. Adams. Russell paused at the steps, uncertain, but Alice waved to him to go on.

"Oh, don't bother," she said. "We have lots of that in this funny little old house! Good-bye!"

And as he went down the steps, she ran back into the house and closed the door heavily behind her.

CHAPTER XXIII

HER mother's wailing could still be heard from overhead, though more faintly; and old Charley Lohr was coming down the stairs alone.

He looked at Alice compassionately. "I was just comin' to suggest maybe you'd excuse yourself from your company," he said. "Your mother was bound not to disturb you, and tried her best to keep you from hearin' how she's takin' on, but I thought probably you better see to her."

"Yes, I'll come. What's the matter?"

"Well," he said, "*I* only stepped over to offer my sympathy and services, as it were. *I* thought of course you folks knew all about it. Fact is, it was in the evening paper—just a little bit of an item on the back page, of course."

"What is it?"

He coughed. "Well, it ain't anything so terrible," he said. "Fact is, your brother Walter's got in a little trouble—well, I suppose you might call it quite a good deal of trouble. Fact is, he's quite considerable short in his accounts down at Lamb and Company."

Alice ran up the stairs and into her father's room, where Mrs. Adams threw herself into her daughter's arms. "Is he gone?" she sobbed. "He didn't hear me, did he? I tried so hard——"

Alice patted the heaving shoulders her arms enclosed. "No, no," she said. "He didn't hear you—it wouldn't have mattered—he doesn't matter anyway."

"Oh, *poor* Walter!" The mother cried. "Oh, the *poor* boy! Poor, poor Walter! Poor, poor, poor, *poor*——"

"Hush, dear, hush!" Alice tried to soothe her, but the lament could not be abated, and from the other side of the room a repetition in a different spirit was as continuous. Adams paced furiously there, pounding his fist into his left palm as he strode. "The dang boy!" he said. "Dang little fool! Dang idiot! Dang fool! Whyn't he *tell* me, the dang little fool?"

"He *did!*" Mrs. Adams sobbed. "He *did* tell you, and you wouldn't *give* it to him."

"He *did*, did he?" Adams shouted at her. "What he begged me for was money to run away with! He never dreamed of putting back what he took. What the dangnation you talking about—accusing me!"

"He *needed* it," she said. "He needed it to run away with! How could he expect to *live*, after he got away, if he didn't have a little money? Oh, poor, poor, *poor* Walter! Poor, poor, poor——"

She went back to this repetition; and Adams went back to his own, then paused, seeing his old friend standing in the hallway outside the open door.

"Ah—I'll just be goin', I guess, Virgil," Lohr said. "I don't see as there's any use my tryin' to say any more. I'll do anything you want me to, you understand."

"Wait a minute," Adams said, and, groaning, came and went down the stairs with him. "You say you didn't see the old man at all?"

"No, I don't know a thing about what he's going to do," Lohr said, as they reached the lower floor. "Not a thing. But look here, Virgil, I don't see as this calls for you and your wife to take on so hard about—anyhow not as hard as the way you've started."

"No," Adams gulped. "It always seems that way to the other party that's only looking on!"

"Oh, well, I know that, of course," old Charley

returned, soothingly. "But look here, Virgil: they *may* not catch the boy; they didn't even seem to be sure what train he made, and if they do get him, why, the ole man might decide not to prosecute if——"

"*Him?*" Adams cried, interrupting. "Him not prosecute? Why, that's what he's been waiting for, all along! He thinks my boy and me both cheated him! Why, he was just letting Walter walk into a trap! Didn't you say they'd been suspecting him for some time back? Didn't you say they'd been watching him and were just about fixing to arrest him?"

"Yes, I know," said Lohr; "but you can't tell, especially if you raise the money and pay it back."

"Every cent!" Adams vociferated. "Every last penny! I can raise it—I *got* to raise it! I'm going to put a loan on my factory to-morrow. Oh, I'll get it for him, you tell him! Every last penny!"

"Well, ole feller, you just try and get quieted down some now." Charley held out his hand in parting. "You and your wife just quiet down some. You *ain't* the healthiest man in the world, you know, and you already been under quite some strain before this happened. You want to take care of yourself for the sake of your wife and that sweet little girl upstairs, you know. Now, good-night," he finished, stepping out upon the veranda. "You send for me if there's anything I can do."

"Do?" Adams echoed. "There ain't anything *anybody* can do!" And then, as his old friend went down the path to the sidewalk, he called after him, "You tell him I'll pay him every last cent! Every last, dang, dirty *penny!*"

He slammed the door and went rapidly up the stairs, talking loudly to himself. "Every dang, last, dirty penny! Thinks *everybody* in this family wants to steal from him, does he? Thinks we're *all* yellow, does he? I'll show him!" And he came into his own room vociferating, "Every last, dang, dirty penny!"

Mrs. Adams had collapsed, and Alice had put her upon his bed, where she lay tossing convulsively and sobbing, "Oh, *poor* Walter!" over and over, but after a time she varied the sorry tune. "Oh, poor Alice!" she moaned, clinging to her daughter's hand. "Oh, poor, *poor* Alice—to have *this* come on the night of your dinner—just when everything seemed to be going so well—at last—oh, poor, poor, *poor*——"

"Hush!" Alice said, sharply. "Don't say 'poor Alice!' I'm all right."

"You *must* be!" her mother cried, clutching her. "You've just *got* to be! *One* of us has got to be all right—surely God wouldn't mind just *one* of us being all right—that wouldn't hurt Him——"

"Hush, hush, mother! Hush!"

But Mrs. Adams only clutched her the more tightly. "He seemed *such* a nice young man, dearie! He may not see this in the paper—Mr. Lohr said it was just a little bit of an item—he *may* not see it, dearie——"

Then her anguish went back to Walter again; and to his needs as a fugitive—she had meant to repair his underwear, but had postponed doing so, and her neglect now appeared to be a detail as lamentable as the calamity itself. She could neither be stilled upon it, nor herself exhaust its urgings to self-reproach, though she finally took up another theme temporarily. Upon an unusually violent outbreak of her husband's, in denunciation of the runaway, she cried out faintly that he was cruel; and further wearied her broken voice with details of Walter's beauty as a baby, and of his bedtime pieties throughout his infancy.

So the hot night wore on. Three had struck before Mrs. Adams was got to bed; and Alice, returning to her own room, could hear her father's bare feet thudding back and forth after that. "Poor papa!" she whispered in helpless imitation of her mother. "Poor papa! Poor mama! Poor Walter! Poor all of us!"

She fell asleep, after a time, while from across the hall the bare feet still thudded over their changeless route; and she woke at seven, hearing Adams pass her door, shod. In her wrapper she ran out into the hallway and found him descending the stairs.

"Papa!"

"Hush," he said, and looked up at her with reddened eyes. "Don't wake your mother."

"I won't," she whispered. "How about you? You haven't slept any at all!"

"Yes, I did. I got some sleep. I'm going over to the works now. I got to throw some figures together to show the bank. Don't worry: I'll get things fixed up. You go back to bed. Good-bye."

"Wait!" she bade him sharply.

"What for?"

"You've got to have some breakfast."

"Don't want 'ny."

"You wait!" she said, imperiously, and disappeared to return almost at once. "I can cook in my bed-

" 'He did tell you,' Mrs. Adams sobbed, 'and you wouldn't give it to him.' "

room slippers," she explained, "but I don't believe I could in my bare feet!"

Descending softly, she made him wait in the dining-room until she brought him toast and eggs and coffee. "Eat!" she said. "And I'm going to telephone for a taxicab to take you, if you think you've really got to go."

"No, I'm going to walk—I *want* to walk."

She shook her head anxiously. "You don't look able. You've walked all night."

"No, I didn't," he returned. "I tell you I got some sleep. I got all I wanted anyhow."

"But, papa——"

"Here!" he interrupted, looking up at her suddenly and setting down his cup of coffee. "Look here! What about this Mr. Russell? I forgot all about him. What about him?"

Her lip trembled a little, but she controlled it before she spoke. "Well, what about him, papa?" she asked, calmly enough.

"Well, we could hardly——" Adams paused, frowning heavily. "We could hardly expect he wouldn't hear something about all this."

"Yes; of course he'll hear it, papa."

"Well?"

"Well, what?" she asked, gently.

"You don't think he'd be the—the cheap kind it'd make a difference with, of course."

"Oh, no; he isn't cheap. It won't make any difference with him."

Adams suffered a profound sigh to escape him. "Well—I'm glad of that, anyway."

"The difference," she explained—"the difference was made without his hearing anything about Walter. He doesn't know about *that* yet."

"Well, what does he know about?"

"Only," she said, "about me."

"What you mean by that, Alice?" he asked, helplessly.

"Never mind," she said. "It's nothing beside the real trouble we're in—I'll tell you some time. You eat your eggs and toast; you can't keep going on just coffee."

"I can't eat any eggs and toast," he objected, rising. "I can't."

"Then wait till I can bring you something else."

"No," he said, irritably. "I won't do it! I don't want any dang food! And look here"— he spoke sharply to stop her, as she went toward the telephone —"I don't want any dang taxi, either! You look after your mother when she wakes up. I got to be at *work!*"

And though she followed him to the front door, entreating, he could not be stayed or hindered. He went through the quiet morning streets at a rickety, rapid gait, swinging his old straw hat in his hands, and whispering angrily to himself as he went. His grizzled hair, not trimmed for a month, blew back from his damp forehead in the warm breeze; his reddened eyes stared hard at nothing from under blinking lids; and one side of his face twitched startlingly from time to time;—children might have run from him, or mocked him.

When he had come into that fallen quarter his industry had partly revived and wholly made odorous, a negro woman, leaning upon her whitewashed gate, gazed after him and chuckled for the benefit of a gossiping friend in the next tiny yard. "Oh, good Satan! Wha'ssa matter that ole glue man?"

"Who? Him?" the neighbour inquired. "What he do now?"

"Talkin' to his ole se'f!" the first explained, joyously. "Look like gone distracted—ole glue man!"

Adams's legs had grown more uncertain with his

hard walk, and he stumbled heavily as he crossed the baked mud of his broad lot, but cared little for that, was almost unaware of it, in fact. Thus his eyes saw as little as his body felt, and so he failed to observe something that would have given him additional light upon an old phrase that already meant quite enough for him.

There are in the wide world people who have never learned its meaning; but most are either young or beautifully unobservant who remain wholly unaware of the inner poignancies the words convey: "a rain of misfortunes." It is a boiling rain, seemingly whimsical in its choice of spots whereon to fall; and, so far as mortal eye can tell, neither the just nor the unjust may hope to avoid it, or need worry themselves by expecting it. It had selected the Adams family for its scaldings; no question.

The glue-works foreman, standing in the doorway of the brick shed, observed his employer's eccentric approach, and doubtfully stroked a whiskered chin. "Well, they ain't no putticular use gettin' so upset over it," he said, as Adams came up. "When a thing happens, why, it happens, and that's all there is to it. When a thing's so, why, it's so. All you can do about it is think if there's anything you *can* do; and that's what you better be doin' with this case."

Adams halted, and seemed to gape at him. "What —case?" he said, with difficulty. "Was it in the morning papers, too?"

"No, it ain't in no morning papers. My land! It don't need to be in no papers; look at the *size* of it!"

"The size of what?"

"Why, great God!" the foreman exclaimed. "He ain't even seen it. Look! Look yonder!"

Adams stared vaguely at the man's outstretched hand and pointing forefinger, then turned and saw a great sign upon the façade of the big factory building across the street. The letters were large enough to be read two blocks away.

"AFTER THE FIFTEENTH OF NEXT MONTH THIS BUILDING WILL BE OCCUPIED BY THE J. A. LAMB LIQUID GLUE CO. INC."

A gray touring-car had just come to rest before the principal entrance of the building, and J. A. Lamb himself descended from it. He glanced over toward the humble rival of his projected great industry, saw his old clerk, and immediately walked across the street and the lot to speak to him.

"Well, Adams," he said, in his husky, cheerful voice, "how's your glue-works?"

Adams uttered an inarticulate sound, and lifted the hand that held his hat as if to make a protestive gesture, but failed to carry it out; and his arm sank limp at his side. The foreman, however, seemed to feel that something ought to be said.

"Our glue-works, hell!" he remarked. "I guess we won't *have* no glue-works over here—not very long, if we got to compete with the sized thing you got over there!"

Lamb chuckled. "I kind of had some such notion," he said. "You see, Virgil, I couldn't exactly let you walk off with it like swallering a pat o' butter, now, could I? It didn't look exactly reasonable to expect me to let go like that, now, did it?"

Adams found a half-choked voice somewhere in his throat. "Do you—would you step into my office a minute, Mr. Lamb?"

"Why, certainly I'm willing to have a little talk with you," the old gentleman said, as he followed his former employee indoors, and he added, "I feel a lot more like it than I did before I got *that* up, over yonder, Virgil!"

Adams threw open the door of the rough room he called his office, having as justification for this title little more than the fact that he had a telephone there and a deal table that served as a desk. "Just step into the office, please," he said.

Lamb glanced at the desk, at the kitchen chair before it, at the telephone, and at the partition walls built of old boards, some covered with ancient paint and some merely weatherbeaten, the salvage of a house-wrecker; and he smiled broadly. "So these are your offices, are they?" he asked. "You expect to do quite a business here, I guess, don't you, Virgil?"

Adams turned upon him a stricken and tortured face. "Have you seen Charley Lohr since last night, Mr. Lamb?"

"No; I haven't seen Charley."

"Well, I told him to tell you," Adams began;—"I told him I'd pay you——"

"Pay me what you expect to make out o' glue, you mean, Virgil?"

"No," Adams said, swallowing. "I mean what my boy owes you. That's what I told Charley to tell you. I told him to tell you I'd pay you every last——"

"Well, well!" the old gentleman interrupted, testily. "I don't know anything about that."

"I'm expecting to pay you," Adams went on, swallowing again, painfully. "I was expecting to do it out of a loan I thought I could get on my glue-works."

The old gentleman lifted his frosted eyebrows. "Oh, out o' the *glue*-works? You expected to raise money on the glue-works, did you?"

At that, Adams's agitation increased prodigiously. "How'd you *think* I expected to pay you?" he said. "Did you think I expected to get money on my own old bones?" He slapped himself harshly upon the chest and legs. "Do you think a bank'll lend money on a man's ribs and his broken-down old knee-bones? They won't do it! You got to have some *business* prospects to show 'em, if you haven't got any property nor securities; and what business prospects have I got now, with that sign of yours up over yonder? Why, you don't need to make an *ounce* o' glue; your sign's fixed *me* without your doing another lick! *That's* all you had to do; just put your sign up! You needn't to——"

"Just let me tell you something, Virgil Adams," the old man interrupted, harshly. "I got just one right important thing to tell you before we talk any further business, and that's this: there's some few men in this town made their money in off-colour ways, but there aren't many; and those there are have had to be a darn sight slicker than you know how to be, or ever *will* know how to be! Yes, sir, and they none of them had the little gumption to try to make it out of a man that had the spirit not to let 'em, and the *strength* not to let 'em! I know what *you* thought. 'Here,' you said to yourself, 'here's this ole fool J. A. Lamb; he's kind of worn out and in his second childhood like; I can put it over on him, without his ever——' "

"I did not!" Adams shouted. "A great deal *you* know about my feelings and all what I said to myself! There's one thing I want to tell *you*, and that's what I'm saying to myself *now*, and what my feelings are this *minute!*"

He struck the table a great blow with his thin fist, and shook the damaged knuckles in the air. "I just want to tell you, whatever I did feel, I don't feel *mean* any more; not to-day, I don't. There's a meaner man in this world than *I* am, Mr. Lamb!"

"Oh, so you feel better about yourself to-day, do you, Virgil?"

"You bet I do! You worked till you got me where you want me; and I wouldn't do that to another man, no matter what he did to me! I wouldn't——"

"What you talkin' about! How've I 'got you where I want you?'"

"Ain't it plain enough?" Adams cried. "You even got me where I can't raise the money to pay back what my boy owes you! Do you suppose anybody's fool enough to let me have a cent on this business after one look at what you got over there across the road?"

"No, I don't."

"No, you don't," Adams echoed, hoarsely. "What's more, you knew my house was mortgaged, and my——"

"I did not," Lamb interrupted, angrily. "What do *I* care about your house?"

"What's the use your talking like that?" Adams cried. "You got me where I can't even raise the money to pay what my boy owes the company, so't I can't show any reason to stop the prosecution and keep him out the penitentiary. That's where you worked till you got *me!*"

"What!" Lamb shouted. "You accuse me of——"

"'Accuse you?' What am I telling you? Do you

think I got no *eyes?*" And Adams hammered the table again. "Why, you knew the boy was weak——"

"I did not!"

"Listen: you kept him there after you got mad at my leaving the way I did. You kept him there after you suspected him; and you had him watched; you let him go on; just waited to catch him and ruin him!"

"You're crazy!" the old man bellowed. "I didn't know there was anything against the boy till last night. You're *crazy*, I say!"

Adams looked it. With his hair disordered over his haggard forehead and bloodshot eyes; with his bruised hands pounding the table and flying in a hundred wild and absurd gestures, while his feet shuffled constantly to preserve his balance upon staggering legs, he was the picture of a man with a mind gone to rags.

"Maybe I *am* crazy!" he cried, his voice breaking and quavering. "Maybe I am, but I wouldn't stand there and taunt a man with it if I'd done to him what you've done to me! Just look at me: I worked all my life for you, and what I did when I quit never harmed you—it didn't make two cents' worth o' difference in your life and it looked like it'd mean all the difference in the world to my family—and now look what you've *done* to me for it! I tell you, Mr. Lamb, there never was a man looked up to another man the way I looked up to you the whole o' my life, but I don't look up to you any more! You think you got a fine day of it now, riding up in your automobile to look at that sign—and then over here at my poor little works that you've ruined. But listen to me just this one last time!" The cracking voice broke into falsetto, and the gesticulating hands fluttered uncontrollably. "Just you listen!" he panted. "You think I did you a bad turn, and now you got me ruined for it, and you got my works ruined, and my family ruined; and if anybody'd 'a' told me this time last year I'd ever say such a thing to you I'd called him a dang liar, but I *do* say it: I say you've acted toward me like—like a—a doggone mean—man!"

His voice, exhausted, like his body, was just able to do him this final service; then he sank, crumpled, into the chair by the table, his chin down hard upon his chest.

"I tell you, you're crazy!" Lamb said again. "I never in the world——" But he checked himself, staring in sudden perplexity at his accuser. "Look here!" he said. "What's the matter of you? Have you got another of those——?" He put his hand upon Adams's shoulder, which jerked feebly under the touch.

The old man went to the door and called to the foreman.

"Here!" he said. "Run and tell my chauffeur to bring my car over here. Tell him to drive right up over the sidewalk and across the lot. Tell him to hurry!"

So, it happened, the great J. A. Lamb a second time brought his former clerk home, stricken and almost inanimate.

CHAPTER XXIV

ABOUT five o'clock that afternoon, the old gentleman came back to Adams's house; and when Alice opened the door, he nodded, walked into the "living-room" without speaking; then stood frowning as if he hesitated to decide some perplexing question.

"Well, how is he now?" he asked, finally.

"The doctor was here again a little while ago; he thinks papa's coming through it. He's pretty sure he will."

"Something like the way it was last spring?"

"Yes."

"Not a bit of sense to it!" Lamb said, gruffly. "When he was getting well the other time the doctor told me it wasn't a regular stroke, so to speak—this 'cerebral effusion' thing. Said there wasn't any particular reason for your father to expect he'd ever have another attack, if he'd take a little care of himself. Said he could consider himself well as anybody else long as he did that."

"Yes. But he didn't do it!"

Lamb nodded, sighed aloud, and crossed the room to a chair. "I guess not," he said, as he sat down. "Bustin' his health up over his glue-works, I expect."

"Yes."

"I guess so; I guess so." Then he looked up at her with a glimmer of anxiety in his eyes. "Has he came to yet?"

"Yes. He's talked a little. His mind's clear; he spoke to mama and me—and to Miss Perry." Alice laughed sadly. "We were lucky enough to get her back, but papa didn't seem to think it was lucky. When he recognized her he said, 'Oh, my goodness, 'tisn't *you*, is it!'"

"Well, that's a good sign, if he's getting a little cross. Did he—did he happen to say anything—for instance, about me?"

This question, awkwardly delivered, had the effect of removing the girl's pallor; rosy tints came quickly upon her cheeks. "He—yes, he did," she said. "Naturally, he's troubled about—about——" She stopped.

"About your brother, maybe?"

"Yes, about making up the——

"Here, now," Lamb said, uncomfortably, as she

stopped again. "Listen, young lady; let's don't talk about that just yet. I want to ask you: you understand all about this glue business, I expect, don't you?"

"I'm not sure. I only know——"

"Let me tell you," he interrupted, impatiently. "I'll tell you all about it in two words. The process belonged to me, and your father up and walked off with it; there's no getting around *that* much, anyhow."

"Isn't there?" Alice stared at him. "I think you're mistaken, Mr. Lamb. Didn't papa improve it so that it virtually belonged to him?"

There was a spark in the old blue eyes at this. "What?" he cried. "Is that the way he got around it? Why, in all my life I never heard of such a——" But he left the sentence unfinished; the testiness went out of his husky voice and the anger out of his eyes. "Well, I expect maybe that was the way of it," he said. "Anyhow, it's right for you to stand up for your father; and if you think he had a right to it——"

"But he did!" she cried.

"I expect so," the old man returned, pacifically. "I expect so, probably. Anyhow, it's a question that's neither here nor there, right now. What I was thinking of saying—well, did your father happen to let out that he and I had words this morning?"

"No."

"Well, we did." He sighed and shook his head. "Your father—well, he used some pretty hard expressions toward me, young lady. They weren't *so*, I'm glad to say, but he used 'em to me, and the worst of it was he believed 'em. Well, I been thinking it over, and I thought I'd just have a kind of little talk with you to set matters straight, so to speak."

"Yes, Mr. Lamb."

"For instance," he said, "it's like this. Now, I hope you won't think I mean any indelicacy, but you take your brother's case, since we got to mention it, why, your father had the whole thing worked out in his mind about as wrong as anybody ever got anything. If I'd acted the way your father thought I did about that, why, somebody just ought to take me out and shoot me! Do *you* know what that man thought?"

"I'm not sure."

He frowned at her, and asked, "Well, what do you think about it?"

"I don't know," she said. "I don't believe I think anything at all about anything to-day."

"Well, well," he returned; "I expect not; I expect not. You kind of look to me as if you ought to be in bed yourself, young lady."

"Oh, no."

"I guess you mean 'Oh, yes'; and I won't keep you long, but there's something we got to get fixed up, and I'd rather talk to you than I would to your mother, because you're a smart girl and always friendly; and I want to be sure I'm understood. Now, listen."

"I will," Alice promised, smiling faintly.

"I never even hardly noticed your brother was still working for me," he explained, earnestly. "I never thought anything about it. My sons sort of tried to tease me about the way your father—about his taking up this glue business, so to speak—and one day Albert, Junior, asked me if I felt all right about your brother's staying there after that, and I told him—well, I just asked him to shut up. If the boy wanted to stay there, I didn't consider it my business to send him away on account of any feeling I had toward his father; not as long as he did his work right—and the report showed he did. Well, as it happens, it looks now as if he stayed because he *had* to; he couldn't quit because he'd 'a' been found out if he did. Well, he'd been covering up his shortage for a considerable time—and do you know what your father practically charged me with about that?"

"No, Mr. Lamb."

In his resentment, the old gentleman's ruddy face became ruddier and his husky voice huskier. "Thinks I kept the boy there because I suspected him! Thinks I did it to get even with *him!* Do I look to *you* like a man that'd do such a thing?"

"No," she said, gently. "I don't think you would."

"No!" he exclaimed. "Nor *he* wouldn't think so if he was himself; he's known me too long. But he must been sort of brooding over this whole business—I mean before Walter's trouble—he must been taking it to heart pretty hard for some time back. He thought I didn't think much of him any more—and I expect he maybe wondered some what I was going to *do*—and there's nothing worse'n that state of mind to make a man suspicious of all kinds of meanness. Well, he practically stood up there and accused me to my face of fixing things so't he couldn't ever raise the money to settle for Walter and ask us not to prosecute. That's the state of mind your father's brooding got him into, young lady—charging me with a trick like that!"

"I'm sorry," she said. "I know you'd never——"

The old man slapped his sturdy knee, angrily. "Why, that dang fool of a Virgil Adams!" he exclaimed. "He wouldn't even give me a chance to talk; and he got me so mad I couldn't hardly talk, anyway! He might 'a' known from the first I wasn't going to let him walk in and beat me out of my own—that is, he might 'a' known I wouldn't let him get ahead of me in a business matter—not with my boys twitting me about it every few minutes! But to talk to me the way he did this morning—well, he was out of his head; that's all! Now, wait just a minute," he interposed, as she seemed about to speak. "In the first place, we aren't going to push this case against your brother. I believe in the law, all right, and business men got to protect themselves; but in a case like this, where restitution's made by the family, why, I expect it's just as well sometimes to use a little influence and let matters drop. Of course your brother'll have to keep out o' this state; that's all."

"But—you said——" she faltered.

"Yes. What'd I say?"

"You said, 'where restitution's made by the family.' That's what seemed to trouble papa so terribly, because—because restitution couldn't——"

"Why, yes, it could. That's what I'm here to talk to you about."

"I don't see——"

"I'm going to *tell* you, ain't I?" he said, gruffly. "Just hold your horses a minute, please." He coughed, rose from his chair, walked up and down the room, then halted before her. "It's like this," he said. "After I brought your father home, this morning, there was one of the things he told me, when he was going for me, over yonder—it kind of stuck in my craw. It was something about all this glue controversy not meaning anything to me in particular, and meaning a whole heap to him and his family. Well, he was wrong about that two ways. The first one was, it did mean a good deal to me to have him go back on me after so many years. I don't need to say any more about it, except just to tell you it meant quite a little more to me than you'd think, maybe. The other way he was wrong is, that how much a thing means to one man and how little it means to another ain't the right way to look at a business matter."

"I suppose it isn't, Mr. Lamb."

"No," he said. "It isn't. It's not the right way to look at anything. Yes, and your father knows it as well as I do, when he's in his right mind; and I expect that's one of the reasons he got so mad at me—but anyhow, I couldn't help thinking about how much all this thing *had* maybe meant to him;—as I say, it kind of stuck in my craw. I want you to tell him something from me, and I want you to go and tell him right off, if he's able and willing to listen. You tell him I got kind of a notion he was pushed into this thing by circumstances, and tell him I've lived long enough to know that circumstances can beat the best of us—you tell him I said 'the *best* of us.' Tell him I haven't got a bit of feeling against him—not any more—and tell him I came here to ask him not to have any against me."

"Yes, Mr. Lamb."

"Tell him I said——" The old man paused abruptly and Alice was surprised, in a dull and tired way, when she saw that his lips had begun to twitch and his eyelids to blink; but he recovered himself almost at once, and continued: "I want him to remember, 'Forgive us our transgressions, as we forgive those that transgress against us'; and if he and I been transgressing against each other, why, tell him I think it's time we *quit* such foolishness!"

He coughed again, smiled heartily upon her, and walked toward the door; then turned back to her with an exclamation: "Well, if I ain't an old fool!"

"What is it?" she asked.

"Why, I forgot what we were just talking about! Your father wants to settle for Walter's deficit. Tell him we'll be glad to accept it; but of course we don't expect him to clean the matter up until he's able to talk business again."

Alice stared at him blankly enough for him to perceive that further explanations were necessary. "It's like this," he said. "You see, if your father decided to keep his works going over yonder, I don't say but he might give us some little competition for a time, 'specially as he's got the start on us and about ready for the market. Then I was figuring we could use his plant—it's small, but it'd be to our benefit to have the use of it—and he's got a lease on that big lot; it may come in handy for us if we want to expand some. Well, I'd prefer to make a deal with him as quietly as possible—no good in every Tom,

Dick and Harry hearing about things like this—but I figured he could sell out to me for a little something more'n enough to cover the mortgage he put on this house, and Walter's deficit, too—*that* don't amount to much in dollars and cents. The way I figure it, I could offer him about ninety-three hundred dollars as a total—or say ninety-three hundred and fifty—and if he feels like accepting, why, I'll send a confidential man up here with the papers soon's your father's able to look 'em over. You tell him, will you, and ask him if he sees his way to accepting that figure?"

"Yes," Alice said; and now her own lips twitched, while her eyes filled so that she saw but a blurred image of the old man, who held out his hand in parting. "I'll tell him. Thank you."

He shook her hand hastily. "Well, let's just keep it kind of quiet," he said, at the door. "No good in every Tom, Dick and Harry knowing all what goes on in town! You telephone me when your papa's ready to go over the papers—and call me up at my house to-night, will you? Let me hear how he's feeling?"

"I will," she said, and through her grateful tears gave him a smile almost radiant. "He'll be better, Mr. Lamb. We all will."

CHAPTER XXV

ONE morning, that autumn, Mrs. Adams came into Alice's room, and found her completing a sober toilet for the street; moreover, the expression revealed in her mirror was harmonious with the business-like severity of her attire. "What makes you look so cross, dearie?" the mother asked. "Couldn't you find anything nicer to wear than that plain old dark dress?"

"I don't believe I'm cross," the girl said, absently. "I believe I'm just thinking. Isn't it about time?"

"Time for what?"

"Time for thinking—for me, I mean?"

Disregarding this, Mrs. Adams looked her over thoughtfully. "I can't see why you don't wear more colour," she said. "At your age it's becoming and proper, too. Anyhow, when you're going on the street, I think you ought to look just as gay and lively as you can manage. You want to show 'em you've got some spunk!"

"How do you mean, mama?"

"I mean about Walter's running away and the mess your father made of his business. It would help to show 'em you're holding up your head just the same."

"Show whom!"

"All these other girls that——"

"Not I!" Alice laughed shortly, shaking her head. "I've quit dressing at them, and if they saw me they wouldn't think what you want 'em to. It's funny; but we don't often make people think what we want 'em to, mama. You do thus and so; and you tell yourself, 'Now, seeing me do thus and so, people will naturally think this and that'; but they don't. They think something else—usually just what you *don't* want 'em to. I suppose about the only good in pretending is the fun we get out of fooling ourselves that we fool somebody."

"Well, but it wouldn't be pretending. You ought to let people see you're still holding your head up because you *are*. You wouldn't want that Mildred Palmer to think you're cast down about—well, you know you wouldn't want *her* not to think you're holding your head up, would you?"

"She wouldn't know whether I am or not, mama." Alice bit her lip, then smiled faintly as she said:

"Anyhow, I'm not thinking about my head in that way—not this morning, I'm not."

Mrs. Adams dropped the subject casually. "Are you going down-town?" she inquired.

"Yes."

"What for?"

"Just something I want to see about. I'll tell you when I come back. Anything you want me to do?"

"No; I guess not to-day. I thought you might look for a rug, but I'd rather go with you to select it. We'll have to get a new rug for your father's room, I expect."

"I'm glad you think so, mama. I don't suppose he's ever even noticed it, but that old rug of his—well, really!"

"I didn't mean for him," her mother explained, thoughtfully. "No; he don't mind it, and he'd likely make a fuss if we changed it on his account. No; what I meant—we'll have to put your father in Walter's room. He won't mind, I don't expect—not much."

"No, I suppose not," Alice agreed, rather sadly. "I heard the bell awhile ago. Was it somebody about that?"

"Yes; just before I came upstairs. Mrs. Lohr gave

him a note to me, and he was really a very pleasant-looking young man. A *very* pleasant-looking young man," Mrs. Adams repeated with increased animation and a thoughtful glance at her daughter. "He's a Mr. Will Dickson; he has a first-rate position with the gas works, Mrs. Lohr says, and he's fully able to afford a nice room. So if you and I double up in here, then with that young married couple in my room, and this Mr. Dickson in your father's, we'll just about have things settled. I thought maybe I could make one more place at table, too, so that with the other people from outside we'd be serving eleven altogether. You see if I have to pay this cook twelve dollars a week—it can't be helped, I guess—well, one more would certainly help toward a profit. Of course it's a terribly worrying thing to see how we *will* come out. Don't you suppose we could squeeze in one more?"

"I suppose it *could* be managed; yes."

Mrs. Adams brightened. "I'm sure it'll be pleasant having that young married couple in the house—and especially this Mr. Will Dickson. He seemed very much of a gentleman, and anxious to get settled in good surroundings. I was very favourably impressed with him in every way; and he explained to me about his name; it seems it isn't William, it's just 'Will'; his parents had him christened that way. It's curious." She paused, and then, with an effort to seem casual, which veiled nothing from her daughter: "It's *quite* curious," she said again. "But it's rather attractive and different, don't you think?"

"Poor mama!" Alice laughed compassionately. "Poor mama!"

"He is, though," Mrs. Adams maintained. "He's *very* much of a gentleman, unless I'm no judge of appearances; and it'll really be nice to have him in the house."

"No doubt," Alice said, as she opened her door to depart. "I don't suppose we'll mind having any of 'em as much as we thought we would. Good-bye."

But her mother detained her, catching her by the arm. "Alice, you do hate it, don't you!"

"No," the girl said, quickly. "There wasn't anything else to do."

Mrs. Adams became emotional at once: her face cried tragedy, and her voice misfortune. "There *might* have been something else to do! Oh, Alice, you gave your father bad advice when you upheld him in taking a miserable little ninety-three hundred and fifty from that old wretch! If your father'd just had the gumption to hold out, they'd have had to pay him anything he asked. If he'd just had the gumption and a little manly *courage*——"

"Hush!" Alice whispered, for her mother's voice grew louder. "Hush! He'll hear you, mama."

"Could he hear me too often?" the embittered lady asked. "If he'd listened to me at the right time, would we have to be taking in boarders and sinking *down* in the scale at the end of our lives, instead of going *up?* You were both wrong; we didn't need to be so panicky—that was just what that old man wanted: to scare us and buy us out for nothing! If your father'd just listened to me then, or if for once in his life he'd just been half a *man*——"

Alice put her hand over her mother's mouth. "You mustn't! He *will* hear you!"

But from the other side of Adams's closed door his voice came querulously. "Oh, I *hear* her, all right!"

"You see, mama?" Alice said, and, as Mrs. Adams turned away, weeping, the daughter sighed; then went in to speak to her father.

He was in his old chair by the table, with a pillow behind his head, but the crocheted scarf and Mrs. Adams's wrapper swathed him no more; he wore a dressing-gown his wife had bought for him, and was smoking his pipe. "The old story, is it?" he said, as Alice came in. "The same, same old story! Well, well! Has she gone?"

"Yes, papa."

"Got your hat on," he said. "Where you going?"

"I'm going down-town on an errand of my own. Is there anything you want, papa?"

"Yes, there is." He smiled at her. "I wish you'd sit down a while and talk to me—unless your errand——"

"No," she said, taking a chair near him. "I was just going down to see about some arrangements I was making for myself. There's no hurry."

"What arrangements for yourself, dearie?"

"I'll tell you afterwards—after I find out something about 'em myself."

"All right," he said, indulgently. "Keep your secrets; keep your secrets." He paused, drew musingly upon his pipe, and shook his head. "Funny—the way your mother looks at things! For the matter o' that, everything's pretty funny, I expect, if you stop to think about it. For instance, let her say all she likes, but we were pushed right spang to the wall, if J. A. Lamb hadn't taken it into his head to make that offer for the works; and there's one of the things I been thinking about lately, Alice: thinking about how funny they work out."

"What did you think about it, papa!"

"Well, I've seen it happen in other people's lives, time and time again; and now it's happened in ours. You think you're going to be pushed right up against the wall; you can't see any way out, or any hope at all; you think you're *gone*—and then something you never counted on turns up; and, while maybe you never do get back to where you used to be, yet somehow you kind of squirm out of being right *spang* against the wall. You keep on going—maybe you can't go much, but you do go a little. See what I mean?"

"Yes. I understand, dear."

"Yes, I'm afraid you do," he said. "Too bad! You oughtn't to understand it at your age. It seems to me a good deal as if the Lord really meant for the young people to have the good times, and for the old to have the troubles; and when anybody as young as you has trouble there's a big mistake somewhere."

"Oh, no!" she protested.

But he persisted whimsically in this view of divine

error: "Yes, it does look a good deal that way. But of course we can't tell; we're never certain about anything—not about anything at all. Sometimes I look at it another way, though. Sometimes it looks to me as if a body's troubles came on him mainly because he hadn't had sense enough to know how not to have any—as if his troubles were kind of like a boy's getting kept in after school by the teacher, to give him discipline, or something or other. But, my, my! We don't learn easy!" He chuckled mournfully. "Not to learn how to live till we're about ready to die, it certainly seems to me dang tough!"

"Then I wouldn't brood on such a notion, papa," she said.

"'Brood?' No!" he returned. "I just kind o' mull it over." He chuckled again, sighed, and then, not looking at her, he said, "That Mr. Russell—your mother tells me he hasn't been here again—not since——"

"No," she said, quietly, as Adams paused. "He never came again."

"Well, but maybe——"

"No," she said. "There isn't any 'maybe.' I told him good-bye that night, papa. It was before he knew about Walter—I told you."

"Well, well," Adams said. "Young people are entitled to their own privacy; I don't want to pry." He emptied his pipe into a chipped saucer on the table beside him, laid the pipe aside, and reverted to a former topic. "Speaking of dying——"

"Well, but we weren't!" Alice protested.

"Yes, about not knowing how to live till you're through living—and *then* maybe not!" he said, chuckling at his own determined pessimism. "I see I'm pretty old because I talk this way—I remember my grandmother saying things a good deal like all what I'm saying now; I used to hear her at it when I was a young fellow—she was a right gloomy old lady, I remember. Well, anyhow, it reminds me: I want to get on my feet again as soon as I can; I got to look around and find something to go into."

Alice shook her head gently. "But, papa, he told you——"

"Never mind throwing that dang doctor up at me!" Adams interrupted, peevishly. "He said I'd be good for *some* kind of light job—if I could find just the right thing. 'Where there wouldn't be either any physical or mental strain,' he said. Well, I got to find something like that. Anyway, I'll feel better if I can just get out *looking* for it."

"But, papa, I'm afraid you won't find it, and you'll be disappointed."

"Well, I want to hunt around and *see*, anyhow."

Alice patted his hand. "You must just be contented, papa. Everything's going to be all right, and you mustn't get to worrying about doing anything. We own this house—it's all clear—and you've taken care of mama and me all our lives; now it's our turn."

"No, sir!" he said, querulously. "I don't like the idea of being the landlady's husband around a boarding-house; it goes against my gizzard. *I* know: makes out the bills for his wife Sunday mornings—works with a screw-driver on somebody's bureau drawer sometimes—'tends the furnace maybe—one the boarders gives him a cigar now and then. That's a *fine* life to look forward to! No, sir; I don't want to finish as a landlady's husband!"

Alice looked grave; for she knew the sketch was but too accurately prophetic in every probability. "But, papa," she said, to console him, "don't you think maybe there isn't such a thing as a 'finish,' after all! You say perhaps we don't learn to live till we die—but maybe that's how it is *after* we die, too—just learning some more, the way we do here, and maybe through trouble again, even after that."

"Oh, it might be," he sighed. "I expect so."

"Well, then," she said, "what's the use of talking about a 'finish?' We do keep looking ahead to things as if they'd finish something, but when we get *to* them, they don't finish anything. They're just part of going on. I'll tell you—I looked ahead all summer to something I was afraid of, and I said to myself, 'Well, if that happens, I'm finished!' But it wasn't so, papa. It did happen, and nothing's finished; I'm going on, just the same—only——" She stopped and blushed.

"Only what?" he asked.

"Well——" She blushed more deeply, then jumped up, and, standing before him, caught both his hands in hers. "Well, don't you think, since we do have to go on, we ought at least to have learned some sense about how to do it?"

He looked up at her adoringly.

"What *I* think," he said, and his voice trembled;—"I think you're the smartest girl in the world! I wouldn't trade you for the whole kit-and-boodle of 'em!"

But as this folly of his threatened to make her tearful, she kissed him hastily, and went forth upon her errand.

Since the night of the tragic-comic dinner she had not seen Russell, nor caught even the remotest chance glimpse of him; and it was curious that she should encounter him as she went upon such an errand as now engaged her. At a corner, not far from that tobacconist's shop she had just left when he overtook her and walked with her for the first time, she met him to-day. He turned the corner, coming toward her, and they were face to face; whereupon that engaging face of Russell's was instantly reddened, but Alice's remained serene.

She stopped short, though; and so did he; then she smiled brightly as she put out her hand.

"Why, Mr. Russell!"

"I'm so—I'm so glad to have this—this chance," he stammered. "I've wanted to tell you—it's just that going into a new undertaking—this business life—one doesn't get to do a great many things he'd like to. I hope you'll let me call again some time, if I can."

"Yes, do!" she said, cordially, and then, with a quick nod, went briskly on.

She breathed more rapidly, but knew that he could not have detected it, and she took some pride in herself for the way she had met this little crisis.

But to have met it with such easy courage meant to her something more reassuring than a momentary pride in the serenity she had shown. For she found that what she had resolved in her inmost heart was now really true: she was "through with all that!"

She walked on, but more slowly, for the tobacconist's shop was not far from her now—and, beyond it, that portal of doom, Frincke's Business College. Already Alice could read the begrimed gilt letters of the sign; and although they had spelled destiny never with a more painful imminence than just then, an old habit of dramatizing herself still prevailed with her.

There came into her mind a whimsical comparison of her fate with that of the heroine in a French romance she had read long ago and remembered well, for she had cried over it. The story ended with the heroine's taking the veil after a death blow to love; and the final scene again became vivid to Alice, for a moment. Again, as when she had read and wept, she seemed herself to stand among the great shadows in the cathedral nave; smelled the smoky incense on the enclosed air, and heard the solemn pulses of the organ. She remembered how the novice's father knelt, trembling, beside a pillar of gray stone; how the faithless lover watched and shivered behind the statue of a saint; how stifled sobs and outcries were heard when the novice came to the altar; and how a shaft of light struck through the rose-window, enveloping her in an amber glow.

It was the vision of a moment only, and for no longer than a moment did Alice tell herself that the romance provided a prettier way of taking the veil than she had chosen, and that a faithless lover, shaking with remorse behind a saint's statue, was a greater solace than one left on a street corner protesting that he'd like to call some time—if he could! Her pity for herself vanished more reluctantly; but she shook it off and tried to smile at it, and at her romantic recollections—at all of them. She had something important to think of.

She passed the tobacconist's, and before her was that dark entrance to the wooden stairway leading up to Frincke's Business College—the very doorway she had always looked upon as the end of youth and the end of hope.

How often she had gone by here, hating the dreary obscurity of that stairway; how often she had thought of this obscurity as something lying in wait to obliterate the footsteps of any girl who should ascend into the smoky darkness above! Never had she passed without those ominous imaginings of hers: pretty girls turning into old maids "taking dictation" —old maids of a dozen different types, yet all looking a little like herself.

Well, she was here at last! She looked up and down the street quickly, and then, with a little heave of the shoulders, she went bravely in, under the sign, and began to climb the wooden steps. Half-way up the shadows were heaviest, but after that the place began to seem brighter. There was an open window overhead somewhere, she found, and the steps at the top were gay with sunshine.

THE END